The Inner Immigrant

Mihkel Mutt

THE INNER IMMIGRANT

Translated from the Estonian by Adam Cullen

DALKEY ARCHIVE PRESS

Originally published in Estonian by Fabian as *Siseemigrant* in 2007.

Library of Congress Cataloging-in-Publication Data
Names: Mutt, Mihkel, author. | Cullen, Adam, 1986- translator.Title: The inner
immigrant : stories / by Mihkel Mutt ; translated by Adam Cullen.
Other titles: Short stories. English
Description: First Dalkey Archive edition. | Victoria, TX : Dalkey Archive Press,
2017. | "Originally published in Estonian by Fabian as Siseemigrant in 2007"
Identifiers: LCCN 2017005016 | ISBN 9781943150151 (pbk. : acid-free
paper)
Classification: LCC PH666.23.U8 A2 2017 | DDC 894/.54533--dc23
LC record available at https://lccn.loc.gov/2017005016

EESTI KULTUURKAPITAL

This book has been supported by the Estonian Cultural Endowment, Traducta
programme.

www.dalkeyarchive.com
Victoria, TX / McLean, IL / Dublin

Dalkey Archive Press publications are, in part, made possible through the
support of the University of Houston-Victoria and its programs in creative
writing, publishing, and translation.

Printed on permanent/durable acid-free paper.

CONTENTS

MY FAIR SLUM

THERE WAS JUST enough time. The hour agreed upon was just far enough into the future to get off the bus a few stops early instead of riding around, and walk directly through his dear little slum. It boosted his spirits, gave him the strength to keep living. Especially on this day, and in this mood. Fabian was unsettled by the unnatural harmony of broad, linear streets; by the sprawling squares. The glass hurt his eyes—just like the bright light it let through. The duralumin and modern building materials unnerved him with their fake optimism. Fabian liked the slum. Naturally not as a source of aesthetic pleasure, but rather because of its mindset; because of the phenomenology of the spirit that streamed forth from it. Fabian did not for one second believe that the faded, dilapidated tenement houses built at the beginning of the century were lovelier than the Estonia Theater, the new headquarters of the Central Committee of the Communist Party of Estonia, or the pretty little tobacco shop on Saiakang Street in Tallinn's Old Town. Yet urbanity as such, as the quintessence of the city, presented itself to Fabian *here*; not in the Old Town, which pointed too far into the past—into the simpleminded burghers' Middle Ages, but also not in the new micro-districts (as people generally believed), since no human relationships, urban or non-urban, could develop in the isolation of its residents. However, the dense population and multi-faceted interaction right here favored those relationships in every way. And Fabian regarded the new type of human relationships precisely as the most important achievement of urban life—a new freedom, morals, and way of living.

Walking among the sun-bleached, two-to-three-story wooden houses, peeking into the somewhat filthy backyards, Fabian felt the distinct aura of urban life. He had lived in the city all his life. This was his home. In the country, Fabian felt rootless and was gripped by anguish. The country was not human; it was an alien not-I. He was glad when he got back into the city. He hated Rousseau, who called people to nature. The grounds for Fabian's fondness at the same time remained pure of banal pleasures, since his love for the city was under no circumstances tied only to mundane and material comforts. He had spent his entire *youth* in a house with woodburning stoves. Heating it in winter was downright onerous (on top of that, firewood was perpetually being stolen from their stack). It was cramped and communal like a dressing room in the public baths, and it held just as many unpleasant aromas. In the middle of the yard was a well that produced bad-tasting water (being situated too close to a cesspit). Fabian certainly understood it objectively, but time and time again, he was amazed at the reactions of his acquaintances to trips to the countryside; how they would bicker and bribe, and do almost anything at work to obtain sanatorium passes to the mountains, and even to the valleys; how they would dream of a trip to the coast along a blue sea still far off in the future, and would extol the ennobling effect of nature. According to an unwritten law and under the threat of ostracism, the compulsory reaction to this was one of sentimentality and awe; long-winded speeches on rural life tended to be forcefully sacred. Upon exiting a bus that drove you out of the city, you were pretty much expected to lie down flat on the ground and kiss the dirt, wave to a lark up in the heavens, inhale deeply through your nose the smell of ammonia rising from the fields, and just frolic, frolic, frolic.

Man becomes simpler in the country. That's right. The country is simple, the city is complicated—there's something clear-cut about that short and sweet contrast. And given that in certain social circles simplicity was still seen as something that made a person more appealing, it was no wonder that everyone wanted to go where they could become attractive. Fabian's film-actor friend, who had recently made it into the San Moreno Film Festival and who was seen as a member of the Moscow elite, once told him about a time he attended a multi-day party at someone's apartment. Before leaving, the actor asked one of his steady companions: "Listen, old man—tell me: who the hell *are* you, anyway?" The companion replied: "Misha." Afterward, it turned out that he was a contender for the Nobel Prize. To this day, the actor is still elated whenever he tells the story, exclaiming, "Just an exceptionally simple old man, he was!" which, coming from his mouth, sounded like the highest compliment. But as Fabian saw it, the relationship between simple and complex could also be assessed differently. The country takes away much of what makes a person interesting; it robs him of his masks, complexes, and poses; forces him to be "himself" against his own will. That awful, awful country living! It acts like insulin, even more so since a city slicker who has been skulking around cafés has gained a ton of weight on fatty foods. What's there to extol, then? Fabian found that most people are depressingly simple *anyway*, so why simplify them even more? They should try to become a little more complex—if they can!

Fabian remembered how his first-year college class had gone to a cabin in early fall. There, they ate, drank, gambled, and danced from morning till night on both Saturday and Sunday, and started walking to the train stop around dawn on Monday morning so they'd make it to their first lecture. One boy had sat quietly by himself the entire time, observing wide-eyed what was happening. He had grown up in a village, was the son of elderly parents, and had seen very little of life, so the sordid and erotic atmosphere that takes hold on such nights was probably too unfamiliar for him to enjoy. But by the time they were on their way to catch the train, he was already considerably drunk. And so, he hopped along the railroad ties, his white-blond bangs fluttering in the breeze; his wide, plain, honest, freckled country-boy face glowing like a young and healthy god. Occasionally, he would cup his hands around his mouth and hoot loudly, making the whole forest echo back. Birds were chirping and the sun was starting to rise. Fabian was no less drunk than the boy (even more so, rather), but he couldn't imagine feeling such freedom and naturalness, not anything anywhere *near* it, even if he were to have drunk ten times as much. The boy's utter immersion in nature astounded him. Later, Fabian mused that the boy must certainly know the language of the birds and the beasts; must feed the boars and the bears from the palm of his hand. From then on, whenever he ended up in the country, he felt that people there expected the very same kind of behavior from him: that he should hoot, do cartwheels, drawl, and speak without using loanwords (and where possible, abandon articulation entirely, pointing to his mouth, shrugging, or gesturing toward his crotch instead); that he should greet the morning in a jovial mood and not lie around in bed half the day; that he should eat a lot, and consume simple but healthy foods. Fabian almost never smoked in the country. He didn't need to. He didn't even *feel* the need to, because a city slicker smoking doesn't fit with the country landscape. How ridiculous the slender white Marlboros, Kents, or even Silvas looked against the majestic scenery of Haanja, on its undulating curves, standing on a romantic hilltop in the evening, your chest swelling, and your mind filled with thoughts of rebellion. But even less fitting was a bottle of champagne in a meadow or on a barren limestone plain; liqueur in a hayloft or beside a bale of hay. So, it was just about the same with drinking. The fact that country folk themselves did both the former and the latter didn't count. They were *them*. To them, it was all natural. The men passing a bottle around in front of the village store never wiped the mouth of the bottle clean with the side of their hand. And just this morning, when Fabian had wanted to make a call, an obese old woman had been using the payphone booth before him, and when his turn finally came, he saw that the earpiece was damp from the old woman's sweaty ear. Fabian had wiped it clean with his sleeve, and on top of that, he held the receiver away from his ear, so his friend on the other end of the line finally shouted: "Can't you hear me?" Consequently, when a guy like him boozes in a village, it's equivalent to driving to your teetotalling, respectable childhood home on your parents' silver wedding anniversary with some random floozy in tow, or masturbating during the national anthem.

In the country, one melted into his environment; was at one with his surrounds. It was unthinkable to be two entities; there was no alternative. In the country, people behaved calmly, with dignity; they didn't struggle or squirm, or make long and complicated life-plans like in the city. In the country, a person lives a day and says thank you for it; lives his or her little lifetime to the end, and even then doesn't let their feathers get ruffled. In the city, everything goes differently. When Fabian entered social life four or five years earlier, he thought he saw devil-may-care types living on a grand scale everywhere; an elegant indifference about the moment to come. Bohemianism still seemed enchanting and romantic to him back then. Yet soon enough, he learned to discern something much more intriguing beneath the mask of carefreeness. It was all bluff, and each and every person had a great fear of death. Some secretly went jogging, some played handball regularly, some popped pills. And overall—if you left health out of it as well, then *everyone* ensured a future for him- or herself; a few without keeping it secret, but most of them inconspicuously, *comme il faut*. Some quietly wrote dissertations, some saved up money, some became Communist Party members. Some went to church on occasion—who knows what awaits you after death. In any case, not a bad choice! Some had children. Maybe *they'll* come in handy some day; maybe you can even live on in their blood!

Of course, Fabian privately acknowledged that his super-urbanist attitude was a façade to some extent. He certainly didn't scorn pastoral life as much as he pretended to with others. Nor was he disgusted by fruits, berries, or mushrooms (organic matter in *general*), as he loved to claim during his exaltation of refined goods. (He had even gone fishing a couple of times.) It was all a conscious whetting of himself; the soul's challenge to the nature that had borne him; a son's war against his *Urvater[1]*. *Likewise, it was to throw down the gauntlet to a public opinion that preferred the latter. (Why did Voltaire passionately protest against the collapse of the countryside?* was Fabian's favorite argument for the curious crowd that often surrounded him—listeners upon whom he unleashed his thoughts with flippant superiority like stones rolling down the face of Mount Olympus.) The drowsy femininity of a midsummer midday, an elegy about golden leaves on autumn trees, a frigid snow queen imagined upon a wintry expanse, and ultimately also spring as the saddest time of the year, when the "Underground Man" nesting within Fabian perceives the painful contrast of how far his inner world is from the renaissance of nature—*that* intrigued him. Hamsters and butterflies—in addition to the privileged status of flowers, crystals, and seashells (and quite a few other things in nature)—*were* good enough. And yet, yet—he remembered very clearly how, having spent an entire week at a friend's summer cabin, tanning for days on end to the point that his consciousness narrowed, he returned to the city, unlocked his complex system of door locks (Swiss, Finnish, and a padlock) with multiple keys, and lost himself in peeking at passersby through the peephole for ten minutes. While vacationing, he had dropped his glasses on an anthill and didn't dare try fishing them out of the swarm.

---

1   Forefather (German)

Fabian's eyes had adjusted quickly, and before long he was even able to distinguish solitary birches in a copse in the distance, and individual cows in the kolkhoz's herd. Yet what was the joy of his sight being restored next to the happiness of being able to spy on fellow citizens while remaining unnoticed himself! The "eye" in the door was a wonder of civilization; no less than the satellite and, in any case, much more important. All we can do is wait for someone, some national hero, to invent an "ear" and a "hand" for doors as well. (Several times upon hearing the doorbell ring, Fabian had crept up to the door in his socks, peeked at the distorted shape of the caller through the tiny opening, and then retreated just as quietly, because he hadn't felt like engaging in social niceties at that moment. He had exercised his free will. It was *his* choice whether he wanted a guest in his home or not. Absolute freedom. The city air liberates— our ancestors already knew that fact. You can do anything in a city, even exact revenge unpunished. When he was jostled by a crowd of mindless passengers in the bus or someone cut in line in front of him at the store and wasn't rebuked for it, then Fabian would burn through more electricity than he needed at home and flush the toilet a number of times unnecessarily. That was his revenge on society for its indifference.) And when he discovered also that his battery-powered desk clock was still ticking, he turned downright emotional. How much *better* that little timepiece was than an ordinary wall clock with its pendulum! A country clock can stop ticking—that's no big deal; the change of the seasons and night and day is enough in the countryside, and some times of the year, you can use the sun for determining the hour. In the city, the electric motor purrs on, as if to prove that nothing falls apart there when you leave.

Loving the city properly is a very complicated task. It's not worth seeking what you *can't* be here. You don't have to love what is marginal. Fabian had a girlfriend one time, a passionate tree hugger from the backwoods, who despised big cities with all her might, delivering incredibly clichéd justifications for doing so, such as the impossibility of maintaining your own personality, the absent calming effect of greenery, and people's indifference and heartlessness. But since she loved Fabian deeply, his attempts to change her mind appeared to bear fruit, and six months later, the young woman claimed outright to *love* the city. Fabian was overjoyed to hear it. Only some time later did he ask the girl what she specifically liked about the city. The girl started to describe how beautiful and full of shade the city's parks are, noting that you can feed the squirrels there; how incredible it is to approach the sleeping city at dawn from a distance, at the hour when the churches' golden cupolas are gleaming in the strengthening sunlight; how birds sing their songs in the copses of the garden suburbs; how you can gather champignons from the green squares in the new residential neighborhoods. Fabian didn't allow her to say any more.

Nevertheless, there are external similarities between the love of urban life and rural life. For example, Fabian would often go on strolls around the city, just as a fan of nature might wander across meadows or go and enjoy ancient river valleys. He would tirelessly and systematically comb through entire blocks, and although he didn't keep count, he definitely had some decent mileage under his belt. In the end, he knew the streets even better than taxi drivers did. He had determined his favorite side streets, which he would miss and sometimes travel a much longer distance to see, even coming from the city center. He found ever more confirmation of his long-held intuition that the city's street names are governed by order; as if a huge, peculiar configuration of dominoes had been set up there. Ash, Birch, and Oak streets ran close to one another, while another location held Tuglas, Koidula, and Eino Leino streets in store (named after prominent writers). When Weasel, Polecat, and Badger were already close at hand, you could discover Coypu or even Mink after searching carefully. If an additional street were to be drawn between Sickle and Hammer, reducing the hectarage of the plots that fell between them, then that new street could be named Blacksmith or Vises. Accordance with these rules was almost absolute. For example, Hedgehog and Belinsky, or Mole and Schopenhauer *never* ended up intersecting.

Fabian was well acquainted with the Old Town's complex system of closed courtyards, where he staged chases or pursuits in his mind, and was confident that no one could capture him. Next, he planned to take on the roofs, which in certain locations stood so close to one another that it appeared as if you could get quite far along them. He knew a lot about the city in general, committing everything to memory on his raids, just as a hiker remembers the freshwater springs, primeval riverbeds, and stumps. Fabian knew which hallway was decorated with a rare ceiling ornament; on what street corner a bourgeois secret-police officer murdered a communist revolutionary by treacherously shooting him in the back; in which building the Russian Emperor's mother-in-law stayed one night on her way to somewhere; where art-nouveau elements could be found; where the religious fellowships were located; where the medical dispensaries and the secondhand shops were situated; and finally, where the cafés were—those true citadels of urban life. *You* know what makes a desert beautiful. But a slum? Probably the little café that you come across on random wanderings! Fabian knew all the cafés. As soon as he moved to Tallinn, he picked up a phone book and looked up every last café, bar, and pub. By now, he had sat and observed the public in each and every one of them, enough to be able to recite in his sleep where the writers convened, where the brokers went, where German-occupation-era broads reminisced about their glory days, where lustful old men go to snack on their daily cream pies, or in which backrooms of run-down wooden houses and gazebos men met their lovers.

Fabian's mood was improving with every street he traversed. Before he knew it, he was pretty much at his destination. Separating him from the pub was just a negligible patch of greenery. Under the trees and on the benches rested pretty young mothers wearing jeans and mohair jumpers, whiling away time in the weakening August sunshine. They were chatting, smoking, and sometimes leisurely rolling their extremely elegant, brightly colored strollers back and forth whenever the racket coming from them swelled to inhuman levels. Playing before them in a sandbox were small children, who by their very existence caused Fabian to recall one of the most famous nostalgic sighs of our time: we all come from our childhoods—from our childhoods, like from some far-off city.

FABIAN THE STUDENT

FABIAN SLEPT IN even later than usual that morning. When he grudgingly pushed himself up to a sitting position on the edge of his bed at nearly noon (after having woken up several times earlier), opened and closed his dry mouth thirstily, and remained there staring at nothing, it was still so dim in the room that he had to turn on the light right away. It was fall once again, and the thermometer showed a mere ten degrees Celsius indoors, though that certainly could not be right. The thermometer had been lying for some time now. The clock was running slow, his electric razor chafed his neck, and the fuses blew constantly, so he couldn't watch television and use the electric blanket at the same time. Fabian was reminded of his first mother-in-law's words: "A house needs a *man*." I don't know how to do anything, Fabian thought miserably.

Consciousness gradually returned to him, and some kind of boundary formed between the cheerlessness of dreams and the true-to-life events of the previous night. Still, it was better to leave analysis of his personal shortcomings for later—let worry wait till evening. Fabian had long ago figured out that the farther away you push your cares, the longer you can be carefree. He took the key from its hook on the wall and went outside to see whether the postman had been. It was banal. Mornings began with banality. But he reassured himself: sometimes, every cynic would like the morning mail to be an event and to bring something new and uplifting. If anything were to come at all anymore, then why not by post? What was the mail system for if not for that?

Other times, Fabian even felt as if his entire life thus far had merely been a disguised preparation for rising to some higher level, without him knowing for certain what was meant by "higher"—whether in terms of career, transcendence, wealth, or great passion. Fabian certainly knew that such a feeling indicated weakness, just like buying lottery tickets, but from time to time (this morning, for example), he wanted, for a moment, to forego the path of the strong and allow weakness to overpower him. On occasion, anticipation could offer amusement just like any sort of banality: like idleness, like commercial culture (on the waves of which it was so pleasant to be rocked), like reading a fashion magazine, with a dumb hit song playing in his head, holding a sweet red sherry in his hand, and a dumb—who?—at his side. But this for only a moment. Just a few days ago, Fabian had been knocking discs around a *koroona*[2] *table for three hours. What a mindless game. A banal game. But he derived pleasure from it. Afterward, he read Fichte's letters to Kant; only, he felt no pleasure from it. Instead, they put him to sleep. And yesterday, he observed— for close to a half an hour, like a snot-nosed kid—an excavator doing its job. He watched how deep it dug. Now, he was analyzing himself to see if it was possible to descend even deeper. It is*, almost certainly. What *had* that rock-and-roller friend, Schasmin, said? "Let's drive out to my cabin for a couple of days, forage for mushrooms, walk along the beach, look for birds' nests, heat up the sauna, light a bonfire, and hit on village girls till dawn. You won't have to think about anything complex," (for some reason, Schasmin thought Fabian was still thinking complexly), "you won't have to exert yourself and be on your guard all the time. No one will be coveting your social position, nor will there be anybody to win over with your wisecracks; village chicks don't get them. Let yourself relax, forget your foreign vocabulary, be *yourself,* allow life to flow through you."

That time, Fabian had stared intently at Schasmin for a long

---

2   A game closely related to pocket billiards.

while and announced that he *certainly* wouldn't go buddying up with a guy the likes of him. But now, it seemed even *that* wouldn't be impossible. If not on the prowl, then in any event to a cabin. He wanted something great and simple. Today, he would like something that brought about a turn; that would change fate or at least give him the strength to keep living. He'd like to write on today's page of the book of life in big, handsome letters; or if he wasn't permitted that, then in any case to write without inkblots. Fabian remembered unhappily that he still hadn't written himself into the building register yet, even though he'd been living there for a month and a half already. Interaction with the building administration was just more than he could handle. No doubt they would track him down themselves one of these days; *they* don't let things slide.

There was only a thin evening newspaper poking out of the mailbox attached to the gate—the only publication that Fabian still subscribed to out of routine, since he read others (the obituaries, the sports items—those were something *concrete*, at least) in passing at work in order to force himself to hang around there, if only for fifteen minutes a day. Of course, on some out-of-the-way street in a slum with a bad reputation, in the city's dark-blooded vein—a place people who were looking to change apartments indicated in their classified ads as "anywhere but there," it didn't pay to wait for the delivery of an invitation to speak in Heidelberg. He hadn't even been invited to attend a summer festival in a long time. What had happened to the summons from dark forces to consecrate a Thursday night? Where were the poltergeists and the faerie-like spirits, the *aos sí*? His flirtation with them was long over. In the meantime, Fabian had tried to learn how to play chess and take the devils seriously, but too much interest had to be feigned for both the former and the latter; too much pointless overexertion. To hell with them. Forces of darkness—they are our yesterday. Far worse was the fact that the mailbox didn't hold any money orders for larger amounts or any fan mail; no court summons or ball invitations, formal letters of congratulation or anonymous threats. *Those* are stable, objective reality. Perceptible. Truth. Practice. The world hadn't run out of money, and even if it had, then in the worst case, at least a counterfeit money order could arrive. The same went for fan mail: no doubt they had transferred their admiration to someone else. Courts are carrying out their plans, the season for balls and receptions had certainly begun, and there was enough honor and threats to go around—only *he* had been left out of the game.

But why? For how much longer? When will true life truly *begin*, then? Fabian wondered in panic in the bathroom doorway, a towel shipped from Singapore wrapped around his waist.

When he picked up the ne wspaper again, an envelope fluttered gracefully to the floor from between its pages. A solitary rowboat and white swans floated on an artistic sea drawn above the zip code, and the sender's address was missing, just like the rower. Every letter is an opportunity; thus, Fabian donned his bathrobe, and rushed over to the desk, where he impatiently tackled his quarry. Looking at it again from front to back, he tore the side off deftly and neatly, and plucked out its prized contents.

"Fabian, old pal, we're getting together again . . ." it read, typed through who knows how many duplicate pages at once, so that in some places the letters were rather faint, making it hard to understand whether the word should read "*saame*" or "*joome*"[3]. Although no one was watching, Fabian wrinkled his nose for a while, smirked ironically, and even raised his eyebrows for a brief moment due to the unpleasant feeling. This here was not Heidelberg or Oxford, and not even a summer festival. The form of address spoke for itself. In Fabian's opinion, "old pal" belonged to the lexicon of the kind of social element that

---

3   "get" or "drink" (Estonian)

would get someone's attention with a whistle on the street: first sticking his fingers in his mouth, afterward slapping high-fives. The kind of people who eat with their mouths open, and who leave greasy splotches when kissing someone's hand. When someone points it out to them, they say "par-*don*" and laugh, showing their frothing gums. And after that, they start getting too touchy. And if angered, they'll whack you in the middle of the night (or whatever people say). These expressions and images caused Fabian almost physical pain. There should be absolutely no interaction with those kinds of people without the utmost need to do so. May a thousand razors chafe your neck, may all the clocks run slow, say a mother-in-law what she might.

It was a crummy invitation. Although, judging an event merely by the paper requesting your presence was questionable. The money order he had been longing for wouldn't be all that much more imaginative either, but "one hundred rubles" sounded somehow better.

The prospect of going on a bender again frightened Fabian. "Participation fee: ten rubles. Don't disappoint your old classmates!" was written on the invitation. Yet, rationality told Fabian that this momentary revulsion was probably caused by the profusion of orgies he'd experienced recently. That's how it goes. Before Buddha abandoned his castle for the eternal meagerness of the wide world, he had spent time, to the point of disgust, with forty dancers. Such was the case now: what does a hangover know about bottle cramps? Is the answer blowing in the wind? That night, he had gotten back from an incredible reception following a lavish funeral, which toward the end resembled more of a pagan Midsummer's Eve bonfire. Now, the undersides of his fingernails were as dirty as they always were after an ordinary binge; the sacral circumstances didn't count one bit for physiology. Strange—the undersides of his fingernails were always dirty after heavy drinking. But even stranger was the fact that the smudges wouldn't disappear even if he took a couple of days off drinking afterward. He would have to find his tools and pry the way open. This obligation was becoming ever more burdensome for Fabian. For quite some time now, he couldn't be bothered polishing his nails with a piece of chamois leather like he used to, and had swapped a nail file for scissors ages ago. Now, he simply took care not to look too much like a predator.

His clothes reeked and his own breath made him turn his head away. He wouldn't be able to kiss anyone today. As if those opportunities ever rained down on him! Temptations would be cancelled for today. Fabian couldn't stand kissing; he hadn't been able to for a long time. In any case, not on the lips. He always felt weird then. Why? A refined man wants to know everything, and observes himself in corresponding situations. Fabian realized that when he was kissing, he imagined all the things that are done with mouths—what passes through them. Food, for example. But eating, if one doesn't happen to do it very nicely, *is* a little vulgar.

Yet, breath changes just like the direction of the wind. What's more, the reunion was in the distant future. Fabian sensed instinctively that new needs could manifest over that time. He knew himself.

Moreover, his conscience was starting to trouble him. While he could otherwise stand to have his share of vodka every three days, the one time that he should drink for a cause and from good intentions, when the distant ringing of the school bell calls him to the playgrounds of his pubescent years, he fails to answer it, using the hypocritical excuse of abstinence. Why was he refusing to clink glasses with an old schoolmarm? It wouldn't be good form. He was behaving like a gigolo who, exhausted from activities elsewhere, can't be bothered to pull himself together and sleep with his legal wife; who is like a heartless brute; a discourteous dude who hasn't even heard of what "keep smiling" means.

Why *should* he go? He had no dear memories of school. He didn't associate it with his early development. Preschool, school, college—in hindsight, it all melted into one, flowed as a homogeneous stream in his memory, like the famous last moments of someone drowning or being hanged, which stretched out into an eternity. How is it for the executioner? Did the rest of the hanging victim or the drowning victim's life materialize before him?

On the one hand, Fabian's gut feeling was that not going would be better as such things were not for him. A man must know where he belongs so as not to become the one who ruins the game. A cheater will be forgiven, but the kind of man who doesn't participate at all, who jeers from the sidelines—people treat a man like that harshly. One must be aware of where his upper and lower limits of tolerance run. If you start feeling odd in a restaurant, then go to a train station buffet and gorge on the entire display case if you care to. If you don't love banter, if you ask someone "what did you really mean by that?" after each and every elegant statement blurted out, if you ask "what's so funny?", then go pick your nose and memorize the daily news from a newspaper—you'll find *more* than enough clarity there!

Fabian possessed his own peculiarities: he didn't want to go to sauna parties as he abhorred slippery masculine frames; hikes in the woods to gather mushrooms and berries drove him crazy with boredom at first, but later even made his nerves curl; he was averse to weddings, where guests were required to chop dolls in half with an axe and participate in other Estonian folk traditions; the same went for theater performances where the audience wasn't allowed to enjoy itself in the dark in peace, but was instead buffeted by attempts to be dragged into the action at any cost. He cared just as little for alumni reunions. But, on the other hand, there was a lot that he couldn't be bothered to do or that he didn't like to do. A journey into the past, in the

midst of fossils in the teachers' lounge, into that restricted area
that to this very day was still a mystery to him, was something
entirely different from taking out the recycling, for instance.
You can't decide it in a single go. Although Fabian had let his
hand that was holding the letter drop theatrically into his lap,
it was purely for show. He should give consideration to the
matter. Instead of shaving in front of the mirror, tidying up his
look, ignoring the dry roof of his mouth, and vigorously getting
down to work (or, on the contrary—pouring himself a hair of
the dog), Fabian sprawled unaesthetically on the corner of the
sofa, resting his bristly chin in his palm.

Yesterday, some young pup had sidled up to him and shown
him a magazine clipping in which a pale man was pleasuring
himself in front of a pretty picture. The kid had wanted a ruble
for the porn. Now, Fabian started to reminisce about his old
class, whom he had been with for eleven years in a row, all the
while secretly hoping to become just the slightest bit emotional;
to wind himself up just a little. What could he really remember
about all of it?

The young teacher's lush lips read aloud a poem in front of
the class. She's a ribbon gymnast! the sixth-grade boys would
whisper ambiguously, one hand in their pants pockets. In retrospect, Fabian realized that the young teacher had actually been
very charismatic, but back then, they had called her a witch. She
lacked the patience for her job and would scream herself ugly
at them. They had a class gathering one evening. She brought
her husband along. The man was dignified, technocratic, and
spilled his glass of juice. Why did she bring him along? One
other teacher brought her two small children everywhere she
went. She had no one else with whom to leave them. Did the
pretty teacher not have anyone with whom she could leave her
husband? Now, a dozen years later, Fabian had spotted them
at the theater. The teacher didn't recognize him, of course. She

herself had gotten much older—there were wrinkles on her fore-head, tiny red pimples under her lower lip, loose skin on her neck. But her husband still looked exemplary, clapping lazily, coolly supercilious while his wife bashed her hands together almost hysterically. That poor teacher!

What else could he remember? Someone's chalk-dusted hand solving an equation on the chalkboard. How sickly sweet the cafeteria smelled. And what were the floors coated with there—some kind of a moist film? His revulsion toward locker rooms originated back then—intense scrutiny revealed spores growing there. Loud music playing in the dim assembly hall; tightly clinging couples, but the teachers looking the other way—they feel somewhat unsure of themselves. What's being done on the dance floor is not exactly moral when taken one way, but on the other hand, they lack instructions for how to punish the guilty parties, so better to pretend not to notice anything.

Sometimes on rare occasions, when he saw someone's more or less familiar face and nodded just in case, he tried to remember afterward—did it belong to a boy from the eighth grade, a classmate who flunked after their first finals, an activist from the Palace of the Pioneers, or rather some distant relative? What had become of their Class 11B? Dunno, dunno. A year after graduation, Fabian would hear rumors here and there about who had continued studying (even knowing what and where); some had certainly headed here to Tallinn as well, but the capital was a big city and Fabian couldn't say anything for sure. How were they doing? From time to time, familiar names *would* pop up in the newspaper or be read out on the radio, but how many "Sepps," "Tamms," and "Rebanes" were there in Estonia? Even "Schmidts" and "Bachs" were plentiful. How could one be certain that they were *them*?

Fabian suddenly recalled that he did know precisely the fate of one young girl. She died of a lung infection two years after finishing secondary school. Fabian had read her obituary in the paper at the time. The first feeling he had when seeing a familiar name bordered in black was the fear that someone might come wanting wreath-money from *him*, too. He'd been quite poor back then. The mailman brought money orders even less frequently than now. Later, they said that their teacher had given a speech at the funeral. Who knows what she said. No doubt she strove to find an excuse for herself. Perhaps she was ashamed of still being alive. There really has to be *some* system up and running. It's pure perversity when a daughter dies before her father, a chick before the chicken, a student before the teacher.

The whole situation gave Fabian the chills. He had felt a dull prick in his own heart one time. The stab of pain came one night when he drunkenly ran from a cabin to the city. Seven kilometers. He no longer remembered whether he was running from or to someone. Probably the latter, because one other show of exertion soon followed the run. The prick in his heart had come a couple of hours later that night, toward morning. He seemed to hear the ringing of a bell at the same moment, but couldn't be sure of it. It's possible that it was just a phantom sound, since he'd read about a large number of cases in which a dull ache in one's chest was followed specifically by hallucinating the ringing of a bell. Maybe it had been the exact opposite: he *did* hear a real ringing noise, and merely imagined that heart trouble had preceded it. That was then. But everything changes, everything grows louder, daylight becomes ever brighter. One fine night when someone makes a racket on the square or a siren starts screeching—doesn't it feel as if he *is* dead, then?

The next day, Fabian had lounged around on the couch at home, and sank into a depression. His heart had sabotaged him at the most inappropriate moment. It was the last day to get a copy of *Varamu*, the monthly classic novel series. But Fabian would not risk leaving home. And what's more—he'd been invited to a wedding that evening; an old friend of his was taking a husband. Why should he be a no-show at a nice little opportunity for masochism? But instead of a sharp thrill, he checked his pulse. One should worry about his health, and Fabian feared the very worst. He thought about death, naturally. What kind of an educated person wouldn't, at least every once in a while? Now and then, more or less. He lounged around and read *The Blue Bird*. Maeterlinck's heaven, where little boys and girls wait in line to be sent to their fathers and mothers on Earth, formed a symmetrical vision in Fabian's mind: Death receiving wrinkled elderly people in his yard. Fabian fell asleep, but the vision continued in his dream: the yard suddenly bore a strong resemblance to a paper recycling drop-off. A *Varamu* edition or a *Leatherstocking Tales* novel was provided to every old person.

Death itself sent its greetings. Fabian was sprawled out with friends in the plush purple side room of a café. Death walked up to them and scolded him: "Pull in your horns, life!" Fabian woke up and fell deep into thought. He felt as if he'd been put on a list somewhere. The dull prick actually meant that an interest in his soul had been felt for the first time. Now, yet another living soul could be sure that he hadn't been overlooked. It would take more time: pale, translucent fingers will lift your file from one stack to another on numerous desks; bluish lips on a bloodless face will repeat your name; but the procession can already be seen at the opposite end of a very long street—a wonderful funeral is in reach. It's possible that your mother-in-law herself will toss three handfuls of dirt into your grave, and that the bell toller will be your own paternal uncle.

Fine, Fabian reasoned, a few of my pals definitely have to be alive. At least the one who came up with the idea of convening the others, but likely all the rest of them, too. He tugged open a desk drawer and removed a leather box, in the bottom of which were yellow-blotched school report cards; certificates of achievement; photographs with sentimental dedications (received from boys, by the way, which confirms the observation that pre-pubescent love is genderless); sports certificates (for types that are only practiced in school, such as dodgeball); a heap of souvenirs and relics, including a perfumed round stone given to him by a girl who had hoped it would bring him luck, and which Fabian used to use as a paperweight when he was airing out the room; and a love letter with a sprig of wild thyme attached to the margin with medical tape.

Fabian engrossed himself in the pictures, reading the names on the back that had been contorted into "signatures" carefully practiced at home. Sometimes, the same name had been written in different styles on the back of a photo and on a class picture, while others had written both their name and a signature, as if they *were* two different things.

The once familiar faces now seemed hopelessly strange. What *was* it? Fabian wondered, not being able to wrap his mind around it at first. Why did they suddenly seem so bizarre? It's certainly clear that every person feels a little strange upon seeing him- or herself and others when they were young. It's completely natural. Still, there was some additional oddity to those pictures. Only then did he realize what it was exactly: they differed from his peers today not simply physically, but *in principle*. In terms of atmosphere, style, aura, coloration, timbre—however you want to put it. To the same extent that the photos of Fabian's class lined up on the school steps were dissimilar from Fabian's father's old gymnasium pictures, both were unlike the colorful spring photos of today's brats. Photographs are unique in every era—the difference doesn't depend on technology alone, something is different in all of them, but *what*? The epochal mystery is indeed manifested on paper, but in the language of some other mystery. Yet does that mean the present moment is easier to express in words than the preceding moments? All you can do is repeat that every era deserves its photos.

No doubt the spirit of the age is hidden behind it, Fabian mused. He set himself to tracing changes in the few individuals who had stayed in the same class as him since the beginning, to discover in their faces the societal transition over the course of eleven school winters, but soon grew bored. The only difference he discovered in the two boys he selected as test subjects manifested in the acne that appeared on their smooth faces in eighth grade, remained there during the following year as well, and then unexpectedly vanished. Fabian now drew his own conclusions from this kind of a metamorphosis, which he definitely would not have been able to come up with back then. In any case, society didn't have all that much to do with that sort of cosmetic transformation.

Who might he hope t o meet in Tartu in a couple of weeks? Everyone. All of them might randomly be in the mood to attend. Just as he might. Yet it was more likely that he would primarily find two types of people at the reunion—the simpleminded and the masochists. Both would hope to gain one thing or another from the alumni night. For the first type, there would be the joy of finding one another again; the delight of reunion. They would take the occasion as a natural happening, just like everything else in the world. A get-together with former classmates—that's just *fantastic*, that's how it should *be*, people have *always* been overjoyed by those. Old friends reunited once again—people sing about that in songs and draw the scenes on wine labels. Let *us* sing and dance now, too. At the first few reunions, the participants' behavior in their old school building is just like at ordinary parties. And indeed—what difference *is* there? But the older they become, newer, stranger trends emerge in their behavior; the more the reunion turns into theater.

Here, Fabian was reminded of a class taught long ago by an unpleasant male student teacher. In Fabian's mind, all student teachers could be divided into two groups: the females were unhappy and the men were unpleasant. In this particular case, he had been irritated by the man's imprecise diction, broad shoulders, and habit of cracking lame adult jokes to the girls in the class. Fabian didn't like male teachers at all except for older ones, at least fifty years old. Fabian could understand their mental world and respected them. It was harder to take the younger ones seriously, even though he knew that schools were sorely in need of men. Why had they chosen a field that brought neither fortune nor fame? There were two possibilities. Of course, it wasn't out of the question that surviving within them was the spirit of the national awakening; the "salt of the earth" mentality; guiding principles and fatherland. However, there also existed a much more banal and likely reason: that radio and television, newspapers and publications, institutes and all kinds of other better-quality companies simply didn't want them because they lacked proficiency. The student teacher had asked Fabian something, but he dodged the question (he lacked his own viewpoints even then), and in order to draw attention to himself (he was already vain back then), Fabian asked in turn how he *could* answer openly when a bald, elderly inspector who was supposed to evaluate the student teacher's instruction was hunched over on a bench in the back of the room. The student teacher then enjoyed perhaps the one and only rosy second of his life, and repeated Fabian's question loudly, addressing the inspector. This is called "creating teaching methods from the materials at hand." The inspector turned watery-eyed and started to reminisce about his own old class's regular five-year reunions. The previous year, only seven of them had gathered at their nineteenth-century village school in South Estonia. Seven—all who were alive, as the others were already below ground; only one lived far away in Australia. "We sat down on those very same benches and became kids once again for a moment," the inspector said, wiping his eyes from under his glasses. He spoke for fifteen minutes, until the bell sounded. Then, he picked up his binder from the bench, slowly made his way up to the teacher's desk with the gait of an old man, took the student teacher gently by the elbow, and led him away. Doubtless the old inspector, who had held his job throughout all kinds of eras, wanted to be a father figure to the young man at that moment. Doubtless he had gotten the impression that the student teacher was a master at making the strings of children's souls sing. In any case, the teacher earned the highest possible score from him. Was praised. Maybe made a career for himself to boot, thanks to that instance. Maybe his salary is higher than mine right now, Fabian thought crossly. Fabian *himself* had been the one who inadvertently played such a brilliant opportunity into that doofus's hands.

The proper old inspector might have envisioned everything in a very lovely, outright Apollonian form. But reality is something else—the picture he paints distorts into a rather revolting carnival that replays itself according to the same scenario. Fabian's classmates will arrive and want to turn into kids again, too. They'll come and sit on the school benches, pretend to be in physics class, and reminisce about how instead of calculating torque, they would use a pocket mirror to flash sunlight into the eyes of the student answering questions at the chalkboard, and shoot spitballs at him. About how they would copy answers from the "teacher's pet" and band together to beat up the weakest classmate. Afterward, they would run across the benches, throw the chalkboard rag at one another, go to the restroom to smoke cigarettes *in secret* and marvel at their own cleverness, and come up with other uninspired, anachronistic jokes, all the while slapping each other on the thighs and sighing—"Right, boys?" and "Huh, girls?"

For what would they really have to talk about? They had all long since belonged to different environments; their roots were in different soils. If they weren't aware of it before, they would experience it now. Even their lexicons were entirely unalike, just like everything else—the books they read, their sexual habits, and their diets. While they will be overjoyed at first by finding that they have retained something similar and common—something that still dates back to the old days, while their former group spirit will feel like a collective mystery ("Right, boys?!"), before long, they will be cheered even more by recognizing that they are sufficiently different; then, they will be glad that there are dissimilarities—*I'm not like them*. And vice versa. No doubt some refined lady there will be afraid to admit that her husband is a mason. If she only knew how many masons her former girlfriends needed for building chimneys and fireplaces in their new private houses! She would become acquaintance number one in a flash.

Fabian would go and see that some were worse off than others. Not all had made it in life. But some would still be holding out bravely. Some would be left by their husbands, some single mothers. All of the ugly girls would have children. Ugly people always have a plethora of offspring. Perhaps some would gain new courage from that reunion; new motivation to begin once again, to find self-affirmation and faith. And why not? Perhaps those of whom nothing even close to motherhood was expected, already *were* mothers.

Some of the guys would most definitely have a white nylon shirt sticking out from underneath their jacket collar. And when they remove those jackets later in the evening (and they will, without fail), blue wifebeaters will glow beneath the shirts. A couple of prim women will have brought along dark, poorly-cut, home-sewn cloth pants for when they went to sleep on mats on the floor—so that no one would cop a feel under their waistbands. That's how simpleminded joy consecrates its reunion.

There is one other type of person, who has an own axe to grind with the past; entirely different urges turn their thoughts toward school. Even they go to find enjoyment in their own way, but what they enjoy is the sense of personal anguish—this in the form of the memories that are stirred within them by every dusty whitewashed wall, every dark corner, the occasional draft, and the dull shine of a stone stair there in a massive box built in the fifties, which they perceive as a magic castle in retrospect. Like an old rentier (two brick houses downtown back in the day) who, interrupting an official busy at work in the office of a newly founded institution, wanders into the apartment that was seized from him by the new regime—into a room where his silk wallpaper has not yet been torn from the walls and expensive parquet still lines the floor—and sighs surreptitiously, remembering that a mahogany bed once stood in the spot where there is now a fireproof safe. And although the partition walls have been torn down, the former owner recognizes the invisible contours of the bidet where the spittoon now stands. This is the same manner in which many of the former students will search here, between these walls, for their own success, fame, and passions that were once bafflingly lost—things which together make up a life worth living.

Who are those shadows of former times who are uplifted by pure nostalgia? First of all, a certain type of girl whose life has lurched from one extreme to another. The period of innocence lasts until fifth grade, but this period gives rise to monstrous relationships. For a long time, the girl who studied well and participated in volunteer Pioneer activities had been seen as beautiful. And the opposite. It would benefit society if this kind of an assessment of a person endured beyond the fifth grade. Small children *tirelessly* put into practice a principle by which literature and art were guided just a few decades ago: I love the exemplary worker and I disavow the lazybones in manufacturing. In retrospect, those spiritual assessments, the sympathies or antipathies that manifested mainly in eye contact—"who is looking at whom" (Who is eating what? Who

is eating whom?)—seem downright comical. Back then, they
existed as the truth of last resort. It was impossible to look past
them; that is where nostalgia *comes* from. For time passed, and
after one summer, boys gained secret knowledge: the "teacher's
pet" no longer caused them any anxiety, and the attention of
those scamps—their eyes now opened to the flesh—was drawn
instead to the tight blouse and round skirt of a female Pioneer
member; formerly seen as a blemish. How did the subjects
themselves, the diligent and unattractive young girls, understand
these things? Why was, all of a sudden, some girl who got bad
grades, who didn't attend Pioneer meetings or ever even learn
how to tie knots properly, preferred over them, the exemplary
ones? What marks did this abrupt change in market price leave
upon the subconscious of, for example, the girl sitting third
from the right in the second row? Was it equivalent to being
banished from paradise? The past is nice and unattainable;
everything that follows inevitably goes downhill. Somewhere
far away is "the memory of what our soul once saw when it
walked together with God across Heaven and looked down
from above upon what we now call the present, and thus truly
'submerged' into being." Inadvertently, their path had crossed
something bewildering and unsuitable for a practical life—like
a telescope, love, or a genius; something that would disturb the
rest of their life, like a peasant girl's primae noctis. Who knows
what kinds of residual memories formed? How could you not
remember and long for the manor lord's feather mattress!

The subjects themselves are hardly likely to be so closely
conscious of it all, but they will already start packing their bags
today, two weeks before the designated date. Already today,
upon receiving the letter, they will be dazed by fever, they'll rub
their cigarette butt out in the sugar bowl, and crookedly iron
the pleats on their baggy-bottomed black pants.

An identical zeal should be exhibited by the faceless girls
who, by some stroke of fate, became points of interest even later

at school, so as to capitalize on everything they had to offer and thus arouse attention. Fabian remembered that most of his school's ugly female activists went out with one boy or another, and not just to do official business. For many, this probably remained their life's sole requited feeling, taking the form of flirtation four or five times a day between classes. Everything disintegrated after the last bell—the coquetry that had come from status was relinquished together with their social position. Or if the relationship *did* actually last longer, then the end came some other way; for instance, by it turning out that they were different kinds of people, since the boy was interested in Finno-Ugric languages, but the girl had enrolled in the Institute of Oil Chemistry. The boy sobered up and thanked his good fortune.

The souls of young girls like that have to find affirmation by varying those same memories in thousands of different ways for the rest of their lives, compensating for their long years devoid of intimate relationships like the defensive myth about "the groom who booked it for Sweden in '44." Whoever was dumped for forever as a high-school sophomore definitely treasures the wise saying: what you learn young, you've got for the long run.

This endurance of feelings inspires respect in those around you—people with attention deficits are amazed by it, like how a happy-go-lucky soul is secretly jealous of a cretin's bookkeeper-like consistency in miniscule matters; how someone lacking even the slightest sense of music is astounded by an orchestra's machinelike precision. Quite a number of sentimental young men fall in love with elegizing old maids. A great, unclear past experience ennobles one like a fashionable disease. The experience itself becomes ever more important in the eye of its possessor; the person weaves more and more poetry into the story, since it's certainly nice to think that a pretty big fish got off the hook; that the groom didn't hightail it to the neighboring village, but rather across the sea. One can bring history into his own game in this manner; can hold the whirlwinds of time

responsible for a bony chest or bad breath. The subject herself
doesn't understand all that well anymore whether she really *wants*
to experience something or not, since what is an average woman
next to a legend in whom she *herself* has ultimately started to
believe?! Whoever goes to a diner no longer gets the itch for a
milk bar. No—she recalls the restaurant's soft seats, the velvet
variety-show curtains, and the glint of bottles reflecting in the
display case within the dimness of the bar. She commands fate
in order to see those who were present that time. *That* is why
those women tend to flock to an alumni reunion. But their
crooked smiles resemble quite tritely a widow's visit to the grave
of her early departed.

Crazy thoughts can certainly be passing through such
girls' heads. And not only theirs, but the heads of everyone
who underwent a great *Liebe* during their school years. Take
for example those two ponytailed ones from the front row,
wearing ribbed white stockings around their pretty calves, both
famous, fortuneless lovers, who are now anxiously checking
their calendars, calculating all possible days, making red circles
around them with markers, and turning red themselves as well.
Some are *still* hoping for something. Who hasn't seen how old
couples surface at reunions and coo at each other, nose to nose,
in the dimness of the hallway. And not *only* them.

Even devout mothers want to put aside their strict bearing at
least once a year; want to forget the ties that bind them. Then,
neither their status, their morals, nor their code count for anything. They won't necessarily pull anything off that night—it
might happen that they get hammered and play the "get out of
jail with a kiss" game or send ambiguous little notes by "Cupid
mail" at a masquerade—but that doesn't count; on the inside,
they're out on the town. Principle is what is important, and that
principle has a classic ring to it: the readiness is all. Afterward,
they'll transform back into practical little housewives who are

content until the next time, almost a year later. Venues suitable for that one very necessary occasion might include a carnival, a chance overnight at a spa, a training seminar (although a ski camp or a sanitarium will also do in a pinch), but *especially* a school or class reunion. Everything there is far simpler than it is with complete strangers. There isn't the pointless stress of getting something going, and one doesn't have to waste precious time for sinning on the ritual of acquaintance. Former ties materialize seemingly on their own; quite a number of suppressed or entirely forgotten passions reawaken and rage cheerfully onward. Oddly, there is even a moral justification for it. All in all, it *is* our old class; we're among friends, not strangers—we are as we were then. Old couples, although long since married, forget effortlessly upon entering the school that two, four, ten, or even more years have passed in the meantime. Old nicknames reappear, unaided, and expressions once used are put into play. A forgotten catchphrase is the best start for infidelity. Fabian recalled the names they had for subjects in schoolboy slang, and wrinkled up his nose. He'd have to wait and see whether their class treasurer would let him near her if he pulled her close on the dance floor, brushed the hair away from her ear, and whispered suggestively: *alge, chemmy, histo.*

Fabian picked up the leather box, placing it on his lap once again, and rummaged through it until he found what he was looking for, fixing his eyes on the black-and-white picture. Here were those girls—wearing uniform skirts and bows, cosmetics-free and still multivalent. Every one of them still had a marshal's baton under her dress or up her sleeve. Whose baton did they have *now*? Now, they're ready, weighed up, put in place; now, they're "real." Fabian unexpectedly realized that all of those twenty-or-so girls have probably long since become women. Am I *really* worried about that? was the next thought that crossed his mind.

I am indeed, he admitted honestly. To this very day, he was

unable to forgive himself for that triviality having once seemed so important to him; for that whole circus having meant so much. Things had certainly been rough with those girls. It appeared as if the whole world revolved around them. For as far back as Fabian's memory could extend, one of his eyes (and it was certainly the same with the other boys) had always been looking sidelong at girls. And vice versa. Long before any sort of puberty or opposite-sex love, one sex meant a horrifying reality to the other. Proportionately, such tensions took up just as large a part of school time as did mathematics, for example. Did it seem that way purely because of his highly refined intuitions? Even back then, had he subconsciously arrived at an unshakable conviction that was simultaneously neither provable nor disprovable—the conviction that his enjoyment of love is twice as sharp and superb as that of others?

For a moment, Fabian suspected that perhaps he was going too far—that perhaps, the sphere of intimacy was even *more* important than mathematics in his treatment of it. If this were true, then their class should not have disbanded after the graduation party that had been held one summer night, but instead should have entered into a group marriage. On top of that, there is something else even more important than passing-period flirtation. Not all of the class-reunion masochists had steered their love lives onto the reefs during their school years and not all would be attending the event specifically out of nostalgia. There were those who had experienced the pinnacle of their lives during their student years, but had done so in some way other than with affection. That was easy to understand. School is a little world of its own. Like a ship on the sea or a prison camp, where the same relationships and tensions that exist in wider life outside are present on a smaller scale; where there are unique laws, chiefs and subordinates, leaders and the led. Whoever had been the big cheese in school wanted to be it afterward, too. A young pup picks up new tricks easily. But many were invited, few were chosen. Schools number many, while lives—if not one, then fewer than schools, in any case. You can't make it in life as easily. If you could get back to school even for just a *moment*, there'd almost be something left; you'd *feel* a little again, you'd get that old feeling.

And that's why that lanky little boy, who sticks out a half head taller than his companions in the third-grade picture, will try to finagle a business trip from his boss for the given day. He was absent a long time during the second winter of school, was held back, and thanks to having harder fists than the other younger boys, became their indisputable leader. That is, until the others hit growth spurts a couple of classes later and the gap disappeared. Thanks to the chicken pox, there were a couple of years of power that may never come again in the rest of the man's life; years that will no longer be gifted. Everything—the grandeur and authority—is forgotten over time, but the thorn is still lodged in his soul. Everything must be paid for. Those couple of years aren't gifted.

Or take that smooth character right in the center of the picture, at the teacher's right-hand side, who played in a beatnik band, was on the volleyball team, danced, and recorded radio programs. Teachers would trust him with make-up lessons. He was made senior prom king. People predicted that he would have a superb future and a speedy ascent. Yet, there was no word of him in college. Later, when Fabian met with one or another of his college classmates, he found out that people had started to call the boy a "high-school peaker" and, according to general opinion, he had "something missing."

All the head honchos of cohorts and crews, the generals of children's crusades and playgrounds, and the non-portfolio ministers of temporary governments will have come to seek what they had lost. If Fabian arrived at the school that night, he could hope to find standing there before him the Chairman of the Group Council, the Chess Pro, the Valedictorian, the Class

Conscience, the Soul of the Café Club, the Ace, the Girlfriend, and many more. Not *every* small functionary becomes prime minister, not every sports team captain's favorite marries a world champion later. Why did the lucky forerunners' triumph come to a halt? What becomes of key leaders when they fall from their thrones, anyway? Some start to drink, some go kamikaze. In such an instance, what became of the legendary dorm boozers and the jocks; the famous bohemians, whose favor had been an outright honor at one time? Every milieu deserves heroes who surface from its midst. Once highly influential, they simply didn't stick out later; they vanished into oblivion. Life swallowed them.

Fabian constantly caught himself sympathizing with people. At the same time, he scorned them a little. There were two possibilities that interchanged equally for him. At times it seemed that, taken separately, he could be capable of loving every person; he would be prepared to display heartfelt sympathy for them, to help them, even to lend them money. But as a whole, humanity formed a mass—dark, inert, and hostile, with unpleasant characteristics that the individual lacked. In the second possibility, things were the opposite. He sympathized with humanity as a whole. He felt sorry for *man*, as Strindberg's Indra had sighed, treading the Earth as a mortal woman. But upon closer acquaintance, he discovered vacuity and banality in every member of the sympathetic race, which was in complete harmony with bleak existence. Pity was *unnecessary*. This was exactly how he felt today.

He felt sorry for his class as a whole. But he knew that in no way could he do anything about it; could not change a thing. Everything is just as it is. A person can always sympathize with another person. No doubt you can find reason. You can spend your entire life pitying, just as professional wailing women and Samaritans do. Yet, he didn't have the strength to sympathize with *everyone*; could not count the tolling of every funeral bell as his own. When would he live his own life, then? One therefore *shouldn't* let everyone in need come too close. You shouldn't let anyone come close *in general*; otherwise, you might torture yourself to death. Keep your distance, cost what it may. If he were given a certain distance, then he could be capable of loving the whole world. But as that chance won't come, it's better to stand on the edge—just as he was doing here in this class picture, as if wanting to imply that he ended up there by complete chance, from a different dimension; as if he was unable to take something called an eighth grade seriously. And he *was* unable to.

Fabian looked for the magnifying glass in his nightstand, and studied his image intently. He looked nice, young, and unworn in the picture. The skin on his face was almost femininely delicate, a mop of hair lay across his forehead, and he was displaying a dismal expression.

The visage that stared back in the mirror right now wore a wry grimace from endless nights spent staying up and overworking, with bags under its eyes that had turned grayish-yellow from smoking. There was something to be *missed*. Yet, nothing would fully lure him back into the photograph-time. There were too many apprehensions back then, and the impressions from those apprehensions were still too fresh.

He didn't feel a calling back to any time. Although mournful yearning for the past, the desire to spend time in places worthy of memories, to pick up with benevolent skepticism a book that had enthralled him in times of storm and stress—reminiscing like that is occasionally even more important than life itself. However, not a single time he had lived so far was entirely worth repeating. That time still lay ahead. If someone were to say that what's to come *has* come, that his peak is already at hand and his time to shine is gone, he couldn't even bring himself to be angry at such foolishness. Although Fabian had long ago given up moving a single muscle to ensure his future, he believes in it all the more firmly. He believes in the future, full of outwardly dispassionate and self-confident optimism. His optimism appears naive at first. In reality, it is a desperate, last-ditch optimism. For there is no other option. Staying in place right now would be pure suicide. Everything must continue to move on the same upward slope, and it *will*. Inertia is unbelievably strong. Whoever ends up at one end of the tunnel once will get to the other end on his or her own; even if it takes a draft. The rooms in his hotel of life have already been booked.

Most people miss their childhood. Fabian doesn't; he never has. On the contrary, he remembers with certainty that he always wanted to be an adult. And he hasn't been disappointed. He doesn't remember what came before his wish to grow up, and therefore, Fabian would occasionally harbor quite serious doubts—without any poses or audience—that he was really born an infant and went through the natural stages of development; that he was fed from a bottle, washed, and diapered. All of that is so distant from him. It felt as if he was immediately complete, and that he stayed that way. So what that he hadn't been a wunderkind in school; that he had scorned lovely music in favor of Estonian folk tunes and beautiful paintings in favor of uninspired caricatures; that he had seemed duller than he does now. He was *still* already complete then, in a certain sense. He perceived the flow of time differently than the other children did. He *never* became identical to himself in their manner.

He felt not the slightest association with that creature there on the pages of the family album with its average, amateur photographs; impassable black holes fell between. It was impossible that he was only imagining everything, deceiving himself, thinking things up in retrospect and anachronistically projecting himself into his early years. Fabian remembered his desires from that time just as clearly as he did last night's dark cravings. Otherwise, his fantasy wasn't so vivid; even today, creating new worlds was not his strongest suit. But back then, he had possessed quite a precise understanding of what it meant to be an adult; had sensed the great and minor secrets of a man's life. He was as far from naive as could possibly be, because when he grew up, he didn't, in truth, have to be disappointed by anything; didn't undergo any sort of disillusionment. Strangely, he had even imagined the female question quite precisely. He even sensed the female's great and minor secrets.

Fabian grasped from the very beginning that grown-ups hold all the cards. Childhood is a time you sleep through; a period of pre-consciousness. What has he gotten from it? He hadn't even inherited any interesting complexes from that period; complexes from which he could now reap the rewards, because he liked women, men were physically disgusting (he was sometimes even repulsed by himself), and he loved his grandfather slightly more than his mother, but neither one of them all that intensely.

Fabian realized that the keenness he felt from his exceptionality could certainly be reduced, claiming that his desire *wasn't* actually all that original; that almost everyone yearned to grow up when they were a tot (to eat what they want and to not have to go to bed at ten o'clock). And he understood that later, everyone has sighed: time came o'er land and the sea, not half as dear to us would it be[4]. That was just it: Fabian had never shed a tear over his boyhood. Sometimes, rarely, he would have a dream about the time when the gift of a rooster-shaped marzipan candy or the funny face made by a strange man secretly visiting his mother would be enough to intoxicate him. The time when a knocked-over Venetian glass mirror or a

4   From the poem "Kodu" (Home) by Estonian writer Lydia Koidula: *Aeg tuli. Maa ja mere peal / silm mõnda seletas – / ei pool nii armas olnud seal / kui külatänavas!* (Time came. The eye discerned / a number of things o'er land and sea –/ not half as dear was it there / as on the village street!)

puddle on the floor caused primal fear. And upon waking, he would shake his own hand in joy and smile in the dark because he was able to escape "from there." He had his own reckoning with those years. To this very day, he's incapable of forgiving the little boy of whom he is still ashamed, because he let bad grades or notes in his assignment book derail him in grade school. He took idiocy seriously, and can't think about that time calmly. And more likely than not, he won't be able to do so for a long time; until one day, as a senile old man, he forgives his former bullies. Then, nothing will matter.

He wasn't worth a dime back then. No wonder that he didn't like himself as a child. First of all, there had been nothing wunderkindly about him. It is, of course, great to emerge from youth when no miracle has happened yet, because then, you maintain the hope that a miracle might occur at some *other* age. Secondly, Fabian had been deprived of the so richly ascribable supernatural capabilities that come with the tenderness of good older men and women toward children. The myth of childish charms is indeed founded upon those capabilities. Fabian certainly didn't intuitively recognize whether a person was good or bad, and allowed himself to be hoodwinked without much effort. Yet isn't that natural? Why should he in particular, a little boy, have had to discover the war criminal under the mask of a kind older man? Fabian had not "understood everything" as a child and often said foolish things, which the well-meaning people around him should not under any circumstance have taken as allegories. What mundane essays he had written! A dowsing rod in his hands didn't start quivering above a hidden treasure or water vein. He once nearly fell into an open cesspool. Was he even always genuine (that most marveled quality of children)? Sometimes he certainly acted sneaky, sometimes quite nastily; he would be obstinate, tell on others, snivel, wet his pants, and whine for sweets, just like all the other children, which is indeed natural, but hardly praiseworthy.

Now, he is much more genuine. This for a very simple reason: he can't be bothered to lie; doesn't make the effort to pretend. Because, to be quite objective: every lie, every instance of pretending requires effort; it demands ambition. But who's worth that much exertion? The only kind of person for whom it's worth putting force into play is one who somehow sits right with you; upon whom something depends; who might be beneficial or detrimental, or whom you can respect all the same. But how many of these kinds of people are there? They're becoming fewer and fewer. And that's precisely why Fabian customarily says everything frankly and bluntly—no dodging or diplomacy. He probably even has a reputation as a non-conformist; he's someone whom people call "incorruptible." Yet he's no seer like Electra, simply a lazybones who can't be bothered to dodge things or to butter anyone up.

If things carry on this way, he'll become entirely open-minded one day; like a child of nature, whom you can read like an open book—like some kind of a Dersu Uzala. He'll certainly progress. It's not as if he became the way he is now overnight. He pretended all of the time when he was a child. Nothing else. Including during puberty. He remembers details that make his stomach turn, because his memory is especially selective. He mentally records all kinds of vulgarities in order to break into a sweat of angry shame over them ten years later, while lying alone on the couch.

He was often especially reminded of his diary. He'd kept it for four or five years in a row, writing entries in it every day. How many hours were wasted upon it! Perhaps that was the very reason his knowledge of literature was so patchy now. Not a single shred of truth could be found on those pages filled with fine handwriting. To a large degree, he made himself veritably more interesting lying about his nonexistent success, adventures, and intentions. For example, he copied down from a popular magazine that, at the age of thirteen, he had intercourse with a morally degenerate young woman four years his senior, and he was presently afraid as his interest in the opposite sex was starting to dwindle. He fibbed about trying out for the Soviet Union's Olympic team and claimed to have ties to the criminal underworld. Now, he knows why he wrote those things, of course. Although he hid his diary under his mattress, he nevertheless hoped someone would read it, and was delighted by the possibility in his imagination. One time, he took his notebook to school and accidentally "forgot" it in a desk drawer. That day the hall monitor became his favorite girl. Oh, those follies of youth!

Before long, he progressed; he acquired the right outlook on life and feelings of superiority and skepticism. When Fabian was still flirting with his first wife, she initially criticized him for not being natural. Fabian replied that he couldn't be bothered. He knew that if he let himself relax, he would leave a very bizarre and unnatural impression on those around him. And vice versa: if he got ahold of himself, strained himself, then he could also have been the type of man who corresponds to the female perception of naturalness. In order to appear natural, he had to be unnatural. But who will make the effort to do that? Why should he alone do it? If eight out of ten won't take the time to strain themselves and rise to a slightly higher state of mental existence, then why should he have to get ahold of himself as a result of their low level of tolerance? That was how little he cared about his first wife already then.

Things had become difficult with women in general. In a certain sense, he treated them like men. He couldn't bring himself to fabricate anything for women in order to achieve his own goals, even though he knew that was exactly what was expected of him. He knew that women don't believe what men say anyway, and that castles in the sky need to be erected for an entirely different reason: to show that one respects his partner. He knew all of this, but still couldn't be bothered; he said what he wanted straight away, but wanted immediately to acquire what would have followed all on its own in time. For him, women had to be like gypsies, who are visited by boyars wearing beaver-pelt collars, riding on troikas, making merry, drinking bucketloads of champagne, dancing with bears, and then disappearing into the blizzard just as suddenly as they came. No blind man's bluff or postlude.

He had missed out on much in life thanks to laziness. During Fabian's junior year of college, he was offered the opportunity to travel abroad for free. He very nearly got his registration papers in order, even though it posed him unbearable hardships. Only one more signature was needed. The documents were due early the next morning. The assistant dean's office hours were over, and therefore Fabian would have had to call on him at home for the signature that evening. Anyone would have managed the task. But he couldn't be bothered. He serenely failed to show up. Halfway there, he turned back and went to a restaurant instead. He got pretty hammered that night. From then onward, he only traveled within the Soviet Union. His relatives and acquaintances couldn't understand it. One of his cousins, for instance, wanted to travel abroad *all* the time.

Be "abroad" what it may, one could still fathom a craving to go there. With a particular consistency, Fabian despised the kinds of enterprising youth who find romanticism in hitchhiking. If you were to travel at all, then it should always be in a manner insured against all unexpected turns, Fabian believed; exclusively with reserved hotel rooms, round-trip tickets, guides, and acquaintances coming to meet you at your destination. People "thumbing a ride" were enticed by the game of chance; by not knowing where they would lie down for the night. Yet, why travel to another city, or as far as Latvia, in order to experience that feeling when you could get the same here in Estonia, too?

If you were to imagine Fabian sitting on a park bench and a little boy running up to him—the boy being he himself at the age of six—then he would put himself on his lap for barely five minutes, and *that* more for the sake of appearances. It'd be just like with relatives—good form calls for visiting them, but for no longer than a minimum of etiquette requires. For he and the boy would have nothing to talk about; he wouldn't interest himself. He would stick a ruble in his palm and send himself to the cinema or to get ice cream, just so as to get rid of himself faster. Other kids the same age would interest him even less. He wouldn't even give them a ruble. Wunderkinder made him particularly uneasy. An infant who plays chess or bridge—in Fabian's opinion, such children were evil; were an outright aversion; were an abnormality.

Fabian considered those close to him. What sort of a timid, stuttering mamma's boy his friend Mauri might have been as a tot—Mauri, whose current personal charm was rooted specifically in his blunt aggression, his banging of taboos on the head; Mauri, who was already brazenly making out with girls in courtyards and stairways at high school. How could a runt with Lelian's facial features, wearing a sailor's outfit and a green Tyrolean hat upon his straw-blond locks, compare to the man's glittering, lofty intellect? A true kitsch little kid, who constantly begged his mother for a clean handkerchief, and ran after passersby that walked along the round pole fence that bordered the other side of their villa property, his little buckled shoes pounding against the ground, responding to the nice strolling vacationers' questions with dumb silence. And who, upon receiving candy, didn't thank them, but instead darted into the depths of the yard with his quarry. Would anyone have wanted to know Oskar if he weren't the intellectual with fine taste that he had become through intense self-analysis during a period of reconsideration in the 1970s? He was said to have even been quite a dull individual in college. But now, our intellectual life is enhanced by his brilliant interruptions from the left wing of parliament. Everyone becomes interesting in his or her own way. Just like how people used to go crazy.

Or take Nonna, for example—a fetching music teacher with the shadow of a mustache and golden peach fuzz on her shanks, who displayed aesthetic intarsia works at youth exhibitions—could any sensible (insensible) person bring themselves to exchange that kind of a midday-fairy, the exceptional symbiosis of a hetaera and a creative artist, for some brassy young sprite?

May everything exist and come in its own time. Just as there is no glee in imagining *today's* young lovers forty years from now, the pre-identity stage of current friends is not of interest; a time when they did not yet grasp Logos, did not possess reflections, and had no table manners. Fabian was wonderfully aware that he was posing a little, because he didn't feel any kind of active animosity toward children—he had a couple of his own, and got along quite well with kids if you didn't count infants, whose irrational behavior repulsed him. Nevertheless, his principles differed sufficiently from the generally accepted norms.

As a result, he had often mulled over his childhood during honest self-analysis in order to bring clarity to the grounds for such an attitude; however, he hadn't come up with anything. Everything about the environment in which he grew up seemed to be in order. An intelligent, upper-middle-class home, progressive conversations during dinner, guests, classic children's books and boys' magazines, a community swing set on the other side of the street, buddies from his own neighborhood, and forbidden games with the neighbor girls. He had no physical defects, was able to pronounce the letter "s" already by the age of two, and was given a five-ruble allowance by his father every payday.

The numerous conversations with acquaintances, during which he had guided the subject onto corresponding rails while himself remaining smartly silent, had deepened Fabian's uncertainty even more, as he found relatively few solid rules between the supposed reality of his first ten years of life and the halo they had acquired in retrospect. He would personally have exchanged, without hesitation, two or even three years of his own (at least seemingly) fully fledged childhood for each one added now. At the same time, some kids had been belted every other day when they were boys; their first pair of pants were stitched for them at the age of seven, and even those were made of coarse linen; yet now, those men sigh at every possible opportunity: "Oh, Mother, return me my childhood for half an hour; I want to hear your soft lullaby until the middle of the starry night!" Where is the logic here?

Tradition plays something of a part: in the West, the child is always placed before the adult. But that is an external factor. Essentially, it should be about weakness. Estonians' slave blood was speaking here, Fabian decided—a yearning to yield to authority, the enjoyment of inevitability and not being held responsible. There is an *abundance* of those who would like to be a blade of grass, a caterpillar, or a cloud—no matter what, if they could only escape their obligation to be human; if they didn't need to exude activeness, to impose. They reckon: a cat has a great life; it doesn't need to study trigonometry. It isn't proper to really *want* to be a cat, it's not regarded as polite— seeing a profane animal as being ideal! But a child is almost like a person. He or she doesn't have to do anything either, and that's why some people ache for childhood.

Fabian felt a little stiff. He stretched and stood up, then tied closed the flaps of his plush yellow bathrobe, which had fallen open. The cloth was greasy, but Fabian couldn't be bothered to take it to the cleaners. It was rather late. He'd been lounging here on the couch for over half an hour. Half an hour—a few years back, he wouldn't have forgiven himself for such torpor. Half an hour—that's an *extremely* long time. Thirty minutes. All the things you could manage to do during that time! That amount of time shouldn't be frittered away. Someone could pull ahead of you in that thirty minutes. They could read fifty pages more and synthesize the outcome completely differently. They could discover or put into words something half an hour earlier than you do. Fabian absentmindedly touched his jaw. It was coarse. He could see stubble in the mirror. He should shave. But he couldn't be bothered to shave every day. He couldn't even be bothered to wash his face and his hands properly every day. They were going to get dirty, anyway. Just like the undersides of his fingernails. Ten, no—even six years ago, he rinsed his hands a good dozen times a day. He'd kept himself extremely clean and didn't want to touch a single object outside of his home. In his pocket he carried a little bottle of eau de cologne that he would secretly rub into his hands under the table. Now it felt as if there was no point. He was unable to withstand it, anyway. The epic battle that should be waged day after day was beyond his means. I can't do it anymore, Fabian thought. There's an infinite number of germs, anyway; everywhere is full of them and they do as they please. If I survive, then it'll be purely by their grace—that of the almighties. He started to pity himself. The letter disappeared under his desk pad. Doubtless, time would tell what he would decide. He might even *go* to Tartu. It could easily be the case that he would feel a nameless anxiety on the evening of the day marked on the invitation; that his mind would be empty, but fixations would manifest—not a single activity would sit right with him, he would feel like he should in fact *do* something; those people two hundred kilometers away there seem so mundane, of course, but at the same time, a great class patriot would be budding inside of him. Alas, it would be too late— only a chartered plane would save him. Because arriving at a party of drunk, nearly complete strangers after midnight on the last bus—no, thank you.

Things would be much simpler if the opposite were to happen—if he went just in case; for even if something made him so fed up at the last moment and he couldn't be bothered to rattle along on a regional bus to the schoolhouse that was located far from the city center and he dismissed the entire undertaking, then he could always find some way to pass the time in a city the size of Tartu. It'd even be stylish. That way, he could—in a very genteel sense—have "not attended the reunion."

Even so, Tartu had emptied of his acquaintances. A few friends had stayed there after graduation; a few residents, with whom he could stay while on business trips, or where he could go just to let loose. For the most part, they were tied down in Tartu by their in-laws' apartment or a lucrative job. The better part of *those* friends had relocated to Tallinn, or else had lost contact. Yet, the power of habit is strong. Fabian still feels as if something is waiting for him in Tartu, and when he glimpses the first outlying structures from the train window, he is always overcome by lame emotion; his heart swells in his chest and even a small sensation of a vague debt pangs somewhere within him, but not one of a debt *so* great that it should be repaid.

When he walks across Chapel Hill into the city center, he starts visiting the cafés and pubs where he and his group of friends once spent their time and acted out a golden youth. He stops and stands dourly on the threshold of the city's watering holes, his disdainful expression saying, "Where on Earth have I ended up?!" and is amazed when he doesn't find his friends waiting before him, despite the fact that they had dispersed to a different city just the other night. When he finishes his round of the pubs, he will most likely start again from the beginning, as if hoping that someone popped up in the meantime, regardless. In this way, he drifts from one place to the next, and is so drunk by the end of the day that he is completely indifferent to his non-existent friends and to himself.

The faces that would stare back from across the tables would be so alien, like those from the photos he had just put down. It would appear that everything in their lives is different. And in five years' time, one can expect that those who would be rowdy there amid the clouds of smoke would similarly enter from the beam of light streaming through the doorway, and let their gaze flit across the room, but won't have a connection to anyone. And someone before him stood here just like this five years ago, too.

He should scratch the Tartu idea. Sure, he would like to meet up with some of those who were still holding out there, even just to say to their faces one thing or another that was once left unsaid. But what might that be?—absolutely nothing. In spite of this, he would still like to say something to their faces. Some others, on the other hand, should be avoided at all costs. Upon encountering them, he would pull his hat down over his face and cross the street, his chin on his chest. And now that he thinks of it—he has a book that should have been returned to the Tartu Library three years ago. He hadn't even started reading it. In all likelihood, such a rare copy would not end up in his hands a second time.

Fabian had invented a game for himself quite a while back. He would watch the children running around parks and courtyards and count the years—had the generation of girls who didn't even have the potential opportunity to become his wife been born into the world? That boundary had to exist; he was no Goethe, now, was he? The limit was probably at hand presently. Now, they can't anymore. That knowledge was frightful—like a borrowed book that will definitely remain unread your entire life.

It's possible that he really will go. Not one external reason had popped into his head that might hold him back from meeting up with his former companions or the teachers who still worked at the same school. He could go at any moment. He had a clean record. That meant freedom and serious self-confidence. He could ascend the school's grand stairway, and upon opening the door still turn and give a broad smile to passersby. He wouldn't have to creep through the courtyard, keeping his hands in his pockets.

How much a truly inventive person could be ashamed of: to be the first boy in his class to marry and acquire a herd of children, or to be the only one who doesn't have his own personal car to park next to the schoolyard, near the gardens weeded long ago on their class yard-work days; not to have been abroad or to have only traveled to Bulgaria. An unexpectedly early onset of baldness could be an obstacle. Even a one-hundred-and-twenty-ruble salary could come into question. You shouldn't show your face anywhere with a salary like that; not even outside your own home. With Fabian, everything was different, and he could look everyone in the face honestly. I haven't even sold out, Fabian mused, no one's bought me.

He instinctively senses that, yes, he had not merited trust—not in the eyes of the school, of society, or of his loved ones. Specifically, at their graduation ceremony, the faculty dean had whispered into Fabian's ear while shaking his hand that, out of all the graduates that year, *he* was the one from whom the school hoped the most; from whom it expected important acts that would benefit humanity. While he was expressing his desire to see Fabian strutting in the line of their homeland's great sons and daughters, the dean's bristly mustache touched Fabian's earlobe, and Fabian was thrown somewhat off-balance by it. Some kind of logic could be found in the common feeling of the family of educators, since although Fabian studied to achieve Bs and Cs and his behavior was challenging, he would intermittently voice ideas that no one else had heard of. It was hardly likely that any of them even understood the ideas, either. They were simply different from the ideas of others. They *expected* something to come of that. The ideas alone weren't enough anymore; "a manhood rich in the joys of labor was at hand." But that was trivial. Does a robber refrain from creeping back to the site of the robbery purely from knowing that he hasn't become the salt of the earth?

They had hoped in university, too. He recalled his college graduation. Fabian had felt immeasurable relief then! He had longed for the moment since his first semester at university; as soon as he got the taste in his mouth. He awaited his diploma like a serf his manumission. One day, everything would finally be over. An end to the banalities, the obligations, the compulsion, the childishness. Most of the graduates apparently perceived what transpired differently. Many had been terrified; had lost their heads, as if they had indeed been liberated, but were property-less. There was nowhere to keep studying. Live. Spread your wings. The agitation led to excesses in their behavior. Several got dead drunk in the dormitory for the first time in their lives. Their group's treasurer, a mother of three, broke her vow of fidelity with one of Fabian's friends on the night of their graduation. Hello, life! Doubtless that act grounded the participants' tensions; helped them to survive the crisis. To whom should I break my vow of fidelity to survive today, then tomorrow, and all the following days? Fabian wondered. I'm like a kid who doesn't even *have* school break, because he doesn't go to school yet.

He picked up his desk calendar, flipped through the pages that he had missed—non-existent days—and wrote a few words in not his most legible handwriting on the given date. He looked at the clock. Five minutes had passed again. He was still feeling sorry for himself. He sighed, but it was purely for show. He wouldn't give up yet. He would go and shave his face clean.

PULL IN YOUR HORNS, LIFE!

I

"I'M GOING TO get going now," Fabian stated resolutely, and furtively wiped beer from around his mouth with the back of his hand. He wanted to get out of here, and planned to get to work before lunch so that he could putz around for an hour or so, glance at the morning mail, write a few letters, take a few calls; in short—simulate editing a magazine.

"You're leaving me here," Ingo sighed. A little seriously, a little forced. Ingo was never in a hurry. He was a freelancer—his only obligations were tied to social relations with his very elderly mother, who, however, regarded her son's irregular lifestyle with astounding stoicism. Fabian knew Ingo's mother. She was one of the few mothers that he knew at all. His current friends didn't appear to *have* mothers. Just as they didn't have fathers, brothers, or other relatives. Not all of them could be dead; war hadn't come and gone. They were more likely a source of embarrassment. In any case, they weren't made public. They undoubtedly existed *somewhere*, whether in a backwoods cabin or an old folks' home, in another city or working as specialists in developing countries; no matter whether they had disowned their children or their children had run away, only one thing was obvious—they didn't live together, and didn't communicate. True, some relatives could be found here and there. But they were new, not classic ones; not the old kind of blood relatives like maternal and paternal aunts and uncles, cousins on both sides. New relatives formed when one friend courted another friend's sister who had reached adulthood. Or else people whose parents remarried even at the age of fifty unexpectedly became half-brothers. Ingo, on the other hand, had a real mother. Ingo's mother read a lot. *Wochenpost, Morning Star, Za Rubezhom*, and she wouldn't even turn down *Le Monde*. Over the last five years, during which Fabian had ended up at their house a couple of times a month, he could remember Ingo's mother in only one way: sitting by the window in a creaking, woven lawn-chair, her glasses perched on the edge of her nose, and a wide pile of newspapers in front of her. She didn't merely read the articles, but processed them, underlining sections in pencil. "Whose side is your mother on, anyway?" Fabian asked Ingo one time. "The Tories, I suppose," his friend replied.

Fabian was certain that Ingo's mother surrounded herself with newspapers, with the imagined lives and the unfamiliar problems of faraway lands, in order to avoid personal memories that weren't exactly pleasant. Ingo spilled his life story to Fabian one time while drunk, and thus he came to understand why that now-old woman was interested in how many blacks were gnawed to the bone by crocodiles in the Congo River, why she rejoiced over the dollar dropping against the yen—all in order to forget a man who had vanished into thin air two hours after he drove them home from the maternity ward, ostensibly having gone out to buy the young mother a copy of *Soviet Teacher*. From then on, *Soviet Teacher* was the only newspaper that Ingo's mother didn't read, out of principle.

"You're leaving me here," Ingo sighed again. As if *he* was someone to leave! Ingo was being ironic, as always. Naturally, they climbed the stairs and walked out of the café together, strolling side by side for a while and commenting on people they passed by, before Ingo turned off to the left. Where and why—Ingo didn't care to start explaining and Fabian himself wasn't about to ask. No doubt the man knows why he's turning left. And Ingo wanted to be a man—always and in all things.

As usual, they didn't utter a single word to each other upon parting, nor did they discuss when they would see each other again or what they would do. Arriving at an intersection, Fabian glanced back over his shoulder for a moment, but saw that the other man hadn't, so he also spun back around right away. He wasn't satisfied with his friend, and something was bugging him, as always. At the same time, he was embarrassed by his own sensitivity and didn't look over his shoulder again until he reached the bus stop, to see if it was coming. But the bus was nowhere to be seen, so he decided to continue on foot.

Fabian's conscience began to trouble him as he trudged along the boulevard that scaled the hill. Once again, *he* had been the first to desert. For life had taught him that, on occasion, unforgettable events arise out of pub encounters such as that. Just like the chance of you going out to have a small cup of tea in the evening, but arriving home only by the time you've already had your morning coffee. What kind of an impression would he leave by deserting too often under the pretense of work? People will start to think that he wants to live to the age of eighty just so he could be a doddering guru of youth! Fabian was well aware that he had acted with foresight just now, and was in the right. *Someone* has to think with the country in mind, too, and (while personally getting a taste for them) suppress sinful thoughts while still possible. For when no one in a healthy society is capable of standing up at the critical moment and saying "let's call it quits" anymore, then the game is over. Anyway, eventually we start to hate everyone who drinks less than we do. They aren't taken into account any longer. Oh, how they are disparaged! We start to snicker at those who don't feel bad in the morning; who don't imbibe early in the day, peering around timorously, darting in through the doors of reeking beer pavilions in dilapidated neighborhoods; who take ascorbic acid and adaptogens or munch instead on refined gentlemen's morning pills delivered in packages sent from abroad. Of course, already years earlier, their common friend, Per-Ivar, had claimed that every honest person should feel like crap in the mornings. Judging by this, Per-Ivar himself was undoubtedly the most honest of men—the veritable conscience of the age. Yet it wasn't as if *they* fell all that far short of Ingo's great rapscallion proportions. Ingo in particular. Nothing hampered him. Not family, animals that needed care, or his job. He knew no shortage of money. His mother received a full pension and needed not a kopeck more. She sometimes even fed her son and would lend his friends a fiver. Otherwise, Ingo was supported by a well-to-do widow. The widow was a classic; it's a wonder that such could still be found. She was called Mrs. Koit—she was forty-seven years old, but well preserved, soft, and had gold teeth. She lived in a garden suburb, where she occupied the second floor of a private dwelling. Mrs. Koit had apparently earned everything good she had in life by selling frothy beer at the gate to the Hippodrome. Sometimes, rarely, mostly in summer when it was warm (because he couldn't be bothered to heat the studio), Ingo would paint some ultramodern painting that only four or five people could understand, and thus earned a small supplement to what he was given by the widow. After the exhibition, when one or another of his paintings was purchased, Ingo would vanish from her radar together with his earnings for up to a month. Lately, he had painted almost nothing. There hadn't been a need to. The widow was already providing for him. She was completely under Ingo's thumb. So much so that Ingo's visits became more and more infrequent. Fabian realized that Mrs. Koit's availability had smothered Ingo's ambitions and that in the interests of Estonian art, that shameful connection should be broken; however, Fabian didn't feel he had the strength for the act. Sometimes he was jealous of Ingo instead, because the latter was, nevertheless, his own master. Each and every one of his movements radiated freedom; even the way in which he tied his tie. The well-to-do man's sovereignty always distinguished Ingo from the other artists Fabian knew. His friend was all the more deserving of jealousy, since the eye still could not discern any significant marks of wear upon him. Already twenty-eight, he still had a stately appearance without a single gray hair in his beard, not even a single fold hanging over his waistband, a stomach that digested cognac and beer as well as ever, and blood coursing through his veins that brought a glow to his cheekbones. A real Pied Piper! One shouldn't have had to say "let's get going" just now to a top dog like that. Even so, he was in the right in the long term, because Fabian knew that although his friend was involved in painting, he wasn't an evergreen; he was no Dorian Gray. Ingo had simply been a late bloomer; he had a small head start in the form of a decent childhood. He had also been involved in sports and would sometimes brag about having once been Tartu's eighth best in race walking. That won't be enough for long. A few years more, and even *his* first symptoms of degradation will appear. Unwanted nighttime visits and vodka mooching at friends' places, unconscious outpourings of hatred, pointless arguments, and accusations will all begin. He'll start avoiding his friends, because he has taken it into his head that all the bigger parties start with *them*, specifically. As such, he is cold and indifferent toward them, yawning at their amiable conversation, only for him to then sometime later, in a completely different mood, be dangling his arm around their necks and banging his chest. Indeed, he tends to repeat stories to the same group of friends, attempting to get by with his old witticisms. Thus, in ten or fifteen years, he won't allow himself to open his mouth without first making sure he hasn't already told that story.

In order to escape a threatening future or to soften it, to delay it till later or in any case avoid a sharp transition, one needed to make an effort; to say no to temptation. But when one's own mental strength wasn't enough, then it was necessary to seek help from external sources. Many of Fabian's onetime friends had rushed to write down in their notebooks of aphorisms the idea voiced by the humanist Schweitzer, according to whom one must attempt to preserve the ideals adopted during his youth—cost what it may—deliberately clinging on to them and not changing or adjusting to transforming conditions. Ah, so what about ideals, Fabian thought. Something simpler would suffice. Initially, one should preserve, untouched, the daily schedule of a schoolchild. Up early, exercise, cold shower, to work, lunch at a certain time, homework, helping one's parents, outside for two hours, and half an hour of independent thought. Prior to falling asleep and after the completion of one's daily schedule should be a Jesuit-like examination of conscience—an *examen conscientiae*; a summary analysis and evaluation of the day. Separately, this should first comprise the situation with morals; secondly, how things were with work; and thirdly, the plans for tomorrow. One could go far like that.

One simple and reliable opportunity for allowing external form to leave a good impression on you was going to work every day. He believed in an upbringing with a strong work ethic. Work meant a normal connection to life. Even working for a couple of hours. If you aren't able to do a full day's work, then do half and do it honestly, as his teacher Laur had encouraged. Doing a job helped to counter the threat of ruin posed by freedom. Fabian had experienced this personally. Then you didn't have the time for all sorts of strange ideas. He had finally figured out why repeatedly, around midday, he would employ great force to push open the massive, hard-swinging door downtown—it had led to ongoing tenure. *That's* how simple it was. You only had to dare to look yourself in the eyes. There was nothing sacred or noble about it. No guiding principles, national benefit, or mental chivalry. Merely pure instinct. Embarrassing to admit to oneself. Self-preservation instinct.

Four years ago, he had fought outright to attain his current position. Of course, he had been striving for completely different reasons at the time. First of all out of greedy ambition, since it was a renowned position. One with traditions. In the editorial staff of an important magazine. The former members of "Young Estonia"[5] had even walked through the vaults of the old building. It was in those rooms that the intellectual greats had stacked the stones of Estonia's cultural wall. A young man like him being chosen for that position was an outright miracle. Many years before his proper time. Though it was incontestable that he had toiled for it, too. In order to beat his rivals, who weren't lacking the necessary skills, and who possessed a significantly greater number of services performed, memberships, and publications than he did, Fabian had worn down many different doors; had waited for many to receive him; had pandered to the interviewers' personal tastes; had danced away entire evenings with middle-aged ladies at banquets; had brownnosed functionaries; had drunk himself to the point of oblivion multiple times; and had listened to the pointless drivel of boring individuals. The position had seemed worthy of effort. He hadn't been disappointed. He was able to get by without working a side job. Nine tenths of his official responsibilities overlapped with what he would have been doing anyway. If he did anything at all. Why not accept money for it to boot, then? Life was sweet. Especially when viewed from a distance. No one especially kept track of his comings and goings, and he had sufficient free time left over. He could set his own goals, research and write, realize all of his opportunities, and be pleased with his creative work. His first mother-in-law had never understood what kind of a job it really was—one you didn't rush to at the toot of the factory whistle every morning, for which you didn't push your way onto a trolley stuffed with bleary-eyed commuters, but rather one that

---

5   "Young-Estonia" ("*Noor-Eesti*") was a group of young writers and poets that formed in Tartu and was an aggressive movement for social and cultural-political change. It functioned more or less from 1905–1915.

you went to when you were in the mood for it, sometime around mid-morning; one that you left at your fancy. And what's worse, in her opinion—the man asks for quiet at home after the end of the official work day, orders the radio to be turned down, because he wants to continue working! Can a serious man *be* like that? Fabian was downright happy at first. He felt that it was *his* position. He fit there, and that was how it would stay. What more could he want?

But now? Something happened in the meantime. He doesn't want to work anymore. He maintained the job only in order to keep his head above water. Unheard of! Delicacies are devoured so as not to die of hunger; the prima donna's trained voice is ordered to be used as a fire engine siren!

But not just that. He goes to work for other reasons as well. There are quite a lot of things that he is unable to do anymore. Like being alone. Just three or four years ago, he could manage to force himself. Then, he would sometimes not emerge from home for several days in a row, only going to the shop across the street and for a walk in the nearest park. He didn't go to the city center looking for company. And other times, he would ask for a week off from work instead. He'd complete in advance everything that needed to be done at work, and drive out to the country; to the house where his grandfather had put together a valuable personal library long ago. There, he spent time in the company of deceased men of genius, rain pattering on the roof above him, becoming ever wiser. How much he managed to do back then! For he was still living off that old fat to this day. Such a life wasn't easy. No doubt he had yearned for company then, too. Had wanted attention. That need generally varies for individuals. When a film diva receives only fifty fan letters in the mail one morning instead of a hundred, she falls into a depression, believing she's been abandoned and forgotten. Yet for a fanatical, credible researcher hunched over an experiment's beakers at a big research institute, it's enough for his boss to stop at his side and make an encouraging comment once a year. Between these two extremes, Fabian is more the first type. But his will came out on top one time!

Now, he's unable to withstand it any longer. He gives in to passion as often as possible. He knows he doesn't have the strength to spend a single day in solitude. Fabian frequently comes to the editorial office even when he officially has the day off. For he always encounters people here; he sees someone and can speak a few words. Or if he actually manages to remain steadfast in the face of temptation, then his thoughts scatter all over the place, and by evening there's no point in talking about concentrating. He is irresistibly drawn to people's company. The desire only grows by the hour, and in the end, he's indifferent— he's prepared to dash off to the nearest taxi stand at midnight and go to the next place from there; to abandon wonderful isolation for the most lowbrow crowd. You can always find one of those. Even beforehand, Fabian knows what usually goes on there. He won't gain a damn thing from the random company. No one will glow, ordinary quips will be made, and gossip will be shared. Such a level of society won't make him even the slightest bit richer. But how did that knowledge help?! When he returned from the city center, Fabian would berate himself, be angry and disappointed, and vow that from that point on he would only leave his refuge when it was of the utmost necessity—and then violate this resolution two days later.

No longer is he even a *speck* of the type of man who builds an island upon his own soul; a place where he can flee the hubbub of the world, walk around in silence as his own boss, and enjoy the slow pleasures of getting engrossed in himself. *That's* what is called "going deep." Fabian doesn't want to go deep; he doesn't want to find anything within himself, because there's nothing to find—not bliss, peace, or new perception. Everything must always come from elsewhere, from outside! Much of it and the very best! Because working on oneself takes immense effort. Then, one must concentrate. He'd like to get by more easily. Depth makes him queasy. He's jealous and disdainful of people who have a high level of spirituality. They used to provoke his respect; now, they merely make him yawn. And make him aggressive. He'd like, for example, to give a Tibetan wise man a whipping. Or to tempt a saint. Chase a vegetarian down the street with a cane. Now, Fabian enjoyed levity. He had embarked upon an endless path, for the walker of which everything has to come from the surrounding world—more and more, ever more frequently, and in stronger concentration, because lusts sharpen once he gives in and boldly demand their own. My life, that drug! Fabian sighed. Within him temporarily swelled the desire to lose himself, denounce himself, and abandon any kind of responsibility, to the degree that he felt totally prepared to orient toward the outer; to not even think with his own head anymore, but instead brazenly borrow all ideas from elsewhere.

Fabian wanted surfeit. He longed for everything. He didn't want to be a starving man, for whom a crumb of bread seems like a banquet. He dreamed instead of a permanent smorgasbord feast. He wanted to revel in an orgy, and he mentally spat at the electric shock that shoots through a first-time lover when his hand accidentally brushes his platonic friend's soft breast. Fabian despised Maeterlinck, Tagore, and generally everyone who provided little impetus, who needed to be enriched with much more imagination. To fill those gaps one had to draw deep from one's own soul. He loved the elegant and the complex, but not in excess. Now, Fabian abhorred the Eastern way of thinking more than ever—although he had subconsciously been inclined to despise it since childhood. He detested it to the extent that he didn't even know for certain what the detested object meant. He had never even browsed a single book on the subject. As if! He has *other* things to do with his time. Thus, the only sensible thing that came from the East was, in his opinion, polygamy.

At the same time, Fabian himself was indeed divorced from his first and only wife.

But even stranger—the stronger the fear of loneliness swelled within Fabian, the fewer compatriots he wanted to see, and the more certain ones made him nauseous. He became more selective of people with each passing year. At one time, he had forgiven them all. Not anymore. Now, he set the very highest requirements; he put forth imperatives in genius. One-dimensional people who didn't meet this requirement irritated him more and more, although Fabian himself had long been unable to concentrate intensely either. It was unjust, and the awareness of his own injustice added new gall to Fabian's soul. Truly—those who met his tastes could be counted on two hands. The circle of people Fabian spent time with after hours and with whom he didn't suffer delirium tremens, was very tight. However, he had to spend the greater part of his time specifically in the company of other kinds of people. Thus, being hungover became a common condition—it became so natural that he had already grown accustomed to it and shaped it into some kind of absurd attitude toward life.

He desired his own kind of people. Still, there was an array of individuals out there who believed that opposites should attract. That a man should be very manly and a woman very womanly. That it's great when people mutually complement each other. That even in bed, everything is better suited when one likes black, and the other likes white. But why make things so complicated? Life is difficult and complex; isn't it easier to bear it with one's own kind? Why should I have to battle both life and my antithesis? Fabian wondered. Variety was supposed to be the spice of life. But why should I have to exchange good for bad purely out of principle, and then bad for something even *worse* just to keep spinning around in a vicious circle of aversions? However, that's inevitable. Who isn't with us is against us.

What's more: if he asks himself whether anything is a source of sincere joy for him here in this world, whether there are situations that can be regarded as pleasant without any kind of reservation, whether there exists an activity that could be practiced without compulsion, then the honest answer is hidden right here. If he could, then he would do nothing other than sit with four or five friends and converse lazily. He would simply exist, and that would be it. He would enjoy the presence of his own kind. For friends are very much alike. They understand everything. They make plain, elegant references that don't require justification. Because justification is tiring. They comprehend things *without* it. They laugh at the right things and grimace when something is off. For although they are involved in different fields and vary in age, they still have a common background; their conversational code is the same; their keywords are shared—without them, a stranger won't make heads or tails of it.

A casual observer might be amazed at what they, old acquaintances, have to talk about from day to day. Doubtless it springs eternal. And so, there's no point in worrying. And even if there *isn't* anything to talk about at the moment, then such individuals can be perfectly content staying silent. For their shared silence is filled with meaning. Things are even *nicer* that way. Fabian occasionally despised conversation. How much he had spoken in his youth, and what had he gotten from it?! He had earned only misunderstanding, merely ended up in arguments and acquired enemies.

Other times, they truly didn't speak about anything of importance. And they never arrived at any conclusions. However, none of them pursued ends in themselves. *They* won't start making decisions. The truth is said to arise from debates. But whom does that truth interest? Heavens *preserve* us from it. They're not a parliament, naturally. That would be infinitely boring. A serious speech is always tedious. And it readily gives you a headache. Furthermore, isn't perceived inevitability the case here? How could they arrive at even an incomplete conclusion, debate even one point just a quarter of the way toward clarity when every sentence—each one that isn't disproved the next moment or that someone doesn't at least begin to sneer at or joke about—when that little, naked, enduring truth is extremely commonplace. When all the words have been spoken, there always remains a feeling of incompletion. Pure rule breaking. One can't even speak seriously without having the irresistible urge to turn what they said into a joke a second later and to sneer at it. And an inevitability like that only seems awful in the first instance, and primarily to those who relinquished cognitive activity halfway and weren't capable of seeing it through to the end. Because the consequence is of no *importance*. The subject matter under discussion isn't important to them. There is something more important than that. At least for Fabian.

It was recognition, spiritual closeness, a little mystery in which even *he* felt that not everything written about human closeness can be false, and the fact that he *isn't* alone came to him as an epiphany. That epiphany was life.

Yet, the more that Fabian thought about his feelings, the more he started to suspect he was wavering over everything he thought about. Lately, the consciousness of their collective life no longer offered its former certainty. He wavered over whether their similar background, his sole support here in this world, was even half as strong as it appeared in its best moments. How had he come up with that at all? How had he arrived at such an insane idea? Perhaps he so yearned for things to be that way that he'd imagined it? Fabian's erstwhile certainty wasn't disturbed by the fact that they weren't men of the same field; that they didn't stand side by side along the same front. Fabian couldn't talk to his friends about half of the things he was involved in.

His friends didn't know the least thing about them. This was completely ordinary and unimportant. Fabian's colleagues were generally smart people, top specialists in their fields. He could certainly *discuss* things with them. The fact that Fabian and his close acquaintances practiced utterly different lifestyles was of no consequence, either—the fact that a couple of them were big womanizers, but others raised their eyebrows in discomfort at a crude joke; some had children, while others couldn't even look at pregnant women; some loved collecting mushrooms in the woods, while others, on the contrary, would only hike when forced to do so, and even then only in the case that a bottle of something was brought along; a couple of men were interested in foreign policy, while others were unaware of even domestic politics—they simply didn't talk about such differences. One man's quirks weren't mandatory for others. None of this was of principal importance; one thing seemed even stranger.

Throughout all ages, people have chosen their own friends and acquaintances. Some enjoy socializing more frequently than others. And, excluding the exceptions, people have always preferred their own kind. It is in this way that groups of friends, circles, and coteries have formed. This can be viewed in the everyday life around you. The faces of the old ladies who sit nose to nose in cafés have worn into your memory over long years. The same ruffians who gather night after night under doorways along central streets. The smokers in library foyers belong together with obvious ties. Literature, theater, and film brim with examples of human convergence. Fabian had read about the Decembrists, the Freemasons, the Jena Romantics, and the Paul Street Boys; had seen films about the Italian Mafia and plays about the everyday life of the Estonian philatelist club. Hanging on the wall of their school cafeteria was a reproduction of Kristjan Raud's patriotic pseudo-historicist painting reimagining the famous *Oath of the Horatii*. And so on, from which the moral emerged: If you leave aside politeness, because of which neighbors always get along, and inevitability, thanks to which relatives have to converse with one another, and casual encounters, in which people are united by women or drink, then it is natural that people are united by some interest; or, even more importantly—by a similar attitude toward world affairs. True, no one had issued such a law. But what could be more natural than *frondeurs* banding together; nudists becoming attached to one another; numismatists spending blissful hours together; Baptists doing their Baptist things together; just like queers, cooks, and all the rest. When two or more people find a common language in intelligent discussion, then they draw close; rendezvous, card tables, and mutual visits take place, over the course of which they begin to exchange their views more openly. From then on, things could progress this way or that. Their relationship *could* stay on that level of heartfelt neutrality, but it often becomes much more intimate. In any case, back in the day, people would determine who was who first and foremost. Otherwise, nothing would come of it. You didn't dive into water in an unfamiliar place, didn't buy a pig in a poke, didn't just start associating with who-knows-whom. Now, the situation has changed: you sleep with them first, and only check to see who they are in the morning. Something was off in the world.

At least between them. Fabian realized now, in hindsight, that they had drawn close in innocent ignorance; had become friends on the basis of some vague sympathy. The most important element of their relationship had been indefinable. Intuition worked, not sense. Yet how could one bank on instinct, be sure that the internal organ, which in our days stands idle the majority of the time, is not mistaken? But you didn't wrack your brain over such questions. Everything went rather simply: you started to like someone, and allowed yourself to enjoy them. Based on personal charm more than creed. Only afterward might you be intrigued by *why*. Later, it started becoming clear who someone was in particular—what they represented; what they think, believe, and reckon.

Even that "afterward," which could follow in a roundabout way, progressed very cautiously; in an emphatically indifferent form. One wasn't allowed to regard it as being overly important; in the same way that, on the other hand, it would be trite to rigidly avoid talking about convictions and to balk at them. And no matter what the topic—the right man can talk about anything. The topic doesn't ruin the man. The opposite certainly does, though. Even "good morning" sounds bad coming from some mouths. In reality, nothing will ruin the right person. Not even practicing freestyle wrestling or going out dancing. Clothes don't even ruin a man. Everything is allowed. On the other hand, some men ruin everything. Not even walking on two legs suits them. Nevertheless, the exception confirmed the rule in this as well. Poverty was a sin. The only true sin. Fabian had lived a hand-to-mouth bohemian life for many a good year. Now, while dining at a good restaurant, he would wear an appropriate tie, and he would tip. Of course, he wasn't awed by money. He thoroughly enjoyed borrowing it. For his attitude toward debt had long since differed from the time when a borrowed sum was reason not to show your face in public. The attitude toward debt had been very tolerant in Fabian's youth; it was the younger generation's sole great trait. He could still remember how his mother and father had warned him against any kinds of monetary machinations. He was forbidden from taking any personal loans. His parents had tugged at his conscience; had lectured that "neither a borrower nor a lender be," and conjured up visions of some mystical debtor's prison and an auctioneer's hammer. Fabian, for his part, found that a debt belongs purely to the debtor, as he could personally allow himself something with it. The lender could not. When his parents heard that he had borrowed money, he was given the necessary sum, along with a stern and worried look, and was ordered to pay it back at once. Fabian had enjoyed that kind of generosity; he was prepared to pretend that the debt had been a great burden to him, that he understood how dishonorably he had behaved, and was afraid that his father's communal apartment could truly be put up for auction. Once, as a last resort, he had simply lied and said he had borrowed again, because he sorely needed the money. At times, he wondered where such an attitude toward the credit system—a system upon which the entire technological civilization had been *built*—might have come from. Doubtless it was the issue of a small, poor nation. What showed through here was the miserliness of a clever old man, who, gritting his teeth, fed his family with bread and water even in the most fortunate of times, just so that he wouldn't have to give away his hard-earned kopecks. But something had changed. True—now people cared about money just as much as they had before, and the mentality that had inspired oleographic pictures of equally ostentatious old peasant men with bulging coin purses hadn't become a thing of the past. Only—a new manner of ostentatiousness had emerged. A great debt, ennobling one like a genteel disease, had become something worthy of discussion.

Oh, yes—you could talk about anything. That was allowed! And still, it happened apropos of nothing; never under the slogan of opening oneself up, by exhorting: let's go all the way, views on the table! That was polite, but wasn't enough, regardless. And sometimes, when Fabian had gone out into the country again and reread Thomas Mann, Hesse, and Bellow; when the humanist cultural tradition stirred within him and reproachfully reminded him of its presence, just like how a letter from an unjustly abandoned lover found randomly between the pages of a book causes distress; when worldview and fundamental ideas seemed important to Fabian just as they had before, then, he realized with a shock that he couldn't place his hand over his heart and say *who* those people were, with whom he spent his afternoons and evenings in plush red café booths.

Thinking back on it honestly, they had almost never discussed any kinds of principles. Their conversation slid along an elegant surface. *That's* why Fabian lacked certainty: his life was constant readiness. You never know what your best friend might surprise you with one fine morning. Perhaps it will turn out that, in terms of ideals, you've been hanging out with your complete opposite the entire time. That you've been clinking glasses with your foil, your mirror image. It really wasn't impossible. Occasionally, Fabian would sense in the air strange references to backgrounds that were completely alien to him. He found even within *himself* yearnings and thoughts that he didn't dare share with others out of fear that they wouldn't be understood. However, not even the blurring borders of his friendships had been the main cause for Fabian's rising fear. It was something else. Views truly didn't sit well with him. That is—they *did* a little, of course, but something else was much more important. It was in the name of that *something* that he himself affirms everything; that he disavows reason before his heart. That he sacrifices knowledge to faith straightaway (doing so on good faith!), enjoys the personal charm of a louse, and refuses to let a principled friend sit at his table. He isn't interested in what and how; doesn't dismantle a radio to see what's playing inside. He will never ever start inspecting his friends too closely. What for? They could mutually clear everything up, get things straight, and then fall into a heated argument. They could spray truth in each other's faces. But what would the consequence and the return be? Would there be a purification and a clearing up, would they sigh happily, breaking down into tears over how great things were—that there was no longer anything between them? Banal and embarrassing, just like in a mediocre play! On top of that, they wouldn't care to remain principled and discuss serious problems for long, anyway. That wasn't their style. So, is it worth launching into a quarrel over one instance? That would be foolish. Dumb, like confessing a one-night stand to your wife. To what end? The truth? What good is troublesome kind of truth that disrupts living? One should flee it like a rabid dog. And if it comes after you, then club it on the snout! Fabian didn't want to know anything compromising about his friends; not about hidden vices, nor memberships in secret organizations— not a single detail that might harm their relationship. He closes his eyes and his ears when he might hear or see anything bad about them. And if someone came to inform him by force, he would punch the speaker in the face. As long as everything is okay, then don't ask why. Is he afraid of the truth? But he knows his friends' flaws *anyway*. And if he were to learn about new ones, it wouldn't change anything on the whole. No, it had nothing to do with truth; it was far from truth.

He must consciously keep the mechanics of a relationship like that running. Every mistake must be prevented. If, for example, Fabian sensed that a friend wasn't interested in dogs, then he would talk to him about anything else. For why must a friend love a dog? Is a hound truly that important? What would it do for Fabian if the man liked dogs? And is it at all likely that one highly developed personality might be capable of proving to another of his kind, even using measures as fine as might be, that an Airedale or a Boxer is a valuable creature fit for attention? No, you can't instill anything more at that age. An old dog doesn't learn new tricks. You'll only get into a fight. Therefore: if you perceive that a friend, contrary to you, loves brunettes, that in his opinion Dostoyevsky's masochism is old-fashioned, that apart from you, no one goes to the theater, and that you alone respect semiotics, then it's better to remain silent. It isn't worth getting into an argument in the name of science or art. Personal life is more important than art or science. Fabian abhorred those who were prepared to forever quarrel in the name of a scientific or, even worse, an aesthetic argument, all the while banging on their chest and declaring that *they* are filled with true artistic fervor; that art is the holiest of holies to them. Interpersonal ties were much more important. These ties were irrational, but significant enough that if their irrational validity were to collapse because of some truth of rationality, that truth should be banished to hell.

If you join a club, then serve and praise it, but don't undermine it. For no one has forced you into it; no one has ordered you to sing its anthem. Fabian had joined his friends' club, and praised them everywhere. He wanted to be honest. Everyone he knew was good. And vice-versa. Although, he wasn't always entirely sure whether or not they really did deserve that public praise. Fabian didn't fail his own men. He didn't conspire with his friends' wives; didn't breed intrigue behind their backs. He would come up with creative lies to tell their wives, saying they'd been together the previous evening developing pictures or writing a joint manifesto, while his friends had actually been fornicating somewhere or up to some other no-good. Fabian takes onboard his friends' viewpoints about those things he believes they know better than he does. And he believes that others accept his views just the same and will lie for him also, if necessary. Outwardly, everything seems more appropriate that way. But in actuality? *No one* knows how it actually is. Whoever gets too close to another is a fool.

Such are the only people for whom Fabian feels a need. Oh, yes—that's how it truly is, for sometimes in summer, when families took his friends along with them all over the country, Fabian, who stayed behind in the city, encountered a gnawing vexation, which was all the more nasty the less he wanted to admit it to himself, and he could feel his nervous system withering from inactivity. And when his friends finally returned after having fulfilled their filial duties on the sand dunes, Fabian always felt that life got going again. Things were hard without them, regardless how cynical you were. Then, you couldn't find self-assurance at all. Loneliness would kill you. For a long time, Fabian thought it was the same for others. That if he were able to go on a business trip to America for two months, his friends would start to miss him over time. He hoped with all his heart, almost prayed in his mind that his kind of people would earnestly appreciate him. But once, when he spoke to Ingo about his feelings in a roundabout way, claiming that Ingo and two or three other friends were the only ones whom he still gave a damn about in the world, Ingo said that he didn't even give a damn about *them* anymore; that he had grown up. That he could survive without them, too. It could, of course, have been the case that he was making a very characteristically cynical joke and simply teasing the inquirer, who was undoubtedly being very honest at that moment, because such inquiring and such honesty were truly on the edge of being in good form. However, at that moment, Ingo's eyes had been so genuine and cold like those of an owl that Fabian gave up talking about it, and turned what he had said earlier into a jest. And later, the more that Fabian thought about what had happened, the more confidently he concluded that his friend had spoken the truth. It *had* to be that way. For Fabian *himself* had already started to feel that friends were growing somewhat distant from him; that he himself gave less and less of a damn about them. He could already spend entire weeks without seeing them. They were outgrowing him, and not to be outdone, he outgrew them likewise. Proud loneliness remained. Or, what *proud*, really—it was a loneliness that was ultimate, metaphysical, and justified by ideals. A loneliness he had arrived at freely, following his true nature; a dead end that came when he had made the very best of who he was! It was a bit frightening.

The doors at work were locked. Everyone had gone to lunch, or had they not even come in yet today? The only sounds were a tapping noise coming from the typist's office, and from the secretary who was munching on candies and paging through a Russian fashion magazine at reception. Fabian realized that the girl was taking advantage of the opportunity and had ordered a long-distance call to her boyfriend, who was studying at the Estonian Agricultural Academy. A work telephone—so what, it's not on my kopeck! He heard from both the typist and the secretary that he had been especially sought-after today; naturally—it was Friday again. Everyone proper was still itching to get something done in that workweek so that they could spend their days off worry-free. The weekend! They still wanted to shrug off something, some nasty obligation, onto Fabian's shoulders, *today* by all means, or else they wished to ask some favor of him— some job, commission, or favorable contract. Sure! Then they could head out of town. They could don a white turtleneck and a black jacket, and head to the public sauna. Everyone at once, of course—all across the country, all over the land. Like back in the age of community rule. Then, the old men convened, peered at an animal's entrails, and decided: "Now we'll start sowing barley! All at once!" And they did. Nowadays, people decide on Friday: "Now we'll start drinking and fornicating! All at once!" And whoever opposes, we'll decapitate with a farm plow or take away their monthly bonus. Fabian couldn't care less if anyone who'd tried to find him at the office had left a note or asked him to call them. And he never provided information on his whereabouts or asked to be called at home, just in case. Completely the opposite: he didn't give the typist or the secretary time for a reminder, didn't even give them the chance to mention it. As if! He didn't even intend to be accommodating. Before darting into his office, he just asked the typist to tell further inquirers that he wasn't there. That he hadn't been and wasn't coming. That the typist should say he went out to Lasnamäe, the sleeper suburb. Let them interpret it in whatever way they wished. It was a request. He had no right to demand it of the typist. Not officially, since they weren't in a superior/inferior relationship; nor personally, since the typist was a fair amount older than his mother. He had no right at all to force an employee of the editorial office to lie, especially since Fabian's job could suffer directly as a consequence of such dodging. However, when he relayed his wish, Fabian's expression conveyed such unfeigned vacancy and bitterness that the request sounded like an order. Fabian knew that the typist would definitely carry it out. She believed Fabian. She was an old-school dame. She thought Fabian was involved in secret research, looking into restricted Estonian history, or writing a novel to be shelved.

Fabian entered his office and locked the door behind him, but immediately unlocked it again. He wouldn't stay longer than fifteen minutes, anyway. Fresh newspapers and a lone envelope whited out the top of his desk. He skimmed through the letter. He'd been invited to meet with the poetry club of a mid-sized Northern Estonian city. Why not. Nothing seemed outwardly wrong about it. Fabian was counted as being young, promising, and self-justifying; as an up-and-coming critic and poet who had made a name for himself. So, it was a completely natural invitation. Everyone like him was asked to rattle on in front of readers from time to time—for libraries, schools, clubs, and military units. No big deal was made out of it. But Fabian didn't like this kind of an offer one bit. Firstly, the time when such a display of attention might have raised his self-awareness had long since passed. But what intensified his lassitude into a state of irritation was rather a more important circumstance— specifically, the invitation touched a nerve with Fabian. Every such meeting was dreadfully troublesome and tiresome for him, because he would need to speak there personally. He would need to present his views. Where was he supposed to get such things ad infinitum? He *had* nowhere to get them. He's a man without views. Therefore, he isn't fit for public meetings. All the same, appearances and views are part of it. A writer must take an active stance at all times. As soon as something appears or happens, he has to express a personal opinion. Fabian's colleagues seemed capable of staying fresh; they managed to constantly and charmingly come up with new valences. But he couldn't. Hence, something was wrong with him, although by all appearances, he writes his pieces like every other man. And true—some time ago, Fabian had arrived at the conviction that he was in the wrong field. How wrong? Not hopelessly, was it? It probably was, all the same.

Oh, how he would like to blow up in front of the whole world's face, telling them that the majority of things didn't interest him one bit. And that the most obnoxious thing was that he had to hold some opinion about everything. If it were only a few things, then there'd be no problem. Because he *does* have some kinds of views. He isn't *that* sloppy, now! And yet, extremely few things interest him. He carries a couple of great ideas in his head, cradles a few important issues in his heart; he could ruminate on them day after day. For what could be more natural than the desire to deal with only the most important matters in one's sole, miniscule life? To address the intimate truths that have gained life-altering acceleration in the stress field of subjectivity? Nothing else offers tension. One step down, the "simply important"—that's already secondary. Consequently, it should be left aside. On top of that, being capable of speaking one's own mind about every little thing— isn't that insane self-confidence and a waste of time? Regardless, people believed that a critic was capable of it. He had to be ready to strike at all times; charged with new energy; must react in a lively and fascinating way.

When Fabian travels to the mid-sized Northern Estonian city in late September, he will be received by the poetry club's women and a couple of men, who will all be wearing their Sunday best; like when going to the theater. And there *will* be theater—Fabian's monodrama. The audience will hope to hear interesting truths from him. He doesn't know what lies he will tell them. Then, questions will follow. He doesn't know what he will answer. He doesn't like questions. Everyone will strive for seriousness. What does Fabian think about the objectivity of beauty? What are the newest tendencies? When will this all finally end? How much longer? Always toward the deep, always deeper. What is the point of art? Can art be taught? What is the point of life? Can life be taught? What is the point of the universe? What is the point of the point? If Fabian had lived in America, then it's possible that people at such meetings would instead ask: Does he like to sleep naked or in pajamas? What is his favorite food and underwear size? Does he feel the urge to whip it out in public? Surely things would go smoothly in America. It'd be a downright joy! In reality, he could get by quite easily here in Estonia as well, if only the poetry-club audience's interests were just the slightest bit more human. Namely, Fabian knows captivating gossip. He wouldn't start covering up anything on his end. He would promptly disclose all of the literary community's abortion stories, stir unwholesome excitement, unearth dark stories about mixed-up times, whisper about whether there were any illicit acts associated with one writer or another, and what kinds. He would cultivate intrigue over which of his colleagues drank and how much, as well as how much they earned. Being titillating—how easy!

However, those in the Northern Estonian city certainly would not want to know such details. Or if they did, then they wouldn't dare to speak up. Not at first, at least. Maybe later, when Fabian goes to the local restaurant for dinner, a Joe Bob who has worked up his courage will alight at his table between songs, confidentially inquiring whether it really *is* true when they say that . . . But that will be afterward. People ask pointless things in the beginning. Fabian would gladly shout at them: Leave me alone, I don't know anything, I don't want to make any decisions, I don't want to lie to you! But he doesn't have the courage to yell. It's not *appropriate*. He'll have a tie around his neck. And his cufflinks off. Furthermore, you *have* to have viewpoints. What kind of a person are you otherwise?

And actually, everyone *believes* that he has views. A full set of principles. He wasn't dumb enough to go and publicly proclaim that he'd given up thinking, though. In that way, he'd deceived everyone. Only not his wife—Fabian simply didn't care sufficiently to beat around the bush with her. Definitely with others, though. At times, there isn't much of a connection between writing and independent thought. No one knows, even suspects, that although he *is* still writing, he personally doesn't have thoughts anymore. Maybe others didn't either? Maybe they don't have views either? No, they certainly do. At least they did at one time . . . Especially when there is a five- or six-year gap between their ages and Fabian's; when they are a generation or two ahead of him. That's the generation of the sixties, the glory days of universities. Doubtless even *they* have started to waver a bit now—to waver over what was then taken as unconditional truth. However, they're still certain about *something*. There are many reasons for this. Habit, first of all. They can't bear to drop their attitudes. Constructive optimism directs their acts to this day. They'll never get away from that foundation. They're certain, since they have a need to be certain of something all the time. That *is* the habit, at once their weakness and their strength. Back in their day, people thought differently overall; thought much more and . . . more simply. People thought logically, technocratically, and uniformly. They approached things downright systematically! Everything was ascertained! This is also from where the primary difference stems. Fabian had missed out on a noteworthy period of life, in which world affairs are made clear to oneself. But why? What happened to it? Who was to blame? Fabian can definitely recall: he borrowed his ideas at first, because they were in fashion and in circulation. He adopted and combined. Heard a word from

here, read another from there, and added original thoughts of
his own. Other peers didn't even do *that*. Then, he was capable
of droning on and debating. He was seen as being plucky and
verbose, almost as a *public figure*. Now, he knows. He hadn't
believed his own words even then. His words departed from
his thoughts. Truths were not intimate. He only *believed* that
he believed; merely thought that the way he thinks was the way
he speaks. Now, he feels that it's already high time to ascertain
something on his own; to pour a foundation that could later
become a house, where he can build floors endlessly without
the structure collapsing beneath them. Yet, he is already too
skeptical; has seen and heard too much to take something *that*
seriously. He has no powerful memories or primary myths like
those the previous generation took from its puberty, and by
which one can erect a gigantic system that might be used to
pluck concise little replies to questions that crop up at every
step from then on. And he probably can't even be bothered
anymore; no doubt it'll remain unbuilt.

Naturally, he offers up those sorts of principles if he sits on it
for a little while even now, so—all fine and well. But that requires
a good half hour. Without a half hour, there's nothing. A credo
won't hatch without it. If you wake him up in the middle of the
night and ask what he thinks about everything, he'll gape at you
and stay regrettably silent. As if he's burned out. When standing
eye to eye with someone asking a question, he's unable to say
anything. You start explaining one thing, but you already see
astonishment in the eyes of the questioner; you have to make
disclaimers, need to start elaborating your first words, saying
what you meant by them *specifically*. And you get no farther
than that. The discussion is like a Hydra that grows seven new
heads in the place of each one that is chopped off. It's better to
write. That is a *monologue*. When for a moment, while doing
it, *you* are the proclaimer, the sermon-giver, the sovereign. At
least at the moment of writing, before you've shown the result

to others, no one can start refuting you. Then, for even a few mere seconds, you maintain the illusion that something is clear and thought through.

It was because of all of this that he didn't want to attend the meeting. Why go there and lie? He's not *that* bad, really. And nor is the audience. Yet, even if he were to have principles like a cartridge full of ammunition that could be sprayed at the poetry club, and like a drunk cowboy in a saloon proclaim to the residents of that Northern Estonian city what we have to know, what we have to believe, what we have to do, and what reward will come of it—he still wouldn't give his firm "yes" to the organizers then. Why should he have to go and report his (in that case undoubtedly correct) opinions to others?

For Fabian's sense of mission had been diminishing steadily over a long period of time. He knows with his mind and feels with his heart that he should appear before large auditoriums of people more frequently; should be open; should strive *to bring about change*. Both above and below. He should boost the general standard. At the same time, he should foster close ties with lone, talented enthusiasts, and take on apprentices. But he can't. Getting along with people is unbearably difficult. How can you start changing them, transforming them to your likeness when every new acquaintance gives you a headache after already half an hour? He flinches at new people. Young ones in particular. He has a dreadful fear that some greenhorn might start debating with him; crossing mental swords in a deadly serious way. Greenhorns, especially when they're as yet unrecognized, always want to come out on top. They imagine that then they'll be noticed and regarded as promising. That if they whack or offend someone, if they march out triumphantly or cockily drag their feet and exit, the old master will tenderly pick up his leather-bound notebook and jot down their names. That from that moment on, he will start to love them, make them into his protégés, pave their paths, and ultimately hatch plans to adopt them outright. Or that the gray-haired maestro will lie down, and a particularly bright halo and peace will settle upon his head while he utters his last words: "Now, I can die in peace—a successor has been found!" This isn't a vile joke. Greenhorns can think that stupidly. For they are uneducated, filthy, and idiots. Fabian felt with all of his senses how actively he hates the young. They tend to argue like year-old roosters. They argue even when there is not and cannot in truth *be* any kind of an argument; when you say it straight to their face. They don't believe it. They think that an argument must nevertheless exist in some hidden form. They don't believe that there isn't. They want there to be one. That is their only chance.

But how to free oneself of such tedious types? How do you just tell them frankly, try to alternately hide smirks and yawns, try to guide the conversation toward drinking, women, and ice hockey? That's *impolite*. And so, you really *are* forced to suffer. Sometimes you gather up the courage and break off the conversation. Even *that* requires immense effort, because then, you have to overcome yourself. You get stirred up, start sweating, and wind yourself up tighter and tighter until you finally explode. You want to scream in their faces: "Go to hell, that doesn't interest me!"; but instead, you smile and apologize and say you're short on time, that you've got a lot of drudgery to do at work. Afterward, you can't find peace for half an hour; you consider your bravery, plan to change your entire life to come, and smoke a great deal, but your heart "beats at an accelerated rhythm."

And how can you especially blame those squirts, anyway? Not for arguing in and of itself. Everyone has their own tastes. Let them bicker among themselves. But what's unforgivable is the fact that they don't grasp, can't even imagine that there could be people who don't enjoy arguing; who outright abhor it. That there exists a mental attitude that spits upon debating;

according to which he who argues is already an idiot in advance. That you can find people who are tired of arguing for arguing's sake. Who have come to understand that it leads nowhere. That arguing is a stupid substitute for true wisdom. That arguing is technocratic.

After flapping their tongues, the squirts feel as though something just happened. That once again, they seemed to have exercised their spirit, messed around with art; seemed to have once again spoken about culture or about life itself. The ritual had been performed, the box checked. They could just as well mark down in their daily report that they walked around in front of the Writers' House for an hour or sat in the Radio House cafeteria. But the fact that in their squabbling they didn't even brush any of the true issues doesn't seem awful to them. The thought doesn't even cross their minds. They don't grasp that something *else* exists.

Proof alone proves nothing. Everything of secondary importance can be proven, like scientific questions or the odds and ends of everyday life. That it's twenty degrees Celsius outside today, that elephants don't live in South America, that a bottle costs ten rubles, that the sun shines in the sky, that someone jumps two meters, that you'd like some coitus, that unhealthy states of mind dominate among the American youth. Step up to all of it, if you please, roll up your sleeves, and prove it. But not one iota more!

Sometimes, Fabian even doubted what was just mentioned. He was plagued by the suspicion that even the most elementary information didn't reach his fellows when expressed aloud. In the flow of people walking down the street or, for instance, when he wants to exit through a door that has a line of people winding in front of it; when he wants to push through the crowd, he should say, "Please step aside," but he can't get the words out of his mouth; he's afraid that those words will be misunderstood. He clenches his fists, growls in dark rage, and shoves his way through, chest-first. He, a high-principled aesthete, who received money for putting words in order!

In any case, when a conversation takes a turn, as soon as people start discussing what *this* is, this life of ours, or what art or faith or science is, then you never get farther than the first couple of sentences. When different intellects or intellect and non-intellect meet, then it takes such a ridiculous amount of energy and blather to explain the most basic of basics that what follows turns into foolishness. No one can be brought around in terms of what is key if he or she doesn't initially possess prerequisites in the form of a corresponding attitude. But if they do? In that case, they could even be sorted out; then, they could be taken by the hand and led, playing the role of a guide across the intellectual landscape. That's not "proving" anymore. For you have to see *on your own*. A guide leads a person to something and provides explanations. He doesn't prove that standing before you is El Escorial, but merely gestures in its direction. It's offensive to think that something should be proven. Whoever cannot understand without it cannot understand at all. And shouldn't, either.

Fabian has personally walked a long road. In retrospect, it seems unbelievable that once, even he would argue to the point of self-forgetting, doing so especially fanatically with strangers, studying their opinions with the fascination of a naive sociologist. He strove to prove his own opinions to them, convincing and explaining them. He participated in speech competitions and debate nights. All kinds of seminar camps and meetings were a treat for him. Especially in the event that representatives of sundry fields were spending time together, like at young academics' summer camps. He awaited those get-togethers with the excitement of a child awaiting his birthday or Christmas. Even the offer that had fallen into his lap today would have seemed like a heavenly blessing back then. Then, he wanted to get a handle on his life; now, he doesn't even want to catch a glimpse of it.

Back then, he was intrigued by both the individual soul and the collective conscience. He was clever at figuring them out. At one point, he came across a book with a foreword that promised to elucidate how to change your entire life through speech. The book didn't lie. From that book, Fabian learned how to look a partner squarely in the mouth and nod along. He let people talk about themselves; to chat about their own lives. He knew that others enjoyed that. He heard about many new things, including extremely alien, mind-boggling everyday lives in different professions, modes of living, and mental worlds. Yet, it was the *variety* that made what he heard exciting, captivating, and a true cognitive exploration. Now, he only wants to hear what he already knows, or what he's confident he'll like beforehand. If anyone talks about anything else, then he refuses to take it in, absentmindedly scribbling triangles and rhombi on a sheet of paper. When the conversation takes place over the phone, he simply holds the receiver away from his ear. He has already been caught doing it on a couple of occasions, because he completely forgot that he was on a call.

Before, he would zealously make new acquaintances. Communicating intensely, associating with as many different kinds of social groups as possible was a kind of growing pain: speaking with philosophers and poets, criminals and sailors, profiteers and boy scouts, playboys and all manner of people. His immense interests and ambition were to blame. Back then, he loved being clued up on everything. "That's how I synthesize the non-existent unity of my generation," he would boast to his friends. Now, when four or five people in the world would have been enough for him, that onetime, insane ambition was taking its revenge.

Casually formed ties are a pain in Fabian's neck, like a bastard child a girl has before marriage. And if only the matter were limited to the fruits of his former wantonness! He *could* start to gradually shake off those old acquaintances, those mistakes of youth, which had now become bothersome. It's simple. You refrain from replying to someone's New Year's greetings. You don't send someone a card on Red Army Day. You don't greet a friend's wife or are deliberately rude to his mistress. If you encounter some acquaintance for three days in a row, you breeze past him each time, not even stopping for a polite half-minute conversation, only smiling: Look, I'm in a hurry. No doubt the friend will realize he should be offended. When all measures have been applied steadily, then the field will soon be clear and only those whom you personally desire will remain. Only—Fabian won't get off the hook that easily. For who isn't aware that acquaintances make new acquaintances all on their own; our friends' friends are our friends, too. The wheels have been set in motion, and it goes on automatically; you no longer control that chain reaction. Every wretched day, someone could call up your friend and ask him to introduce you to each other at lunch. At any moment, some dilettante could categorically demand that you be brought together *today*; that he has an insatiable hunger to debate with that "guy," meaning you yourself. Certainly right now, some greasy-haired, cross, and unquestionably ugly young 'un is engrossed in a manual of Zen Buddhism in order to come and undermine the scant faith you have left with the granules of thought he has borrowed from that work; to spit on your soul's last remaining sanctities; to upset your already brittle everyday existence. Even some refined woman might bleach her hair in honor of your acquaintance and mentally go over and over her intellectual baggage, which consists of a couple dozen names, ten or so aphorisms by a French writer, and five fresher pieces of gossip.

Fabian's current job crowned his cascade of acquaintances. Here, interaction with people was inevitable; making new acquaintances was indirectly one of his official duties. The readers demanded fresh names, and Fabian had to acquire them. He didn't want to see anyone, but all the same, he had three different kinds of business cards in his wallet in addition to notebooks full of telephone numbers, and representative fees were put together out of the "black till" for him to take guests from abroad out for dinner and drinks.

Fabian could regard himself as "one of our own" in several places. In the city center, there were at least three editorial offices and five private bars where he could go daily to do this and that and drink vodka without consequence. He was asked to discuss things, to give advice, and to tell of any news, although people were glad to see him entering through the door just the same, without any specific reason. Someone was always drinking somewhere; the opposite was never the case. He gave in. He's a man who's unable to say no. He knows how it all began. There was a time when, as a young beginner, he couldn't reject a single invitation. Otherwise, he would have been left out. Work transpired through social life. Like it once did on golf courses or in theater boxes. That was then. The situation has changed. He could retain his status with honor even if he were to forego social boozing. Some are capable of it. And no one declares ostracism against them. Even Fabian has long since been able to choose where to go and where not to go without the threat of future boycott if he refused; without possibly having to drop out of the scene. He grits his teeth. And still, he goes everywhere, he accepts everything. But not because he's afraid that he'll disappoint others with his refusal. Far from it. "No" simply doesn't cross his lips. And it's not as if he'll gain that skill anymore.

Now he's certainly not being entirely honest. It really doesn't pay to justify things, claiming that you're dragged everywhere by force; that you yourself are utterly passive. You can lead a horse to water . . . but it'll gallop there if it's vodka. In moments of weakness and lack of willpower, when he could no longer manage to get anything done, when his mind was empty and his mood had plummeted—when those instants caught him near some familiar locale, then he was irresistibly drawn to step in "just for kicks." And where else *could* it happen? There were simply so many of those places. Other people probably had fewer. In the morning, Fabian—his head splitting—cursed his abundance of acquaintances, but in the evening, it mostly made him glad. When sober, he was jealous of those who had only a couple groups of friends—three or four at the most— with whom they could go out and get wasted. Yet *he* had to go out with hordes of people. Daily partying tended to affect his health. What would happen when the landslide of acquaintances progressed? What would happen when he knew everyone one day? Then, I'll probably be dead, Fabian thought bitterly.

He was incapable of changing himself, but in order to delay such a sad ending, even just a little, he had to act cleverly. Fabian crossed over to the other side of a street more than once a day in order to avoid meeting an individual who might coax him to come along somewhere. He turned a corner and waited until the undesired person passed by. Yesterday, for example, he popped momentarily into a pet store to hide. So far, he'd been lucky. Yet who could guarantee that by concealing himself, he wouldn't end up jumping out of the frying pan and into the fire? That there in the pet store, he might not stumble across a mauve-nosed children's writer who had come to buy food for his hamster, but upon seeing Fabian would sacrifice his pet's interests; would have forgotten the rodent's abdominal chemistry, and decided to drink away the money together at a corner bar?

At work, Fabian had erected an array of lines of fortification. Since he and the typist had a parallel telephone, he would always let the old woman be the first to answer, and then listen to who was speaking. Fabian had instructed the old typist and their young secretary on how to respond to someone when they came to request an appointment with him in person. Who should be lied to, who should be told the truth. It wasn't far off from him giving them a list of physical features and photographs en face and in profile, just like on wanted posters in train stations; not of fugitives in this case, but rather of respected and promising cultural figures, of decent and outstanding people.

He—a successful individual in the eyes of the public, an up-and-coming, herald and hope of his generation—hid himself like a debtor who has borrowed something from everyone. And still, day after day, he returns to his editorial office, straight into the clutches of his lenders, plays hide-and-seek with them in the hallway and in the slim space between the restroom and the offices, because to stay at home "on his own island," to carry out a slow suicide, seemed far more awful.

II

Fabian decided to go to the bar next door for a coffee. It turned out to be a fateful decision, but only later. There didn't appear to be any of his friends at the bar but he had no desire for company. There were relatively few patrons as all the decent people who had come for lunch had already gone back to work, while the evening drunks had not yet arrived. Fabian chose an empty table, looked around in boredom while waiting for the waiter, and discovered that the old sign reading "Merry Christmas!" had finally been taken down. It was the last chance for it, too; they had been a little late in removing it this year, as the calendar already showed an Indian summer. Fabian strove to be on his own, but even so, the topics being discussed at the adjacent tables soon reached his ears as the tables were placed very close together and the patrons at them spoke loudly, like animals in their pens on Christmas Eve. They were discussing how they should go and congratulate the translator Valentin, who was celebrating a little birthday anniversary that night. Hearing this,

Fabian's heart dropped, for the birthday affected *him* as well.
How could he have forgotten! And he'd already hoped that he'd
escaped for today. Now, escape was out of the question. Valentin
was one of his closest friends. Especially before. Lately, their ties
had eased. A large number of new acquaintances had been added
to his life and cast somewhat of a shadow over Valentin's former
special status. But that didn't count. Others could be good, too,
but *he* was Fabian's first. Valentin had done many good things
for him. It would be rude of Fabian not to go over, even though
the group at the adjacent table, gesticulating vibrantly and passionately, would definitely be among the guests. No doubt they
would carry on behaving like demonstrative futurists, breaking
things and deliberately ignoring table manners that night. Poor
Valentin—it would be too bad if he had to get by with only
their company; he, who couldn't bear futurism in the very least!
Fabian realized that the die had been cast. He must sacrifice
himself once again. But he wasn't prepared! Fortunately, he remembered that he had a book in a drawer at work—one on
French-language aphorisms about women (which he had otherwise intended to give to the used bookstore), and that someone's still relatively fresh marigolds were standing in a vase at
reception. He would take them with him when he was the last
to leave the building. Especially since Valentin loved uncon-
ventional bouquets, golden chains, daphnes, chamomiles, and
morning glories. Valentin was still just talking about wanting to
learn French, but his ballerina sister had spoken it for a while.

Valentin lived in a neighborhood that was called "new," even
though it was already starting to crumble at one end. Newer
districts had been completed by now; the whole city had been
encircled by ugly gray symmetrical apartment blocks. Valentin's
neighborhood had been labeled as "new" since the old days. The
best way to get there was by trolley. A taxi would take you even
faster, of course. But Fabian didn't have all that much money

at the moment, though he certainly had time, since it wasn't the done thing to get to a birthday party too early; to be the very first to arrive. He ambled over to the trolley stop. It came immediately—too quickly, like an uninvited guest. At the same time, Fabian wasn't about to skip it for the next one, since it appeared to be relatively empty and he would be able to get a seat soon. Out of the two seats being vacated, he chose the one abandoned by a young woman in jeans. Fabian could still feel the warmth in the upholstery. He put on his dark glasses. It was early September outside and the glaring sun shone with a special cosmetic beauty. Women's arms were bare, but plump and brown, so their pockmarks almost didn't show. People didn't know how to dress—whether according to the calendar or the weather, as always during transitional seasons.

Fabian had traveled that route often; especially when he was a student and Valentin was his sole acquaintance in the capital. Valentin had been the one who brought him into society. To this day, Fabian is grateful to him. He would have ended up in society on his own anyway, too (he never doubted that), but only after four or five years. Maybe faster, though. Or with someone else's help. That didn't matter. It's a big thing when someone nudges you so far ahead of your life's normal schedule, in any case. Fabian had been writing his thesis at the time and was an unremarkable, ambitious young man; one of thousands. The thesis did not go easily. Some of the books he needed were in the capital, some in the country. A number of smart people who could have helped him with advice lived in Eastern Estonia, while another portion lived in the western part of the country and in little forest villages. And so, he traveled from one town to another, not finding peace, and wasting money. Fabian's briefcase, with which he hauled around resources for his ever-expanding paper, was stretched to ugly proportions, and the lining showed through the leather in some spots like pink underwear. There seemed to be no end in sight. Everything in his head was mixed up, and the scraps of paper covered in writing lacked a method and a credo. Ultimately, Fabian ended up visiting Valentin for some book. At that time, a powerful sense of mission burned brightly within Valentin, and he took Fabian under his wing without any further ado. He took Fabian seriously and helped him organize ideas for his thesis. Fabian lived there for a week, eating his food, drinking his wine, and listening to the bits of wisdom that spilled out at the dinner table. Back then, Valentin practiced a very active social life. He interacted with people probably even more intensely than Fabian does now. All manner of people streamed through his apartment over the course of that week! The motliest group of people you could imagine. Valentin introduced Fabian to them as his "young friend"; a representative of the new generation. "Our post-generation!" as he put it. Fabian wore a shy expression and remained silent, since he was unable to say anything that might sound new to them and prove his unarguable belonging to the post-generation. Not that it would have especially interested anyone, anyway.

But one time, a very peculiar guest arrived. He wasn't a simple man—one could see that even from his socks. Not an ordinary actor, writer, designer, or shrink, like those who constantly buzzed around that apartment. He was a pure aristocrat. A stocky man with a reddish-blond mane of hair and wearing a good suit. He was fairly intoxicated, but seemed to have his wits about him. Fabian had no idea where Valentin found him for his collection. In any case, he treated the man with sufficient deference, which he did not always do with the other more-or-less tipsy guests. For Valentin had long since moved from quiet Tartu to the capital city and had already seen a lot, so in truth, nothing surprised him anymore. Cramps, hallucinations, and "self-discovery" didn't have that much of an effect at his salon. Someone said the man's name was Taniel. At an opportune moment, Valentin planted Fabian in front of the guest like a full glass of cognac. "Talk to him," he whispered into Fabian's ear.

Fabian introduced himself and told him what he was doing at present. "And how's it going?" Taniel stooped to inquire. Fabian replied that he was finding it difficult; that he wasn't able to capture what is primary. That there are facts, but still a ways to go before synthesis. "You're right—don't deal in trivialities," Taniel said carelessly. "I was just the same in my youth—my hands were itching, but the water ran through my fingers. At least we had good employment prospects. Those of your generation are less so . . . What kinds of problems do you all have? They're probably different from ours, aren't they? Do you yourselves understand them? Do you even *have* problems?" Taniel cracked his knuckles to the rhythm of his words. "We'll try to achieve clarity on this together . . . Let's start from the simplest: tell me, what do you think about everything?"—"I don't know," Fabian replied with complete sincerity. "Very nice answer," Taniel said, tossing his head back. "Come with me and I'll tell you!" Then he asked what time it was and told someone to order him a taxi. Naturally, he didn't intend to take Fabian with him right away. What he had said just before was promised more in principle, for at the door, he squeezed Fabian's wrist, looked into his eyes, blew a breath into his face, and said meaningfully: "If there's anything—call!" And then he was gone, vanished into the snowstorm, saturated in alcohol but still capable of doing business; in short—a great and intellectually rich personality. When the door had closed, Valentin poured everyone whiskey, launched into a euphoria, scuttled around the room, and said animatedly: "He's one of the leading emotionals of our era. He's even got influence on them *there* . . . He always thinks globally and he has a whole lot of ideas . . . If even a portion of them are realized, then great things can be expected . . . Oohh . . ." He lit a cigarette. With his restive ambition, Fabian resolved to strike while the iron was hot, and asked Valentin to pair them up again sometime. "Certainly!" Valentin thundered. "Now, he took note of you himself. He'll keep you in mind—I know it. No doubt he'll invite you out on his own. You'll go far!"

Taniel was in fact the one from whom Fabian dove into the pet shop for cover; because of whom he was forced to listen to the peeping of white mice and a macaw's ear-splitting racket, his back pressed up against plate glass, behind which a black grass snake shifted from one position to another.

Fabian had traveled the route many times since forever ago, and its familiarity didn't draw his attention. He was accustomed to having a quarter of an hour to himself when riding to Valentin's apartment, pondering a few thoughts or simply letting his mind wander. But not always. If he was unable to sit down, then things were very bad. The other trolley passengers swayed terribly. Women who'd eaten so much that their bottoms had grown to the point of astonishing obesity, as if preparing for winter hibernation, always tried to shove their way to the front of the bus. Likewise, a lot depended on who happened to sit down next to you. There were good and bad seat-fellows. Some were conducive to pondering, others disturbed it. A troublesome neighbor was worse than an enemy—sitting down next to him was more horrific than standing. A tenured public transport user notices quite a bit, and draws his own conclusions from it. Over time, Fabian had observed that younger women and teens sat next to him relatively rarely; only as a last resort. Why? He wasn't overtly unscrupulous, was he? What's more, he could be wearing a filthy nylon windbreaker or a snazzy coat; could be sober or dozing off a little—beautiful women would pass by his seat regardless. It couldn't just be random. Doubtless women at the pinnacle of their reproductive age had a sixth sense even from a distance for the proclivity for destruction hidden within Fabian; instinctively picked up on his dark melancholy. However, a proper woman— as an embodiment of natural continuity and an instinctive affirmation of life—will always resist such a mood or simply avoid its bearer. And so much the better, Fabian consoled himself, since the proximity of young women led his thoughts elsewhere—most often to the women themselves—and disturbed his concentration. The best fellow passengers were thin men in gray, ready-made suits that cost somewhere around twenty-five rubles apiece. They quickly created a conducive and neutral environment because they took up little space in their seat, and even if he made a great effort, there was no basis for dreaming about any kind of adventures in which they might jointly participate.

Two stops had already gone by, but the seat next to Fabian was still free. I made it, he sighed to himself in relief when the bus doors also shut at the third stop and it jerked forward. It was a good start, and now there would follow a line of stops that bore bird names, nestled in the tangle of houses between the new district and the actual city, which very few people were commuting to or from at that time of day. It appeared that the thicket was quiet this time, too.

In vain! He had already counted himself lucky, having escaped once today, and just like that time, things went differently now. The already moving bus stopped again, and the front door shuddered open. Fabian saw a chubby, red-faced man rushing to the trolley stop from a distance, one hand holding down his straw hat so that the breeze whipped up in his great rush wouldn't blow it away. For some reason, it seemed like he was holding a watermelon. Fabian had a hunch the man would sit down next to him. And so he did. When the man settled into the seat, Fabian had to shuffle over to the side a little, even though he always—even when sitting alone—kept precise track of the dividing line. He didn't barge into strange territory, and was dreadfully offended when he was bumped. Fabian didn't tolerate physical contact. Whenever an acquaintance unintentionally placed his hand on Fabian's shoulder or wrapped an arm around him, it was not uncommon for Fabian to emit an outright roar. But sometimes he put up with human contact quite well. Fabian edged even closer to the window, since the first time apparently hadn't been enough. The man pulled a sports paper out of his jacket pocket and shifted in his seat, brushing Fabian again. Fabian edged over once more, but it seemed as if the man was inexplicably *still* rubbing against him all the same. He was a strange seat partner. He puffed up, looking bigger and bigger. The man appeared to spill out like a sloppily heaped haystack or a mass of dough. His body seemed to lap over either end of his seat now and then. In the end, Fabian was able to avoid touching the man's side only if he squashed himself up against the window with all his might. He was extremely irked. His whole body under stress, a stranger's elbow sticking between his ribs like a revolver—you can't mull over things or submit to reflection like that. Fabian would have wanted to ask him: Where's your watermelon? The man sniffled. Maybe the gentleman would like to say something, Fabian huffed to himself crossly, only he just doesn't know how to start; the laconic giant can't find the right expressions? The man turned to the second page of the newspaper, making the page rustle right in front of Fabian's nose. Poe's terrifying razor-sharp pendulum materialized before him. Fabian attempted to make himself even smaller, but was unable to. On top of it all, the man's knee rubbed quite heedlessly against Fabian's own; as loosely as the drooping jaw of someone nodding off. The man apparently felt quite at liberty. Fabian was unable to bear it anymore, so he stretched his elbows and shifted his knees. The man startled and politely made space. He apparently wasn't ill intentioned at all. It was highly likely that he had no idea what was going on in Fabian's soul. He wasn't aware that he was being bothersome. That was surprising. Fabian felt certain that the man was hassling him on purpose; out of pure sadism. For how could it possibly not cross the mind of a person—made of the same skin, bone, and blood as he was—that how you sit next to another man makes a *difference*? That it's not the same as sitting next to a woman. That sitting isn't a natural act that can be done unconsciously, ignoring the outcome. *Nothing* is natural. Everything passes through the court of consciousness: breathing, standing, sleeping. And sitting. Where had the man gotten the idea that you don't have to be aware of yourself when sitting; that you're allowed to relax and not think about your seat partner? Nevertheless, Fabian didn't have the courage to say all this aloud, because he knew that the man might become downright cross if he started instructing him how he's supposed to sit, eat, or stand correctly. He has known how to sit his entire life, but now, all of a sudden, it turns out that he *hasn't*.

The man's simplemindedness was moving. For a nerveless hulk like him—someone whose body doesn't guide sensuous energy, just like a sheet of particle board—getting by in his own life was just a walk in the park. Fabian was even more moved by the fact that he was moved. He thought: I can't be a totally negative person if I'm capable of becoming emotional over prereflective cogito. He felt self-affirmed for the first time in a long while. It was a rather good feeling.

But not knowing the law doesn't ease the punishment. He had been sensitive with quite enough of their kind; had striven to understand them! Fabian turned his thumb downward in his mind, as the fifteen-minute ride had now turned out to be exhaustingly long and his reflections had foundered. Fabian even got off the trolley a stop early in order to kill time by walking. He would probably have done so anyway. He didn't want to arrive at the beginning of the party. Valentin was throwing a big birthday party. All kinds of people would certainly come, including old schoolmates, immediate relatives, colleagues, and translators. Those are usually the first to show up. The guests are quite stiff at first, everyone greets everyone else with a handshake, and the host tries to get them acquainted with one another. Some old woman could end up being Fabian's conversation partner and tire him out with all kinds of moronic questions about his job. The guests will munch on breadsticks and no one will have the courage to be the first to ask for vodka, even though everyone will be dying of thirst. The atmosphere will be sober and dreadfully forced. The situation will change later on. An endless stream of people comes and goes during those open-door birthday celebrations. Some will come after a performance, others had been waiting for their children to fall asleep, and still others were at another party before they arrived. No one bothers to introduce the late arrivals. At some point, three people might come together and hear with amazement that they had all been at N's birthday party, even though no one remembers seeing the others.

Fabian's caution was for naught, all the same. Judging by the guests' faces, the party had been going strong for several hours. He reckons that people get started earlier and earlier every year; on this occasion, it had probably been first thing in the morning. Life goes on and people's demands increase. The impressive restaurant-ordered meat platter bore obvious signs of decimation. A couple of peas had rolled off the platter onto the white tablecloth, and had been squashed under someone's elbow; a lone pig tongue sneered on the platter, as if it were sticking out of someone's mouth; here and there, the rim of a saucer had already been mistaken for an ashtray. The birthday boy was still sober enough to personally receive his guests. It seemed to Fabian as if Valentin was apologizing for the profusion of guests. And indeed: after his greeting, he added in hushed tones that he would gladly speak with Fabian one-to-one; that they hadn't seen each other for nearly a week, but an opportunity for conversation would hardly surface today, as politeness requires him to treat everyone equally that night. Fabian reassured Valentin that he fully understood—that a birthday boy is usually like the groom at his own wedding, always having the least fun out of everyone and being allowed to do the very least of what he personally wants to do. "You don't talk about rope in a hanged man's house!" Valentin said, laughing. He'd been a bachelor in principle since his wife left him five years earlier, running off with an older, poorer, uglier, and less famous man. That was in style lately. Women had gone crazy. "The modern *Perversität*," Valentin himself commented with a chuckle. He translated primarily from German.

Fabian smoothed back his hair, checked to make sure the bottom button on his vest was still undone, and gradually strolled into the din of the living room, which felt quite small seeing as how it was filled with tables from wall to wall. There was a gap between two older women near the door. Fabian pushed his way through, mumbling hellos and apologies, trying to draw as little attention to himself as possible. He had glimpsed friends at the other end of the table. "It's been a long time, good to see you," Ingo said without lifting his nose from his plate. Perched on the tip of Fabian's tongue was the question: why hadn't Ingo said a word that day about intending to come here in the evening? Why hadn't he reminded Fabian that today was Valentin's birthday? He would have wanted to grab Ingo by the chest, shake him, and yell: "Why didn't you tell me you were planning to come and get hammered here tonight, you good-for-nothing?" However, he realized that by doing that, he would be violating some kind of rules known only to them.

Fabian looked around leisurely and observed with great satisfaction that all of the guests' initial awkwardness had passed. He slammed down a couple shots of vodka, waiting patiently for his body to begin tingling. Busy young women who smelled of cake, frizzy clumps of hair plastered against their flushed foreheads, immediately brought him a clean plate and a fork. Fortunately, Fabian had just eaten, and wouldn't necessarily have to heap his plate with food from the platters, since it's not at all courteous to be spreading mustard on aspic while others are sipping coffee from dainty cups as exquisite as owl eggshells. Fabian couldn't stand the smell of food, particularly when it came from the mouth of a conversation partner, and not counting when he himself was presently dining. Food had a worse aroma than alcohol, in his opinion. It was strange that most people thought the opposite. True, it also depended on the brand of beverage. The stench of ether was undoubtedly worse than the smell that wafted from the windows of a bakery. Still, eating is a vapid act overall. Fabian didn't know how to behave, where to put his eyes, ears, and nose when a fellow train passenger piled the compartment table high with small bundles of food and crockery. In his opinion, devouring pastries on the street should be a finable offense. Even eating in places specially designated for the act could trick you miserably. How many people, whom Fabian would otherwise have been prepared to respect to this very day, had lost their status in his eyes as soon as he saw them at the lunch table for the first time, readying the contents of their plate before lifting it to their mouths, their thumbs in their soup, handling their dish, licking their knife, and sucking their teeth with a squeaky sound. Because of this, Fabian had turned cautious. For the most part, he ate alone or with complete strangers. At a banquet with a smorgasbord, he would go around a corner or hide behind a potted palm. He never launched into an eating encounter if he wasn't sure of a positive result beforehand. It wasn't the same as climbing into bed, was it! Otherwise, you might be disappointed and lose your appetite for the future.

Fabian's mood improved even further when he saw how correctly he had acted by sitting where he did. New guests were constantly arriving. The doorbell rang incessantly. Valentin wasn't even able to leave the front hallway, and was already calling for vodka to be brought over to him since he was going to just stay by the coatrack for the rest of the night. No one could fit at the table anymore, and those who were closer to the door inevitably had to get up and relinquish their seats to

others in order to give them the chance to knock back a little
booze. And so, before long, the temporary hostess (Valentin's
ballerina sister) gave the order to break ranks, announcing that
the official part of the evening was now over and everyone could
henceforth move freely, naturally carrying their coffee cup and
shot glass. Many indeed left for other rooms with hopeful looks
on their faces, as if who-knows-what excitement awaited them
there. Luckily there was enough space for all—the apartment
comprised five rooms, including the kitchen. As soon as the
radiola was switched on came the vigorous clomping sound of
heels, so eager were some for rock and roll. Female admirers
clustered around the celebrities—the hour for ambitious young
people to push their way into society had struck. The geniuses
they had selected as springboards had eaten their fill and were
as mild as metabolizing pythons, so it was easy to approach
them. They offered a wealth of theoretical promises easily and
generously. The icy propriety of the top dogs was already starting
to melt, people were already slurping their drinks, and vulgar
words were slipping into the conversation. The masters were
belching, disclosing unexpectedly liberal views, and mentally
disavowing their wives for the first time that night. Sharp eyes
could already discern the first signs of the mind's imminent and
inevitable succumbing to the flesh, and once again, the moment
at which intellectual giants flirt with absolutely every available
woman came one little step closer. Suddenly, an exceptionally
large amount of vodka started flowing.

No one left Fabian's little corner, nor were they in a hurry
to go anywhere. Sitting here was just as good as sitting at a bar
or a canteen: the same faces were around the table, the same
stuff upon it. Here was even better, since there were no waiters
or bartenders. Fabian couldn't stand them. Especially men who
had filled their bellies, who were flabby and arrogant. It would
be great if he could spend the entire birthday party here. Fabian
wished with all his heart that his friends desired the same.

That they wouldn't go drifting around or making any random acquaintances. That they wouldn't be enticed by the thought that original and interesting people might be sitting in the adjacent rooms. Go ahead and let them be there! I don't even want to know about them! I don't want to see or hear anything, not any news or people, Fabian thought. For they hadn't come to a session of the club of interesting meetings. Whoever wants news, go find yourself some TASS correspondent, and drag *him* around; no doubt he'll chat from the journalistic meridian or speak some other poppycock.

Fabian's friends' jokes became ever hazier and more refined, the backgrounds to them ever more selective. The constant rotation of guests gave rise to a vague general mood—there was no overseer of the table discussion. The host himself had disappeared somewhere; judging by the voices, one could guess that he was entertaining guests in the other rooms. The ballerina was decorating another cake in the kitchen. Fabian and company took advantage of the absence of a controlling hand, and forced their manner upon others. They reacted to the other guests' jokes, stories, and rejoinders so brutally and mercilessly that those telling them soon shut their mouths tight. Although it was highly entertaining to hear, a true dictatorship thus took shape. The others had given up competing with what came from the other end of the table, and although a few perhaps protested in their minds, even *they* laughed along obediently. On the whole, only a pair of gnarled old men (who loved to ramble on about life events contentedly and at length) sat looking sour. Fabian's mood only kept improving. After all, weren't they a great crowd altogether! You can't get *by* without them. Not a single clique can manage without that superior intellectual concentration in the way that *they* express it. So what if all of their energy and creative work, all of those fireworks of cynicism and displays of irony are cast to the winds; so what if their intellectual sparks fly out of the chimney and into the sky! Everything is destroyed at the very same moment it forms; no one is recording them. But in reality, their influence is much greater than it appears. Fabian was certain that the other rooms were more boring. Everywhere in the *world* was probably more boring than here. Fabian didn't want to leave.

Yet, he had already drunk a fair amount of both coffee and booze, and had to get up now to go to the toilet, just in case. He delayed it as long as he could, since he couldn't bring himself to leave out of fear that as soon as he did, some statement that would become historic would cross someone's lips, or a gesture that would be remembered years later would be born; luckily, Ingo reassured him—go right ahead and don't worry, I'll definitely sum up what and how later. They would switch roles afterward. Fabian worked his way toward the door. He had to elbow and worm his way through by force, because although the entire apartment was echoing with jovial voices, all of the spots here around the table were also full. Fabian felt as if he were crawling across someone's lap, then probably did brush someone's head with his stomach, knocked a shot glass that was set too close to the edge of the table onto the floor with the hem of his jacket, and then broke through into the hallway. There he breathed a sigh of relief, wiped the sweat off his brow, and listened. The party was picking up speed. In all five rooms, guests were chortling, guffawing, mewing, neighing, and barking laughter. Young women were tittering somewhere nearby. Fabian hated that kind of laughter. He used to let it disappoint him. Young women who laughed that way seemed very sensitive and receptive at first; very keen on nuance. It appeared as if they understood all the subtleties and particulars behind a text. That impression dissipated as soon as Fabian discovered that they tittered the very same way at the vapidities and banalities that were passed off as witticisms elsewhere. Such a lack of discernment offends him more than the complete lack of a sense of humor. The tittering was coming from his left. Fabian cocked his head to one side in order to hear better, and a large wall mirror happened to catch his eye. Valentin had recently renovated his apartment, had painted and moved furniture around. At first, Fabian didn't even realize that he was staring into a pier glass. Even so, he recognized himself straight away. It was him! He was standing in a cascade of light, as if bathed in golden rain, cast by the modern chandelier in the front hall.

Fabian crept up to the next door. Coming from behind it was the loud rumble of men's conversation. It appeared that they were debating management styles, lasers, sociology, supersonic airplanes, and economic self-administration. Fabian wrinkled up his nose and stuck his tongue out at the door. "Discuss, discuss your world affairs there," he whispered spitefully. Organize your mandatory culture mornings and hold your mock literary trials! Submit your rationalization proposals and hammer your swords into plowshares. Explore public opinion. Get the hell out of my way and off through hardships to the stars! he spat at them in his head, unleashing his harshest insults, annihilating them, and then creeping to the lavatory.

The bathroom door's round Finnish-made latch soon jerked almost noiselessly again. Fabian raised his eyebrows lewdly, inhaled deeply through his nose, and listened to the sounds of the nighttime orgy. He would have liked to do something naughty. He took a couple of steps and already *would* have happily darted back (he was even holding the handle that would open the way to a protective environment), but at that very moment, the door at which Fabian had been listening before opened, and Valentin appeared at its threshold. He was not yet completely drunk, and was wearing a black velvet vest over a white shirt like a gypsy violinist. Valentin asked Fabian to step into the room for a moment—he was actually just coming to look for him. Fabian initially thought that Valentin was joking, and replied rather cynically that, thank you very much, but he'd already been to the zoo that year. Valentin laughed, but appeared serious about his request. "Come on," he said, "there are completely different sorts of people in there than the ones whom you're chatting with in the back room, and whom you see every day to the point of nausea, anyway. It's good to meet people who are unlike you every once in a while. Make my birthday a springtime of experience!"

Fabian gloomily acknowledged to himself that although Valentin was a fantastic, intelligent man, they nevertheless belonged to different generations. There *was* an entire nine years' age difference between them. Valentin has other views, another mentality; from one aspect, he still belongs to a club of fun and inventive people, and is a man who wants to find out about everything and get to know who is toiling and endeavoring, struggling and arguing. Even now, at the age of forty, Valentin had started studying Spanish and practicing karate. A victim of his era, Fabian concluded bitterly. What kind of a guy they'd devoured!

"Come on, you're needed in there right now," Valentin continued. "The men in there are debating the crisis of the generations. You attended university in the period between two generations. You're like a link between them. You have a foggy conception of what was before and what came after. You were *there*. You must have some impressions and memories. We don't have a clue about the new youth. We only know it secondhand. Come and have your say. Bring us illumination!" Valentin said, gradually transitioning to the high style of speech that he ordinarily employed on such occasions. Valentin was thickset, stocky, brusque, and lazy like a groundhog, but when he really needed something (such as right now), then he was able to persuade one exceptionally well, using sonorous expressions like a great orator inciting the plebs at the forum, and being dreamily insistent like a true philanderer.

"I don't have any opinions on that topic," Fabian said, trying to worm his way out of it.

"Do you want to renounce your intellect?" Valentin asked icily.

Fabian explained patiently that there is no connection between aphorizing and intellect; that it was the very opposite—whoever debates is a fool. "Well, then I guess you should prove it to them," Valentin prodded him, and Fabian started to suspect that the birthday boy was drunker than he appeared. All the same, he decided to give it a go in the hopes that he would successfully emerge from the mess unscathed.

"But I've got no idea what the conversation was about; what ideas were discussed. I can't just barge in halfway through and start interrupting. I might start to repeat everything that you've all long since settled; I'll drag your tempo down."

"I'll summarize for you briefly," Valentin assured him very suggestively. Hearing this, Fabian started brandishing his arms hysterically. He declared that he didn't want to make an effort. He hadn't come all the way here to congratulate his friend just to end up arguing with some veterans. Had he known that a "dissertation defense" was underway here, he wouldn't have come. Go ahead, Valentin, and let them know that tonight, his position on the given issue is in a shot glass on the table in the back room. Tell your company there in the room to drink more and speak less foolishness.

"Let's go, then," Valentin said firmly, paying no heed to his tirade, staring right through him with a glassy look in his eyes, and seizing him by the sleeve. Like a vigilante, flashed through Fabian's mind. He broke into a sweat. It appeared things were getting serious. Until then, he had only talked about styles; now, he had to dive right into the water and swim.

Mostly men had gathered in the other room. There were only a couple of flat-chested young women swathed in velvet lounging fashionably on the floor in the middle of them. At first, Fabian thought they were exile Estonians. One or another visited Valentin every day. In reality, they were Valentin's cousins. They had just enrolled in college. Everything had indeed started with them, although a little later; not right away. The men were significantly older, but not yet elderly, belonging primarily to the generation of vim-and-vigor boys of the Valentin Age. Fabian could recall the aftershock of that pleiad, its last representatives, from his early university years. They were highly energetic people. They participated in hobby clubs and flying squads, climbed mountains in winter, worked in volunteer brigades in summer, and discussed politics during lecture breaks. They were brimming with optimism, possessed an extremely positive view of the world, and led the intellectual life of someone from the Renaissance. They were student-like in the generally recognized meaning of the word. They maintained a lively interest in the environment in which they lived, and wanted to reshape it. For instance, they came up with what Fabian thought was an exceptionally bizarre idea: to take upon themselves in dormitories and several places elsewhere the obligations of the official appointed to run it, who would otherwise have received a state salary for his work. They organized debates and meetings, campaigned and sang the complex and melancholy songs of contemporary Estonian poets, accompanying themselves on guitar. They sang a lot in general. They were constantly in a rush. They and their rush were lauded. Someone who held a hundred positions was counted as a first-class cavalier at a party. Fabian certainly wasn't sure whether that really was the case—whether women truly behaved that way. But it was highly likely. Women *do* determine everything. How long could a man force himself to act stiffly according to some guiding principles if that wasn't how women liked it? Fabian had observed in his everyday surroundings how difficult it was to remain intellectual when a woman held a lack of culture as her ideal. Basically, that was also how it was *then*. If a blonde hadn't given herself to an activist, then how long would the activist have been able to stay himself?

Fabian had encountered quite a few of the men in the lobby of the university's main building while they were incessantly rushing off to some secretive headquarters. Fabian remembered that they were treated a little differently than their later leaders. Perhaps they were simply better known; more conspicuous. They'd been trained in living the life of a public figure over the course of their active dealings; had acquired several of that social group's manners. For example, they had great respect for physical contact. They greeted you with a handshake much more than ordinary people—it wasn't uncommon for them to shake the same individual's hand several times a day. They would stand very close to a conversation partner, would put their hand on his shoulder, or wrap their arm around him. While young scholars and artists used the foreign expressions "all right," "okay," "*merde*," or "*so ist das Leben*" to continue a story, they loved to interweave into their speech the words "*dixi*," "*ladno*," and "*khorosho*."

In their subsequent lives, they had gotten involved in very diverse areas, all the while maintaining their reputations as predominantly non-conformist and progressive figures. One thing that stood out was that relatively few of them had become actual Communist Party functionaries. And even *they* hadn't reached the top yet; some kind of a force always seemed to keep them locked in mid-level positions. However, their need for public life had stuck. Very many of them worked as social scientists, foreign commentators, prosecutors, journalists, or a variety of advisors and aides. Another thing connecting them was a sense of general discontent.

Now, the former leaders had tugged off their jackets and taken positions on the floor along the wall. Such was their style. Boys, let's relax! They figured that if *they* reclined, then everyone else would feel like they could act dreadfully casually. The men remi-

nisced about funny episodes from tests and final exams, and told
anecdotes about an absentminded professor. A onetime anarchist
was already plucking at a guitar and starting to hum old Russian
criminal songs. It all set the tune for emotion. And then, completely by accident, it had become clear that the two girls sitting
in their midst were fresh-out-of-the-oven university students.
The two slender young women's endeavor toward intellectual
enlightenment moved the great men to emotion, and they saw
it as their duty to give them their blessing. However, since the
men had received intense schooling and possessed strong social
intuitions, it wasn't long before their conversation advanced to
the place of the university in Estonian culture. The men ardently
drew parallels between the current situation and the conditions
in which they had entered life. Many spoke about the particular-
ities of the moment. The men prompted one another. The young
women were given guidelines. Over the course of half an hour,
they were showered with the entirety of foreign policy, game
theory, all kinds of behind-the-scenes facts from various events,
the significant main stages of how city and country had drawn
closer, and snippets from the Moral Code. The dainty young
women were issued preposterous requirements for the next five
years. The things they had to accomplish over the course of
their studies! It was like Danko yanking his heart from his chest
and letting it radiate above their heads.[6] Inciting the masses.
Working at the gym and in a cellar. Not abandoning practicing
music and dance. Sketching out a rough draft of their future
dissertation. Not forgetting that doctors believe a woman's best
reproductive years fall during one's university age.

Valentin towed Fabian into the room at the same time as
a thin, baby-faced man—the former "brains" of a volunteer
brigade—was speaking to the young women about the
importance of a personal minimum program. "What's that?"

---

6   In reference to the Russian writer Maxim Gorky's short
story "Danko's Burning Heart."

Fabian asked Valentin softly. "Ask *him*," Valentin clucked into his hand. Instead of inquiring, Fabian gave the prettier of the girls the eye. He wasn't hoping to win over the girl's heart at all, didn't believe that she might submit herself to him after that one wink, and above all, he knew that Valentin wasn't, in principle, receptive to those seeking shelter for fleeting love in his apartment. He was conspiring with the girl over the speaker's shoulder only because he had started to feel sorry for the women, since he realized that the men's conversation was Greek even to them, although they didn't dare make a peep. Fabian wanted to hint to them that *he* too understood just as little of it; he yearned to inform them of his solidarity.

However, the "brains" was speaking on about how important a minimum program was right now in particular—at a time when not all youth are capable of speaking out on social issues; are indifferent, indolent, and have limited interest in them overall. That was precisely where the debate over today's youth had begun. Many didn't agree with the "brains." They asked: why so pessimistic? Why such grim tones? Are our youth truly that dull? It isn't true, others answered: they're capable of becoming impassioned, just that we don't *know* them; we've created a myth about them; we've desired phantoms, fashionable clichés.

"You have to say something," Valentin pleaded softly, yet passionately into Fabian's ear. "What?" Fabian shrugged. The "brains's" droning was making him drowsy. The conversation was definitely very interesting in the other room. These men here sure are talkative. How can they argue so much when there's actually nothing to argue about? Fabian wondered. The minimum-program-man wouldn't give up. He claimed that today's young generation differed from all the previous ones by the fact that it practically *wasn't* a generation! There was a generation before it, and one might come after, but at the moment there existed an amorphous group of young boys and girls who lacked a common mindset; who didn't create social values; who were incapable of historical creation; and what's worse—they *themselves* didn't know what they want. Yet, it isn't their fault, because they don't know what they're doing; the whole world, television and other media, the sexual revolution, and other vices of the modern era were to blame. Naturally, this didn't rule out the surfacing of lone, very strong personalities who would manage to penetrate that mire and realize themselves to the utmost extent. Still, even *they* wouldn't develop generational ideals; they always align themselves with earlier guiding principles and adopt the habits of some other generation, which they take up by closely associating with older friends. For, oddly enough—those "catch-uppers" know the very least about their own peers, but despise them the most, and are thus even more distant from them than others. This, in turn, conflicts with the mission that falls upon the shoulders of the "breakthroughers." This group's number is severalfold less than earlier. But there is significantly more to complete than before, since the dimensions widened. Therefore, a manifold obligation and responsibility rests upon each and every one of them. They must lead culture and society as far forward as their predecessors did. The "brains" called on people to align with the "breakthroughers." Naturally, he also regarded the two reclining girls as the latter. "You've got to go and exact revenge for your peers!" the man finally exclaimed hysterically. Then, his nose started to bleed. He had a sensitive and fleshy Armenian nose with reddish nose hairs, and it gushed blood profusely. He bleated for a cotton ball. The ballerina guided him to a sofa in the other room.

Valentin adeptly took advantage of the silence that arose while first aid was being administered to the wounded, asking why indeed they were arguing like medieval scholars theorizing about whether a mole might or might not have eyes—instead of having one of the animals be caught and then seeing for themselves. "Present among us is a representative of the very

generation being criticized and pitied by all of you—allow him
to personally say what he thinks about all of this." And Valentin
spun grandly toward Fabian, as if he were the Super Guest Star
of the show, and nudged him forward (Like he once nudged
me toward Taniel, flashed through Fabian's mind). Valentin
suffered from a "serving-up" disease.

A whisper rippled through the crowd. All eyes turned toward
Fabian. "Is he *really* that young?" someone rasped from the
corner. Fabian was well aware that he looked older than his years.
However, the question still angered him. For in his opinion, the
questioner's own generation conversely looked younger than
necessary. They wore the perpetually slanted mouths of insatiable little boys. They ate an enormous amount—six or seven
dishes a day. Do I have to show you my ID? he wanted to ask.
He was at a loss for words. He couldn't understand how the
conversation concerned him. "Pull yourself together!" Valentin said, tapping him lightly with his foot. He had to speak.
Fabian cleared his throat and commenced. It was unsettling to
hear himself in the silence. His voice tended to waver. That was
even a good thing—that way, people would believe him more;
would think that the words flowing spasmodically across his lips
excite him to death. Fabian voiced the opinion that, in his mind,
things weren't all that bad with the youth of today. *He* personally
didn't feel that the average young Estonian man or woman was
deadened; that they lacked the capability to be invigorated. He
couldn't blame them for a narrowness of interests. Young people
are always the same. They know how to enjoy themselves right
now, and are capable of feeling excitement. For instance, when
a conductor checking tickets enters a train carriage or a woman
enters a pub filled with men.

Fabian was regarded with new expressions. Valentin was
the first to cackle in delight. Gradually, the others started to
chuckle as well. Only a social psychologist, who was studying

the American youth movement, remained serious to the end, claiming that one Chicago professor thought the very same way. That comment was already accompanied by *true* exhilaration. Fabian hoped he had gotten away with it, but hope failed him for already the third time that day. A meek, yet painfully toxic-looking man, who had been silently but sharply observing everything that was going on, asked Fabian very mildly:

"Joking is all fine and dandy, of course. Who of us doesn't love to laugh? But someone said even before me that there's nothing more disagreeable than pointless aphorizing. You dearly love to scoff. You and some others. That's your job. Scoffing isn't bad in and of itself, especially when there's something to scoff at. But you're making a joke out of *everything*. Or am I wrong? Sure—I know that my question seems embarrassing to you; even so, I'd like to know whether you have any values to offer. I'd be interested to hear it from your own mouth—is there anything of worth to you in this world, or isn't there?"

"Come now, Fabian's no nihilist!" a tubby, well-meaning journalist (the special correspondent of a youth paper, who was striving to quash the budding fight in its infancy) exclaimed. However, the rest of the men immediately hissed at him to be quiet, as they hoped they would be able to argue themselves out. On top of that, they were sure that Fabian did really have some kinds of very intriguing ideas in reserve. *These* they yearned to hear in addition to what they already knew; to compare the former with the latter; to analyze and dissect them. Even Valentin egged him on: "Give it to them! Show them what you've got!"

Only Fabian knew that the ideas everyone was hoping for, he didn't have. He didn't know what to say. Everyone would immediately realize that he hadn't been thinking about anything over the last three years. That it's all a bluff, an empty shell, a promising superficiality. Yet, knowing the nearness of being exposed didn't bother Fabian. He wasn't embarrassed. He only felt great disgust. It all seemed unimportant to him. He could sense right away that the questioner was a refined man, wiser than all the rest put together. But why, then, didn't he stay on Fabian's side; why did he jump at undermining his own kind? He's certainly got some kind of inner flaw that made him bad-tempered, Fabian reasoned, maybe kidney stones, or liver disease, ruined by his diet during his college days? That would explain the pained look on his face, too.

But he had to come up with something, all the same. He couldn't stay completely silent, either. The former generation demanded to know: Has the legacy of the fathers been well kept? Fabian was afraid of snickering openly and offending the others. He picked up a shot of vodka and let his usual speech flow. He spoke of passive opposition; of nonviolence; a force that intends evil but manages good; of the impact of denial and its value; of artistic engagement; of liberalism. He had heard or read all of it somewhere. They weren't his words. He wove in terminology from art and psychology, hoping that they would be too foreign to the audience and that he wouldn't need to start justifying their use. The start went well. A whisper rippled through the ranks again. But then the questions started raining down. What did Fabian mean by this claim? What does he mean by that one? What is his own understanding of that concept? Fabian mumbled out a response. He started to stammer. There wasn't a trace of elegance about him. He had exhausted himself, was tired and apathetic. Like after intercourse with a woman whom he didn't love. He strove to break free, pitting the men against one another. The figure with the pained face started debating with the "brains," who had emerged from the other room and declared already while standing in the doorway: "Let's define terminology, let's define terminology!" The tubby journalist wanted to conciliate again—he knelt down before them, laid his hands on their knees, and sighed:

"Oh, boys—those were great times! Times when great deeds

were done! You remember all the places we worked up a storm, old man? Brilliant times those were—weren't they, old man?"

Fabian composed himself slightly and decided to leave a little better impression. His accursed vanity had broken through again, and so he piped up at the end of Tubby's comments, saying that every generation has some kind of a central characteristic that sets it apart from others. Back in their day, youth had had a proper dose of optimism and naivety in their blood. It was particularly thanks to *naivety* (since every global endeavor requires naivety), thanks only to the fact that people harbored a rock-hard belief in it, that the undertaking could come to fruition. Conversely, a spirit of doubt weakens. Skepticism coats deeds in rust. All great men and great nations have been a little naive. So it is with generations as well. There was definitely a romantic simplemindedness to Tubby's generation, in Fabian's mind. Why were such deeds accomplished otherwise; why did people work up a storm, otherwise?

Saying this out loud had been a fatal misstep. The men flared up. In their own eyes, they were very sharp-eyed skeptics, had ironically drawn smirks, were insightful and merciless analysts. "Listen, you really are a fake," the painful-faced figure said. "What do *you* know of our era? Who are *you* to speak up?"

"This, I won't tolerate," a bald university student council leader bellowed in support—a massive, very honest-looking, box-headed man wearing a ski sweater. Incredibly, he was completely sober.

"*Nothing* is sacred to that guy!" Fabian saw the man was gripping a glass of juice so hard that his knuckles were white. Here it comes, Fabian thought in exasperation, it won't wait! And what was worse—you can't explain anything to a person like him; the words won't sink in. It wasn't even worth trying. He has already formed an idea in his tiny brain, and he doesn't plan to rethink it. A true black hole! And then everyone will attack. They'll take off their belts and give him a beating. Their

types could kill you for your ideals, too. He had an inhuman
fear of any sort of physical violence. What's more, Valentin had
just whispered into his ear that he was going to the restroom,
saying Fabian should try to manage on his own meanwhile. As
if *he* would have been any help! He had been gone suspiciously
long by now, leaving Fabian in the midst of those monsters.
Doubtless he had forgotten, passed out, or started hitting on
someone. But perhaps it had been intentional: did Valentin
plan the entire incident? But why? What have *I* done? Fabian
wondered. Did I steal a girl from him? Valentin wouldn't have
been angry about that. A debt? Not especially; and he just owed
me money recently. Maybe Valentin is afraid that I'm hankering
to take over his place? That's ridiculous. Or does he truly want
to bring me together with life itself and boost the relatively
sterile level of my writing?

Fortunately, the men had begun squabbling among
themselves once more, and Fabian was forgotten in an instant.
He took advantage of the opportunity and slipped out of the
room. The toilet was occupied, so Fabian locked himself in the
bathroom, even though he wasn't planning to vomit. Valentin
had a fantastic bathtub built into the floor. It radiated lust
and was lined with light-blue glazed tiles. Why does an old
bachelor need a bathtub like this? Fabian wondered, sitting on
the washing machine. What does he do in it? He felt a little
embarrassed. As if someone had gotten the better of him. He
tried to convince himself that it was of no consequence and that
he should ignore it. Still, he wasn't certain whether anything
about his stance was exemplary or worthy of Valentin's cousins'
admiration. They had kept silent; they weren't even noticed.
Although, it seemed that neither of them had been interested in
the sophisticating.

Fabian was reminded of a girl with whom he had fallen in
love in the tenth grade. Fabian had met her at the Cultural
Center, at a dance for city kids. Back then, the girl had been

of much greater value than he had since she bore a strong resemblance to Monica Vitti, and had successfully courted one of the city's most famous guitarists before being involved with Fabian. Fabian went on a date with her, wearing a cheap green windbreaker and army boots. If we look for a prototype again, then perhaps he only resembled the man from "There is Such a Lad."[7] Nevertheless, the girl still dated him. The situation seemed strange even to himself, not to mention others. Once, young Fabian could no longer stand it, and, having stimulated his own masochism with a couple of shots at the bar, asked her frankly: "Why on earth are you going out with me? I'm not rich, handsome, or even famous yet. You could find yourself much higher caliber of men whenever you want to." Monica Vitti answered shortly and sweetly: "Because you have a beautiful soul." Fabian blushed and coughed. Actually, he was still dumbfounded and happy for a long time after that. Where's my beautiful soul now? Fabian wondered while sitting on the washing machine, having lost the battle for ideas he didn't believe in; having fought those whom he couldn't stand, and he pressed his face into the ballerina's bath towel.

He dozed off, apparently. When he came to again, and cautiously cracked the door open, silence reigned in the room that had just been full of his fears. I bet they're taking a break and counting the corpses, Fabian mused. He entered the room where he had left his group of friends. Odd—it was empty. Every bottle of vodka had been drained, the sofa cushions were jumbled, the tablecloth soiled, and on the rug, an art book was opened to one of Magritte's more gruesome paintings. Fabian cocked an ear. The entire building seemed bizarrely silent. Only a loose four-track cassette ribbon rustled softly, spinning on its reel. Fabian looked at the clock and was startled. He had thought that his trip to the other room lasted half an hour at the most, but the

---

7   "Живёт такой парень," a 1964 Soviet film.

clock hands already showed early morning. The whole night had strangely gone by. Fabian was embarrassed. Everyone had left. No one had any interest in him. Neither Ingo nor the others had been troubled by Fabian's unexpected disappearance at the party's climax. He hurried out. In the hallway, he bumped into Valentin's ballerina sister, who was holding a broken red wine bottle. She eyed Fabian with restrained disgust. She was apparently afraid that Fabian wasn't actually planning on leaving; that he wanted more to drink or to stick his head into her lap and start confessing. When she saw that he wasn't intending to do either of these things, she said quite resignedly: "They broke a bottle right before they left; there are shards everywhere and it'll leave a stain, too."

Fabian left. What more could he do here? Entering the hallway, his first thought had been: where could he go to end the night and continue carousing? But the rising sun was shining outside, and seeing people passing by was enough for him to banish that kind of a delirious idea. He was embarrassed to look passersby in the face, as he had exchanged night for day like an infant. A vision materialized in his head: it was a morning identical to the one now, people are hurrying out of apartment-block doors and to transport stops to board a trolley or a bus. But look—Fabian's acquaintances are also walking here at a brisk pace. Bohemians are pushing their children in strollers or leading them by the hand to the nursery or preschool. Freelancers, who otherwise hardly drag themselves out of bed before noon, are the first ones waiting patiently in line at the door to the milk shop. Vagrants are standing in line at savings banks to pay their apartment rent on time. Playboys are returning from the market, wearing flip-flops at the ends of their pleated pant legs, their mesh bags full of fresh vegetables. Even barflies have washed their greasy hair and changed their oily rags for blue dress shirts. Broads are buying Communist Party newspapers from the kiosk. And walking in the midst of these businesslike people is he, Fabian, who has drunk himself sober, has a cigarette hanging from the corner of his mouth, bloodshot eyes, a couple of stains on his clothing, and the sort of expression on his face that suggests detonating the entire universe wouldn't cost him a thing.

Fabian flagged down an early-morning cab and told the driver to take him home.

This is the dream he had. He is appointed to a very high position. But first, there is a probationary period. He works in a majestic glass palace. He sleeps between two fur coats and eats caviar at a *nomenklatura* buffet. A black Volga awaits him in front of the main entryway. His trial period has ended successfully, all he has to do is pass a medical checkup. He has acquired all the signatures that he needs, even from the shrink, and only the blood test is left to do. He goes to the clinic, checks in at reception, and is led into an office. The room is empty. It's just him and the doctor. The latter seems somehow familiar. A little like Ingo, a little like Valentin, a little like the "brains." Everything gleams and shines, is clean and polished. Fabian sits down, the doctor swabs his finger with a cotton ball, and jabs him. He squeezes his finger, and drops fall onto the little glass plate: one, two, three. Three drops of blood. The doctor smiles, thanking him. Only then does he start drawing the blood into a glass tube through plastic tubing. Flipping through his mail the next morning, Fabian spots a white envelope. It contains a single page with no signature and one sentence at the top: "Annabel Lee is the Baron's whore." On his way home after work, bird droppings fall on his head and he's beaten up by hooligans.

When Fabian got up, he had a headache and it seemed as if it wouldn't pass all on its own. I'll buy some beer and get happy again, Fabian thought. He hated distress and believed that happiness ennobles a person. He felt particularly bad when he stood up. He went into the bathroom and splashed water onto his face. He couldn't be bothered to brush his teeth—instead, he sprayed deodorant into his mouth until he started fearing that he would get drunk again. He sat down at his desk and opened a drawer to take out some money. Rifling through the papers it contained, his hand brushed a letter from his mother. As if everything else wasn't enough! The letter had arrived more than two weeks ago, and he hadn't replied so far. Fabian remembered its opening: "How are you doing? You haven't written in so long, and we don't know anything about you." Fabian squeezed his head between his hands. He knew that if he were to shoot a quick glance over his right shoulder, he might see his own suicide.

He pulled on the first jacket that his hand touched in the closet, clenched his teeth, and unbolted the door. Outside, Fabian immediately perceived a bizarre phenomenon: just as usual on hangover mornings, so now too did his senses sharpen to the extreme. To the brink of outright pain. He could hear previously inaudible scraping and rasping noises in the bowels of the city; could smell the odious stench of excrement throughout the metropolis. And the scenery, the scenery . . . Altogether, his view of the world suddenly cleared. Everything settled into place, and the basic questions of existence became evident in all their authenticity. Fabian reckoned that there was only one true question, something like: is anything important at all, or not? Who determines what it is; who says what truth is? "Truth is the taste of better men," Per-Ivar had told him. Am I a better man? Where is my beautiful soul? Fabian asked himself.

Fabian had once been very fond of the condition he was in on such mornings. It felt romantic. Furthermore, that was precisely when he came up with the greater portion of the good thoughts and worthy ideas that he could utilize in his work. His mind worked inventively. Fabian's friends said the same about their own experiences. Yes, yes—friends; they were still alive. Fabian rummaged in his pocket for the two-kopeck coins that could be found between strands of tobacco and loose pills. He would call Ingo and invite him along. It was too bad that Fabian wasn't a painter like his friend, because then he could take even greater advantage of the sharpness of his senses. True, though—a doctor-acquaintance, to whom he had once confided this condition, had said that the eyes were simply in pain from being up late at night, aching from alcohol and heavy smoke; that there was nothing supernatural about it; that it wasn't God's resolute finger gliding over his eyelids on those mornings.

PARAMOURS

In those moments of leisure—away from work and friends, blissfully lounging in the half-empty carriages of long-distance trains, wandering around dilapidated neighborhoods, in the hours saved by not attending class reunions—during those times, Fabian would read other writers' books, watch films, and go to see plays, interspersed with attending artist-acquaintances' exhibitions. At the same time, however, he would ponder the nature of life; would compare art with what he had experienced personally. The thoughts led him to a dead end; they worried him. For quite some time, Fabian had been bothered by the fact that everything in life had changed. He didn't blame art for the discord, since art was more beautiful, and it's hard to blame what is more beautiful. Life itself had to take responsibility—there was something wrong with it.

One subject that always captivated Fabian and stimulated him at such times while he was musing was that of paramours. Books, both historical and contemporary, were seething with them, as were other art forms. It gave the impression that paramours were always held in high esteem. All it takes is a glance into the past. The list of "women of love" might be thousands of times longer than the endless old romance-novel series of the same name. And not only have rulers, artists, and admirals added the sinful jewel of forbidden love to their lives, but even every cooper or guild master has a matted-haired maid, seamstress, or cook. Fabian had heard people saying that men keep paramours even now. But where? In America? For, oddly enough, when he scrutinized his friends' and acquaintances' relationships, he couldn't find a single paramour. True, you could find men who hadn't registered their partnership and practiced an open marriage. But that wasn't the same! "Open marriage" was just a nice title. In some ways, it was extremely similar to an ordinary marriage. And so, the participants *themselves* forgot their status. A couple of Fabian's acquaintances in a similar situation had only noticed it when they traveled somewhere and were forbidden from renting the same hotel room. Fabian was also aware that, from time to time, men would simply chase chicks at parties and bars; but this was pure horniness, nothing spiritual or exceptional. One time, Fabian himself had even watched a young woman standing in a doorway. It had happened in the Old Town, on Niguliste Street. Fabian was just returning from buying pesticides at the chemicals store across the way. Afterward, he couldn't even explain to himself why his mind started moving down *that* kind of a path when he spotted the woman. Maybe she was escaping from the rain? Had it been raining at all? He couldn't remember. And even so, when he thought back to her, his mind always strayed into daydreams for a few minutes.

Fabian had methodically familiarized himself with the kinds of relationships practiced between the genders in Estonia— from late-night visits to group sex; however, none matched the classic understanding of a relationship with a paramour that Fabian had envisioned. He could be woken up from a deep sleep and asked about paramours, and he would know what to say right off the bat—the way a trained spy remembers the details listed on his false passport.

Everything about a paramour starts with secrecy. One might say that a paramour *is* secrecy plus collusion. One can't just show up anywhere with a paramour. You didn't attend your establishment's Christmas party or a cabaret with her. You would, however, certainly take a paramour to a quiet corner of a café in a tenement house or to a private sauna in the company of intimate friends. You would miss out on walking together in a Song Festival parade, but the two of you could watch the same parade on television that night. Fabian imagined how you might feel being at the parade, and knowing that somewhere nearby your paramour was marching, her feet slapping on the ground. The frisson of tension it would provide; how it would add a spark to the holiday! You don't promenade with your paramour on a square, but rather wander along side streets in a garden suburb. And not at rush hour, but at dusk, when all women look gray. This especially on September nights, when the tepid sunset transitions to twilight in half tones—slowly, like how the lights dim and go out in a classy cinema at showtime. A paramour belongs to autumn in general; she is like a migratory bird, who has been left behind by the flock of women flown off to warm family lands. And if someone scoops her up in the autumn, then doubtless he'll keep her for the winter. What will come in spring, no one knows.

Paramours lack ties—they have no relatives, no past or future. They have no obligations, neither will they have children. A paramour belongs to the world of cars with shades drawn, veils, telephone booths, flower shops, secret slips of paper, passwords, and conspiratorial apartments. To Fabian, it seemed that out of all spheres of society, that kind of setting could only be found in two places: black-market retail and espionage. But mostly in the latter. Fabian had had no personal encounters with espionage. But he respected it. He knew a thing or two about it. Primarily through art: at home, he would often press his ear up against the radio—on evenings when thrilling serial dramas were broadcast. Fabian reckoned that while just a few years ago tropical typhoons were exclusively given pretty women's names, now, one could start classifying paramours themselves according to distinguishing features and work methods, using the more widely recognized secret services as a basis. You would get an array of types in doing so: the Sureté, SAVAK, Mossad, Gestapo, Okhranka, and other types of paramours.

But there were no more paramours. They were a dying breed, the way dinosaurs once became extinct. They died out because of a cold climate. Was the heart's warmth now in short supply? Apparently that wasn't the case not so long ago. Fabian knew of one mid-level office at a ministry he visited quite frequently that was occupied by four fifty-year-old women who still bore the traces of their former beauty. They had been the sunshine girls of once eminent men, worthy of promotion to that office. And how *many* such offices might there number! There they sit, that iron reserve of ours!

But new paramours were needed. Sixty of them, at least. Not for Fabian, of course, but rather to improve the intellectual health of Estonia's cultural community. *They* would put things right. How? But what are paramours needed for in the first place? People usually believe that they're for something flagrant. Fabian's position is entirely different. In his opinion, they weren't needed as objects of erotic affection. A paramour was not an erotic item. That is, they *were* a little, of course; but not primarily. Above all, a paramour meant freedom. For the only type of person capable of keeping a paramour is one who is free; who has enough time and willpower to deal with things himself. Who is a goal unto himself; a one-time goal of the utmost importance, not the means to it. A person who makes his life into a work of art. And the contrary, also: a man who has obligations, who is shackled by life, who isn't free—*he* is not one to keep a paramour. The girders of society, whose personal lives are in the public's palm, can't manage paramours. Neither can those who are the victims of destructive passion; those without independence, like the drunkards, the gluttons, the misers, and the researchers. Rational planners are even more complex. They're deceiving at first since they don't take paramours, either; but not for the aforementioned reasons. They're simply biding their time, banking their hopes on their future lives. The present is merely a preparation for them, solely a springboard.

They shouldn't be thought of as pious individuals yearning to inherit eternal life. No—for the most part, they are skeptics who recognize their abilities and know that unparalleled freedom is not gifted to them as it is to fate's favorites, merely for a smile. No, they have to make an effort to buy their freedom. Fabian had realized long ago that humankind is divided into two groups in terms of lifestyle. One group seizes the day, the other gambles. The first group's formula for life is simple: the more nice days there are, the better. The sum does not change the order of what is added. They are people who are capable of enjoying the moment and not worrying about what will come tomorrow. Others play big hands, sacrifice over and over again, tighten their belts, and suppress their desires in the hope that they will win it back several-fold. Later, when they *are* someone. In order to then have a bigger salary. To be famous. To choose their own apartments, trips abroad, women, and other things.

One of Fabian's former college classmates represented the latter class in quite unadulterated form. Fabian remembered him well: a tall boy with extremely wide hips and a narrow skull; flat feet that made him walk with his entire sole touching the ground, swaying lightly. Furthermore, he would rock his head to the beat of his footsteps. You could imagine him as a peace-loving dinosaur, walking in a primeval forest, munching juicy shoots off trees. That beanpole of a boy did the decathlon in middle school. In the tenth grade, he was old enough to realize he totally lacked coordination, and therefore, he would never become a top athlete. Then he started gaining fame and fortune with chess. Night and day, he would study openings, solve chess problems, and participate in simulations. That was how he reached the second level. It was his limit—pure diligence wasn't enough for more. Then he enrolled in university and tried his luck at knowledge. He intentionally chose an unpopular and relatively dull field, and focused on it with blind, dogged ambition. He soon defended his dissertation. A few years later, he became number one in his field, traveling from conference to conference, and representing our republic. He once admitted in a more intimate setting: "First of all is work, work, and once again work. Later come vodka, women, and other frivolities; when you're an accomplished man." Such a man consciously abandons the joys of life that are traditionally regarded as the privileges of his age. Because right now, his price would be low and his strike weak. He would only get things of his own kind. Still, he waits, ascends higher, and already demands a loftier standard. And if he endures further, he'll reach luxury-goods status. No, that man's thoughts were undoubtedly very worldly.

Fabian admired the literary characters of out-of-touch worlds—bankers' sons, and aristocratic maidens. However, this wasn't so much because of around-the-world journeys, tennis played on board yachts, performances held in royal courts, or other luxuries. No—he was jealous of their chance to deal with themselves uninterrupted, to practice matters of the soul, to arrange personal ties, to make self-sacrifices without finding love in return, or to express their feelings otherwise. It gave the impression that realizing their goals was outright *central* to their life. They knew no other troubles, didn't have to worry about where they'd reap or sow. It was utterly sublime how the petty details that concerned their personality unexpectedly gained importance and affected both their attitude toward life and how they were doing. For example, Fabian was envious of how literary characters could be unreservedly offended. They had the time and the means for it. They could take such offenses seriously and challenge one to a duel. Or hold a grudge for several decades and not get along. And this wasn't just for fun, not apropos of anything, but almost like a calling—a calling to be offended. Ultimately, making amends became a worthy culmination of high-quality self-realization.

But now, everything went quickly—flickering past like a movie-reel frame at a faded theater. Even life's moments of upheaval were staged there. People wed in a flash, had kids like lightning, divorced in passing. There wasn't *time* anymore. Before, a man would wait for hours below his inamorata's window as a sign of fidelity. He would serenade and watch, enraptured, a dark silhouette flitting behind the curtain up above. But now he had to go to work by eight o'clock. Otherwise he'd be written up for an absence to boot. Before, you would cater to a lady for ten years. Now, you had to go doing it in an entirely different location. But if you wanted to stubbornly cater to your lady all the same, you were in danger of being convicted for leading a parasitic lifestyle.

Oh, yes—freedom was necessary. And money, too. A decent sum of money. Wouldn't I like to send a woman an armful of roses every day? Fabian wondered indignantly. Rent her a furnished room? As if! But where was he supposed to get the rubles to buy flowers from old women on the street? And how many cooperative apartments can one person manage to build in a lifetime?

Of course, having a paramour was not the only chance to feel human. What's more, it was one of the most *difficult* ways to do it. Simpler choices could be found. Every voluntary act that didn't benefit anything apart from yourself would do. One could have a dog instead of a paramour, for example. The kind that has to be let outside to run every day. Fabian had observed from the window of his room a man who let his dog out at a particular time to run on the grass in the yard opposite. The dog was large, spotted, as naked as a sausage, and the only thing it did was jump up and down. The man was also large, soft, young, and had a beer belly. Fabian couldn't estimate the dog's age. The man's belly was ugly, but said something about him. The man looked like a floating buoy from the midriff—one placed where a river makes an especially lovely arc. At the same time, the belly hinted at the fact that a gut like that wasn't a problem for that sort of a "big deal." He's too much of an ace for it. He can get by anyway. Let guys who don't possess anything else care about slenderness; guys whose waist and hips are their sole capital. They could perhaps even insure them. *He*, on the other hand, could swell. He could swell to his heart's content. His kingdom isn't from the world of waistlines. The man wore a garish tracksuit and would also hop three or four steps. Then he would smoke in deep concentration. He stayed alert to make sure the dog didn't escape to go and ruin its pedigree with the mixed-blood mutts bounding at a distance.

A dog like that shows that the man takes himself seriously. No one *commands* you to have a dog. A dog takes up a lot of time. However, time is what that man has. He's involved in his own life, not in anything trivial. He doesn't toil mindlessly and haphazardly day in, day out. He doesn't strain to make a career for himself; doesn't stand in lines, doesn't pitch from side to side in a trolley. His affairs are already accomplished. He possesses an identity.

Traveling was an even easier way to feel free. Not traveling along one's daily route to work and back, of course. But every path that was even a little newer was great. Fabian had wandering in his blood. Since childhood, he would be gripped by exhilaration several days before a trip. His heightened spirits weren't connected to the destination. Going to see his uncle, vacationing with family—all of that was important, of course, but not so important that it might overshadow the trip as precious in and of itself. Such was the case, invariably. He was certainly intrigued by new cities and lands, by buildings, people, customs, and setting; however, the state of traveling itself was boundlessly important, all the same. Every mode of transportation was good in its own way. A plane meant a leap in time, a ship enchanted him with its spacious separation amid an expanse of water (even though Fabian feared water to the extreme), a bus was a compact and "team" sort of a thing, a car a more intimate place for conversation. However, a train prevailed over all of them. When he happened to be traveling at a late hour in the middle of the week, when there were fewer passengers and he was sitting in the half-empty dining car, dark emptiness outside the window and just his own reflection in the glass, then Fabian lived a few seconds in which it seemed that everything belonged to *him*; that *that* was his life, that he almost had a hold on himself, was standing on his own two heels. Was this partly because of the fact that the click-clack of train wheels matched the rhythm of his heart? That they were taking the same steps? Who knows whether it was that simple. Even so, it gave him the feeling as if he had rubbed his mitten over the thick frost on a bitterly cold window until it melted, turned transparent, and through the tiny gap he had seen—himself.

Traveling buoyed the soul. Fabian recalled one instance after his first year at university. He was dispatched to do summer work on the hayfields, but his girlfriend was doing an archaeology internship near Tallinn at the same time: Fabian took their separation very hard. Even more so because he knew how promiscuous his girlfriend was. A number of stories about the archaeology-aces' shenanigans had already reached his ears through the grapevine. Who knows how far they went. One weekend, Fabian planned to go to Tallinn unannounced and expose his girlfriend's relationships with the archaeologists. However, that same weekend, the other hayfield workers had planned for a trip to the kolkhoz's summer sauna and cabin, which was nestled in the reeds along the Baltic Sea, near the Matsalu avian reserve. Fabian couldn't resist the temptation, nor did he have the patience to be a no-show. What's more, he subconsciously hoped for revenge for his girlfriend's infidelity. The party lasted longer than expected. The sauna's plumbing was broken, but on the other hand, there was a ton of beer. Only early on Sunday morning did Fabian rouse himself, his head splitting but his spirit prevailing over his body. Fabian crossed the dewy hayfield to the main road. When he had been walking for half an hour, he stopped and looked back. He could still see the sauna; the landscape was flat. The sun was already shining quite brightly. Villagers came from the opposite direction. It smelled like country life. It was good to walk. An exceptional state of restfulness sprung up in his soul. The air was fresh. The main road was right in front of him, and the bus stop within reach. Fabian would have had to wait for the first bus, but he couldn't stand still anymore—he had gotten the taste for walking, and so he strolled and strolled ever farther away from Matsalu, as if he wanted to reach Tallinn on foot. He walked one more long stretch between bus stops to sit and wait for it there—the same bus that he could have boarded sixteen kilometers earlier. He arrived in Tallinn around lunchtime. He was tired, went to the nearest café, and ate. Eating exhausted him even more. He didn't even consider traveling on, to go see his girlfriend, for a single second. He didn't need to fight even the smallest temptation. He sat on a park bench and dozed off for a while. Then, he checked the schedule in the bus station to see when the next one back was leaving, and took it to the haymaking site. He got off a stop early and walked among the fields. He *needed* nothing else. The trip soothed him. Perhaps everything would be fine. He got over it. That little bit was enough that time. He never thought about the girl again. He received word of her wedding without his usual distress.

Movement, paramours, and dogs—actually, they all meant one and the same thing. It was no wonder, then, that his daydreams occasionally fused and formed complete visions. The most noteworthy character in Fabian's secret dreams of late was a young woman with her own car. A paramour on wheels. Fabian lusted for her above all. And once again, not as something valuable in and of itself; not because of her car as property—rather, he'd like the woman to drive him around. She would play the role of a geisha/taxi driver. The woman had to be a skilled driver, but in no way athletic; instead, gentle and poetic. Not smelling of gasoline, carrying a wrench in her breast pocket, or with motor oil smeared under her arms. She had to be a fragile, platinum blonde pawn at the wheel of a Cadillac, who could have a best seller lying between the two front seats— in the spot where men keep their tobacco or newspapers; a woman who would pull up next to Fabian, open the door, and beckon him invitingly, cooing like a dove. That was his dream. Fabian would entrust himself to such a woman's care without hesitation. He would drive with her as far as the gas would take them. That's how far he had managed to detach himself from life!

But at the same time, he himself totally acknowledges, completely admits to himself, that he longs to demonstrate free will; wants to take charge, to be in situations where he would perceive that *he* was acting, and not to just be the engine that was once started up within him, and under the influence of which he does everything, without rhyme or reason, like an Everyman, like "*monsieur tout le monde*," as Heidegger says. But even folk sayings teach: when impulses have been identified and rationalized, then it's much simpler to manage them; even better to tolerate their torment. And sure enough, quite a number of acts that would otherwise have remained a mystery to Fabian now unfolded before him with their dark backgrounds.

One morning, Fabian ran into his friend, Schasmin, with whom he had attended the same event the night before. They had been to the funeral of a sculptor. How glad we always are to see companions from the night before! We even hold long conversations with casual acquaintances, jointly clarify details, restore gaps in our memory, discuss the order and number of different alcohol brands we drank, as well as science's latest word on the treatment of hangovers. That's how very many lovely and long-lasting male friendships are formed. But old friends—you're inevitably drawn toward them on such mornings! Sometimes, we're so utterly exhausted that we gather up our courage and have the secretary call them out of an important meeting, which is being personally attended by the minister's deputy and a couple of foreigners. We might even go to their homes, despite the fact that we'll encounter an extremely angry wife, who is convinced that you and you alone are to blame for what has happened, and who would gladly do anything and everything to end the association between you and her man. Piddling little problems such as this are nothing next to the happiness of sharing that kind of a morning. And Fabian *was* gladdened by the meeting. They drank beer and ate salted nuts in a grungy pub located in a dilapidated neighborhood. The establishment was third-rate, but nevertheless offered a waiter, didn't stink all that much (since a ventilator whirred on the ceiling), and had a derelict cloak room next to the front door, which suggested the place had been more respectable at one time. He wasn't sure if that was the reason, but Fabian seemed to recognize a finer class of people in a few of the clients there—those who wouldn't risk leaning their gray-suited elbows on the moist tablecloth; who had a portfolio set neatly between their feet on the floor or next to the table leg. They also went to the locale out of old habit or because the location was far from the city center, out of the way—it was a good place to stop before going to work. Quite a few of the men had wrinkled faces with craggy features. A lot of them definitely hadn't gone home the night before. A heroic resistance surfaced in their attitude; a resolution to stick it out to the end. They were rebels.

Schasmin finished his summary of the previous night. "And finally, you were going around from one woman to the next, wanting to put your head in everyone's lap." "Why'd I do that?" Fabian asked, even though he instantly realized that he was asking for no good reason. "How should I know," Schasmin replied, shrugging as if in confirmation, and smirking.

Fabian sank into thought. Ever more often lately, rumors had reached his ears about how many of his acquaintances express their desire to lay their heads in some young lady's lap, and fall asleep there when they've run out of steam at their social venue, drunk their fill of booze, and tired themselves out from dancing. Especially famed was one poet, who attempted to act like that in a public place; at a venue they normally frequented together. *He* was apparently the one who had come up with that sort of trick and was capable of turning personal downfall into a style that only spread and spread; though not as a revolution, since every beginning is difficult. At first, some men merely had the courage to fall to their knees, others to drape their arms across the woman's lap, while a third group would lean their foreheads against the couch and concentrate.

That kind of fame for the poet's gesture couldn't lie solely in his poetic talent. Apparently the time was ripe for it. The poet's deed turned out to be a spark in a gunpowder barrel; the last drop that made the rain barrel overflow. The poet particularly loved to shock foreigners. When he was successful in doing so, and some well-traveled Canadian dame or German *Mädchen* looked left and right, perturbed, not knowing how they should behave with the poet's ear pressed up against the zipper of her expensive jeans, then everyone present in the venue experienced a sense of exhilaration. Having lived a lot doesn't necessarily mean possessing experiences! "Well traveled, and for what!" was written invisibly in the air. The big nation didn't understand the language of the little nation's gestures; was naive. And so, one was able to somehow triumph over them; to avenge Estonian culture's hundred-year youth and teensy population.

Up until now, Fabian had furtively laughed at the poet. Yet, he didn't do so maliciously. For even though he regarded a trick like that as just the right amount of novelty, Fabian could smell a culture of capitulation to it. The poet had been drinking a lot lately and wasn't especially picky about his choice of venue. He loved to surround himself with bums, sitting in their midst with

a rose poked through one buttonhole. He was indiscriminate—
the important thing was that he was praised. He had rocketed
into poetry fame as a boy wonder, and hadn't gotten over it to
this day. His manner of behavior dealt a blow to the honor of
his profession, in Fabian's opinion. But if Schasmin was to be
believed, then how was he himself any better now?

"Actually , I do have one theory," Schasmin began. Schasmin
always had many theories. He had apparently noticed that men
would always climb up and stick their heads in larger women's
laps. Such a choice couldn't be accidental: men's foreheads put
on autopilot would search too purposefully for matrons and
Helgas. Therefore, Schasmin believed that such an act was free
of any kind of eroticism. Here lies an entirely different reason
that on the one hand is significantly more innocent, but on the
other is more appalling in its primal nature. For why big women,
all the same? Not because there might be more space in their
lap. Lap size doesn't figure in here at all. How thick is a head,
really? On top of that, it was mostly smaller men (though not
large-headed dwarves) who wanted access to their laps. And you
don't climb into a lap in numbers. Group things are especially
unaesthetic with such an act. As such, what mattered was something entirely different. And namely: a moment of childishness.
The men tried to assume the relationship of little boy and mer-
ciful mother. They simply wanted peace. When a seagoing vessel
is battered, it longs for docking before it sails around Cape Horn
again. When a man is fatigued and exhausted, then he wants to
lean upon a basic good. Before he goes in for another round,
a genius demands that even he be told a healing spell: "magic
mend and candle burn." Most fitting for this is a large woman
who can have a more motherly effect than a petite, pert female
at any hour. It seems to help a little more when she blows on it.

"That first of all," Schasmin said, smirking smugly before he
continued. Secondly, there exists another, much more general

reason, the roots of which stretch out into the cosmos. When a man is having a difficult time, he yearns to be away from the world. He would like to be back at the cellular stage. Instinct tells him that the lap is connected to such a yearning. That's where the cell originates. But if woman has been endowed with the ability to give life, then why not to take it away as well? Thus, the lap is an outright philosophical concept.

Fabian had already read that idea somewhere. Probably in the same place that Schasmin had. Yes, yes—only woman and nature had mastered the art of giving life. Yet for him as a man, the truth was currently elsewhere. He suddenly realized that the roots of the poet's and the group's degeneration lay in the latter. Fabian smiled to himself and no longer paid attention to what Schasmin was saying. To him, it was clear. He and the others before him, everyone without paramours and dogs, they wanted only one thing—they wished to prove to themselves their own freedom!

JACK OF ALL TRADES

Although, on that memorable night, Fabian had confessed to Elen his opinions on beauty and ugliness, and had quite resolutely outlined how worldviews and welfares stem from people's external features, nevertheless, he observed from everyday life that this wasn't quite the case. Not every outcast was a pessimist, and a rather large number of attractive faces had tragic ends written upon them. Likewise, Fabian repeatedly had to concede that in their interactions with women, top dogs and spirited playboys usually lost to men with unimpressive appearances. Fabian had an interest in and admiration for the latter breed of his fellow males. Among such successful types was also his casual acquaintance, Martin Hurja, a TV cameraman and radio actor. He was quite a hideous-looking man. However, Fabian had not yet witnessed him being left high and dry anywhere in a social setting. Of course, Martin's fame was helped by that speck of celebrity that always goes along with radio and television, and which has a magical effect on a broader audience. All the same, there were other, more famous radio and television personalities, so his fame wasn't especially important. What else did he have to offer? He delighted one part of the intelligentsia with the fact that he possessed acquaintances in the empire's capital, who steadily equipped him with gossip about Moscow's bohemians. Just recently, Fabian had seen him holding a notebook full of pages scribbled with dozens of four-line stanzas. They were mini-parodies dedicated to Yevtushenko, Yuri Nikulin, Gherman Titov, and other celebrities, authored by the unknown genius Ben Levin. The paper was splotched with ink, which

betrayed beyond any shred of doubt where it was written. The
sheet was read aloud like scripture in several social groups. The
kind of things they came up with there in Moscow! Yet such
hearsay, manuscripts and anecdotes, weren't enough to bring
luck with young ladies, not to mention also earning the undi-
vided attention and supportive respect of virtuous older women.
For truly—no one thought of him as a skirt-chaser.

Martin Hurja's good reputation was a result of his jawbone,
which possessed an unforeseen force that redirected the
thoughts of those around them away from their true goals. It
even compensated for his external deficits. Anyone who had
even fleetingly heard that Estonians are anthropologically
divided into two types immediately grasped that stumpy Martin
descended from the eastern tribes. Only his eyes (although
white) were sharp and expressive, free of the sleepy Finno-Ugric
substrate.

How did Martin's victories fall into his lap? By way of
great adroitness, of course. He had everything thought out in
advance. He never elbowed his way into the limelight at the
start of a gathering and wasn't intrusive, but rather a polite
and helpful conversation partner. He knew that the less that
was expected of him at first, the greater the impact later. As
such, he listened with slightly naive interest, looked his partners
attentively in the eye, and would gain the trust of all those in a
group, who would then each want to gabber on about him- or
herself. After that, he would keep everyone under his thumb and
give his performance. He had his own stories and conversation
topics. And he was wonderfully adept at selecting just the right
moment to come forth with them. Most often when there was
a pause that was still thick with the previous thought, when out
of the silence that ensued came someone's muffled cough, when
someone sipped their drink, or when someone pensively lit a
new cigarette. The most suitable moments were after they had
discussed literature, death, birth, or something lofty or ethical.

These topics left behind a mood in which Martin could launch his own art. And then . . .

He would stare straight ahead for a while, after which he would thoughtfully utter something like:

"Yea-ah, life is odd; more complicated than we're capable of realizing . . . It's ready to deal all kinds of blows to us . . . Who's protected from them?" And he looked straight at those sitting around him, as if someone had vaguely hinted that he or she *was* protected from the strokes of fate; that they didn't fear plague, wars, or floods. The listeners became attentive. Martin sensed from the silence that had formed that he had hit the nail on the head, and continued:

"Death is always tragic . . . But the Reaper becomes a thousand times more frightful when he steals a person who is close to us . . . The closer they are, the more harshly the old graveyard-walker strikes . . ." He paused for a few seconds again, as if wavering over whether he should keep talking, seemingly struggling over whether or not it was inflicting unspeakable torments upon him. Naturally, no one dared utter a single word. Everyone held their breath; to them, it appeared that what would now transpire would be the painful confession of an extraordinary person. Something was in the air. And they wouldn't be disappointed. After bestowing another rare, genuine look on everyone with his white eyes, as if thus proving that he, Martin Hurja, is a great man, is wise and deep, he continued:

"I've got this girl. Or woman, I guess . . . A 'girl' no more . . . The years go by, don't they?" That was one of his brilliant moves. "The years go by, don't they" always had an effect: Fabian had remarked how exceptionally well talking about time sunk in for even the most passionless, fantasy-poor individual. Time hypnotized, began repeating, and incited temporal madness.

"The years don't preserve us," Martin said, declaring his next truth. "We met the summer before last. It happened in Rakvere. We were filming there." (Fabian had seen the film.

The camerawork was exceptionally poor. On top of that, he got the impression that the entire film crew had been constantly drunk.) "She had a family, a husband and two kids . . . But she and the man hadn't found each other . . . It wasn't love, not even friendship. Their souls weren't mutually bound; they hadn't understood each other's unvoiced desires in a long while. But what is marriage without that? And it's natural for a woman who hasn't had the gentle attention of a man in a long while to thirst for it, the way a field in drought thirsts for the sky's tears. We started dating. She admitted that she had never cheated on her husband before."

By saying that, Martin implied that he was the only one out of thousands whom the woman deemed worthy of the honor. Here, he stretched out his arms forward a little and adopted the serious expression of a primary witness in a film drama. He was entirely caught up in his own story. And everyone kept silent, fascinated. "We dated until just recently . . . I rented a cozy little room on an out-of-the-way street for our love trysts. But one time, she didn't show up. She didn't send a letter to inform me. And so it went for weeks after that, too. I started to get dreadfully worried . . . My heart perceived the worst . . . I drove there . . . I found out that she has blood cancer. She's dying." Martin would then look at his watch. "She could already be dead by now." Everyone froze. Just imagine—blood cancer! Cancer was such an impressive illness! It was as if everyone had some personal connection to cancer. Oohh, yes, cancer—we know about that!

"She's dying . . . And the worst part is that I can't do anything about it!" Martin concluded. Everyone was crestfallen that there was nothing to be done. So much genuine pain rang in Martin's voice that even Fabian would have felt sympathetic for him had he not known that the female in question, if she had even existed at all, had died already, at least five years ago. The man was a magnificent actor. Everyone felt the need to shake his hand. No one even seemed to realize that if Martin's story really were true, then the affair described would have meant years of whoring on his part, since Martin himself was married and the father of three children, who were just as hideous-looking as he was. But not even the most virtuous of the bourgeois old dames thought about *them* while he was telling the story. And Fabian almost believed that even Martin's big and beautiful wife would have been sincerely sympathetic after such a heartrending tale.

Having shut his mouth, Martin slumped against the seat back. Now he was sure he wouldn't have to leave alone tonight. All of the women were prepared to offer the unfortunate man consolation at least once. With their imaginations straining from underload, they put themselves in the place of that woman dying of blood cancer. Thus, even they took part in the lofty and the sublime, with what lies behind the curtains of eternity; their souls were cleansed. *That* wasn't *that* anymore, not at all; going to Martin's place became a noble act, took on the aspect of sacred sex.

Martin had more stories like that. One of the most grandiose and heartrending ones he came up with was about his dog. Martin didn't ordinarily attempt to repeat a story in the same social setting, and thanks to his attentive memory, he made fewer mistakes like that than a number of inveterate joke-tellers did. Nevertheless, the tale had been worn into Fabian's brain down to the last detail. As always, Martin firstly gave it the proper timing. When the suitable moment was at hand, he began his introduction:

"Yea-ah, the soul—that's divine, possessing a soul . . . Yet, what is the soul?" Although none of those present (as usual with over-educated individuals) mentally recognized themselves as inveterate materialists, no one was able to provide an answer to such a frank question.

"Considering the soul, I'm always reminded about my dear old dog. Not the one that we have now," Martin continued with the sort of confidence that takes hold of an actor when he takes the audience into his grasp. "We'd grown up together. He was given to me as a present when I was still quite a young boy, just going to school. Dogs rarely live past the age of fifteen. But at that time, he was already seventeen. He had gotten fat, his teeth had fallen out, he really wasn't able to do anything anymore, but nevertheless—he was alive. We were very close, closer even than most people. It was no wonder, either. We'd been together through thick and thin. He had dragged me out of a hole in the ice, had protected me from hooligans, and I can't manage to forget how I carried him twelve kilometers in my arms when he had broken both of his back legs. We had camped together, swum together, gone hunting together, played hide-and-seek, cops and robbers, and everything that was at all possible. Without him, my childhood wouldn't have been *half* of what it actually was." Martin stared tenderly at a point somewhere far above the listeners' heads (where you could see the opening that ventilated the cigarette smoke). No one dared to move a muscle during such extraordinary, intimate recollections. Coffee cooled in mugs, rolled cigarettes burned down to the filters, aspic and whipped cream melted. Everyone was entranced.

"Alas, his years went faster than mine. I enrolled in the Film Institute and was just starting to live, but he'd grown old in that time. I visited home infrequently back then—a thousand kilometers *did* separate my father's farm from Moscow. An especially long spell away came when my dissertation was successfully defended, I'd graduated from the Institute, and should have rightfully enjoyed a break among my fellows. But it was the will of fate that I'd caught the eye of old Petrov himself, and thus, life offered me independent work at that very junction. The offer was tempting, and—I needn't explain further. It was a youth thing. I felt a calling . . ." Martin pressed his lips together and elevated his jaw resolutely. "There was no other choice than to write home, telling them to wait another

half a year. We traveled to Siberia. We were to film the lives
of the log drivers on the Lena River and the cods' journey to
their spawning grounds. Or was it vice-versa? No matter . . ."
(He himself had no idea what was spewing from his mouth,
either. Even so, his story was having an effect. Oh, it was so very
natural, grand in scale, almost holy. Fabian had long since noted
how the majority of people treat travelers with deference—the
green-jacketed, bearded men who are able to tell a male bear's
excrements apart from that of a female rabbit; who live in
the forest, roam the tundra, and tramp through the swamps.
They emerge from time to time in order to write books for the
public and replicate birdsongs while meeting with readers. They
were great celebrities among women. No, that Martin knew
what repertoire to take!) "But Siberia, you yourselves know,
is no cakewalk!" he proclaimed, his tone turning serious, and
stared almost threateningly at his audience, as if someone had
intended to make a lighthearted joke at Siberia's expense. No
matter that the seriousness of Siberia hadn't the least thing to do
with a dog's spiritual life.

"Mm-hmm," Martin Hurja continued at a brisker pace, as if
shaking himself loose of Siberia's enchantment in order to arrive
at the main point more quickly. "Of course, I was plagued by
homesickness. And so, as soon as the last frame had been shot,
I couldn't take it anymore and didn't have the patience to sit
around and wait for the helicopter they'd promised to send
for us—I started journeying in the direction of the sunset on
my own. I hitchhiked on the main road, but all alone, without
comrades on the highways of Siberia—it's no cakewalk. I begged
for random open seats at airports in order to get back home even
just a day or two earlier. Because to me, sitting unoccupied and
then rocking from side to side on a train seemed impossible. I
finally arrived. I felt like Odysseus returning home. I'd never
been away from my loved ones for so long before that. I can
remember even now how mild and warm the weather was that

day—even now, the chirping of crickets echoes in my ears and I could draw the exact shapes of the scattered, majestic clouds floating in the sky at that moment. I crested the hill near my home and slowed my pace in order to absorb as fully as possible, with all of my senses, the once-in-a-lifetime atmosphere of childhood playing fields.

"My old dog spotted me from the distance. He'd been lying in the grass, warming his old joints in the sunlight. He didn't recognize me at first. His eyesight had dulled and his nose couldn't discern scents. When I opened the gate, he received me with feeble barking. I whistled softly—in the way that he knew only *I* could call him. Oh, how happy he became! How the recognition startled him! He pushed himself up on his paws, started whimpering excitedly, and weakly wagged his furless tail. He wobbled toward me, gathering up the very last of his strength, and then he collapsed. I trotted closer, but there was nothing to be done; no one could have done anything. He was already dying. Only one time, when I patted his snout, did his warm tongue emerge to lick my hand. And if you could have seen his moist button-eyes! Sparkling within them was a look, as if he wanted to say: 'Now I can die in peace, because my eyes have seen you, master!' And do you know what the local doctor, who checked him out afterward, discovered to even his own surprise? The poor mutt died of a heart attack. He perished from emotion! That's a *human* disease! Shouldn't one suppose, then, that the dog is the only creature, aside from humans, that is capable of moral feeling? His old heart burst because of something of the kind that's located *outside* of him! It didn't concern his biological existence. Instinct can't explain any of it, either. More like his excitement was an expression of the divine essence; the goodness and altruism in nature, which dogs have also been allowed to partake in . . . Doesn't that mean, then, that dogs might also have a soul?" And again, Martin, pensive, stared directly at his listeners with the look of a wise man. Oh, what richness of expression sparkled in his white button-eyes! And since his former dog might have had a soul, all of the women around surrendered to him.

Fabian was truly fond of dogs. He'd had several himself. And because of that, Martin's fibbing irritated him. He personally *never* spoke about such things. On top of that, whether consciously or not, Martin wove into his story an impermissible amount of details from the final meeting between Jolyon Forsyte and his old dog Balthasar, which Fabian, as a man of literature, immediately recognized.

On occasion, Martin loved to tell variations of those two favorite stories. Once, it was the paramour's dog who rushed up to meet him; another time, the paramour herself died of emotion and the dog of blood cancer. Sometimes, Martin slipped up and asked rhetorically: "Doesn't that mean that paramours have a sense of divine altruism? Doesn't it prove that they're the only animals that possess a soul?"

If the first two stories weren't enough, every so often Martin would launch into a third. But this was certainly rare. If the aforementioned stories didn't soften up the audience, then something was off, the barometric pressure was low, or the constellations were poorly positioned. The listeners had been given quite a sufficient dose of sentimentality for one time; nothing extra would have saved it. A normal person can only tolerate an extraordinary spiritual life in small doses. Just like with cynicism. Furthermore, the third story was not as banally clear as the ones told before it; not as unambiguous, but rather more complex. It had also been told fewer times, and therefore the performance wasn't as striking as the previous ones. Otherwise, everything followed the same scenario. Having focused attention on himself with the traditional preparations, Martin began with the claim:

"The female soul is complicated. Woman has been, is, and will remain a mystery to me . . ." One need not add that all the women in earshot perked up their ears at such a frank confession. "She's capable of the most curious of acts. What goes on in her mind at those moments? Does she even always admit it to herself? How can *we* know?" Martin inquired hollowly and forcefully. This heightened the general interest, so according to polite custom, no one answered. And Martin got down to business:

"It happened when I was just a beginner. I was studying in the amateur-activity program and taking part as an extra in crowd scenes for films. I was working in a comb factory, though. It was there that I managed to score a pass to a workers' spa in Hungary, since thanks to me, our factory had taken second place in an amateur-activity review. Our group contained a couple dozen people from diverse walks of life. And it was to my great surprise when at the orientation, I met Maaritsa—a young woman who'd been my neighbor for some time down on Saeveski Street. How pretty she had become over the years! I was a couple of years older than her: we'd last seen each other when I was sixteen and she was fourteen—just like Romeo and Juliet! I probably don't even need to say that when I was a young boy, I'd been awfully in love with her . . . Now, I saw straight away that a gold ring was sparkling invitingly on her left hand. Yes, she was married. She greeted me nonchalantly. I really was no one special; just a onetime, awkward neighbor boy." Hearing this, everyone sitting at the table was dreadfully moved, as if Martin were a world celebrity now. "What upset me the most about her, though, was her height. She'd been tall even as a girl: now, she seemed to be the same height as me or even taller and slenderer. How'd she get to be so tall? She sure was big and beautiful, all right! I won't start burdening you with the details. In short, my feelings for her blossomed once more right then and there, and I fell in love again. I wanted to tell her. I wasn't held back by the prospect of being rejected. It'd still be better than keeping everything to yourself. However, there was no opportunity for the confession. We went on excursions during the day, she diligently went shopping from place to place after lunch, and in the evening, everyone danced down in the hotel restaurant. I was a poor dancer in general, since I hadn't been taught yet at the studio, and on top of that, I was intimidated by women taller than me. As luck would have it, she was always wearing extremely high-heeled shoes." The listeners chuckled good-naturedly, as if Martin had grown to who-knows-what height in the meantime. "As it turned out, her height posed no problem in her marriage: her husband (some expert at the lottery office) is apparently one meter and ninety centimeters tall. But even so, I got talking to Maaritsa. And at first, everything went just how I'd imagined it in my wildest dreams. She told me everything. Confessed that she already regretted getting married. We conversed in the hotel lobby on those long nights, so even the porters got used to us and would smile kindly. No doubt, they thought we were young and in love or a newly married couple, who had gone there to spend their honeymoon. Oh, if only they'd known! Our conversation turned less clever with every night and with every hour, and in the end, we were merely swapping fragmented sentences fraught with emotion. Instead of arguing points, we held hands, embraced each other passionately, and exchanged ever hotter kisses. How strange it seems in hindsight! My first time abroad, gorgeous nature and beautiful weather, health, recognizing the strength of my youth, and a great love to boot! I knew already then that for me, that spring would never be repeated. How was it with her? I can't say for sure. Often, it felt like she was experiencing our relationship just as I was, but sometimes she would laugh and hint that it was all an ordinary holiday romance that holds no obligations. In retrospect, I think that she was afraid; she was intimidated by our love, and therefore she held herself back." Martin, his teeth clenched, gestured as if he were trying to slow down a wagon rolling downhill, or at least a wheelbarrow, and continued thoughtfully: "It's strange how a woman sometimes holds herself back . . ." The others nodded fervidly at this subsequent true show of tenderness, since the way that a woman wants to do something but holds herself back felt so deep and poignant.

"Because when our emotion had already grown to such proportions that all there was left to do was to take that one last step, to reach the peak, the supreme thing that nature has put aside for a man and a woman, she changed all of a sudden, would make fun of me, and started teasing me. We didn't speak a single word to each other for the last four days of the trip, and she talked provocatively with the group's guide the entire time. We purposely avoided each other." Martin drew in a deep breath, which meant that the story was reaching its decisive chapter.

"I knew that Maaritsa absolutely had to buy a men's umbrella. It was the only thing her husband had asked for. Back then, a men's umbrella was considered a great rarity. I knew that she hadn't bought it yet by the morning of the last day; I also knew that she still had exactly enough money left for it. The simple and helpful girls in our group found all of this out for me. I probably don't need to add that the whole group was following our love with bated breath.

"Then came the final evening. I was all out of sorts and nervous, drank a couple of shots real quick, and then burrowed into the corner. All of a sudden, I sensed that someone was approaching me and asking me to dance. It was her! My eyesight turned foggy out of immense happiness, so I almost tripped when I was taking the dance floor. I wrapped my arms delicately around her shoulders and cautiously pressed myself against her. She clung to me trustingly. And all of a sudden, I sensed that something was different about her. She was shorter than she usually was. Instinctively, I peeked down at her feet. Maaritsa was wearing short-heeled shoes, cheap and unattractive. She had wasted her last forints on a pair of shoes that she most likely never intended to wear again. They cost exactly the same amount as a men's umbrella . . . I thanked her—I was unable to express how moved I was any other way. And we didn't mention the shoes again. But do you know the strangest part?! There hasn't been anything more between us since that night. In our homeland, she politely but firmly declined my invitations to meet up. I remember her last words on the telephone, when she asked me to forget her. Her voice was feeble, full of tragic love . . ." If you mentally enhanced the scene, you could imagine Martin bursting into true tears. Fabian had seen all kinds of theater, and could say with certainty that Martin used the Stanislavski system when he lied.

"What good was that to her back then—that sort of lovely gesture, wasting all of the foreign currency she had left? I've wondered about it to this day. I've lived to an old age, but haven't found the answer. But *is* there an answer at all? Perhaps an undecipherable enigma lies in every woman's soul?" he asked, entranced, staring off into the distance with a gaze clouded with emotion; looking off toward the corner of the buffet, where a cobweb was suspended under the ceiling. What an incredible person! everyone had to be thinking. How Chekhovian! What lovely life experiences adorn his soul, simultaneously simple and lofty! How complexly such a finely woven spirit experiences even a seemingly banal situation! It was no wonder, then, that the next time Martin's presence was expected in a social setting, all the women would wear low-heeled shoes. And it wasn't uncommon for an evening to end with one having to take her shoes *off* instead; and occasionally her slippers and stockings as well.

Fabian didn't like women who selected partners only by appearance or fame. That was too simple. Consequently, an exception the likes of Martin should have been agreeable to him. The way in which he snatched the better plates away from barrel-chested militia officers and influential barmen; the fact that he packed a greater punch with women than did professional boxers, dock workers, and DJs—men who were renowned for their high demand and whose toughness should have inspired and offered life meaning. Yet, something in Martin rubbed him the wrong way. His fame was too generic. It wasn't limited to some single, gorgeous, and intellectual exception of a woman who might have preferred him to a stud. When an average person's fame becomes the norm, then it's just as repellent as the complete lack of such an opportunity. For at least a load of logic and the approval of public opinion could be found with the latter.

Nevertheless, Fabian also had to admit that women are strange, and their souls are full of mystery. He himself had experienced how bizarre their preferences could be. Often, they chose a much blander man standing in the shadow of an interesting one. This made a man feel awfully powerless. How difficult it was to start proving to females that *you* are actually more intriguing!

Fabian had been sent to an Uzbek poetry festival three years earlier. Also representing Estonia at the event was one other youth journalist. The latter had a reddish beard, and was lean and sickly. He hadn't written all that much poetry (only a couple of emotive lines captioning the newspaper's lyrical fall and spring photos), but he wrote responses to novices who sent their own verses to the newspaper. Those who had turned thirty and a little older could still remember his energetic activist's voice from the radio poetry club. Moreover, it was his duty to manage a youth newspaper's column that addressed sexual issues and intimacy.

The poetry festival officially lasted three days, but the local admirers of Estonian literature didn't want to hear a word of Fabian and Enno leaving so early. They were attended to constantly from the very beginning. Firstly, they participated in a plenary meeting, at which guests from all the Soviet republics paid compliments to Uzbek poetry. On the second day, the two of them visited a factory where young laborers paid compliments to Estonian poetry. Fabian and Enno recited verses from Estonian classics that they could remember from their school days. On the third evening, a banquet was thrown in honor of all the guests. Wedged in between the events were a city tour, day trips to the mountains and to see the eternal flame, as well as an innumerable number of private meetings. They met many new people. The pair of Estonians became close friends with the two writers who had been appointed to welcome and escort them. Naturally, all of the events were attended by a large number of young women, poetesses, and other enthusiasts, including true beauties. They met a few of them more than once. One girl, who said she worked at the literary museum and dreamed of Tallinn, demonstrated especially deep emotion. "Oh, how I love your city of towers!" she sighed to both of the young men, standing quite close to them. Her name was Nyura, and she was curious whether it might in any way be possible to arrange for herself a business trip to the Northern Baltic region with their help.

Fabian was sure that the young Uzbek woman was fonder of him, and therefore stuck his nose up in the air and treated her unceremoniously. He made remarks, sarcastic comments, and mocked her a little. Enno behaved completely differently. He was simple and intellectually helpful. Once, he picked up a fork that Nyura had dropped; another time, he gave her an interlinear Russian-language translation of one completely untranslatable Estonian wordplay-master's poetry. Fabian scoffed at this, was self-confident, and awaited his chance. He decided that only during the final banquet would he show what kind of a man he actually was. The way it went, though, was that Enno was absent from their room the evening before the party started. Fabian shrugged, locked the door, and went downstairs to bring the porter the key. Descending the stairs, he suddenly spotted his companion sitting with the young woman behind a potted palm in the foyer, discussing something. Fabian smirked, walked up to the bar right next to them, sat with his back facing them, and attempted to overhear the conversation. Only scattered fragments reached his ears. Enno confessed: "I, for example, love flowers a lot."—"And I like trees," Nyura replied dreamily. "But do you cry while reading sometimes, too?"—"I sure do," Enno answered with conviction. "When I read, the page is downright soaked."

Fabian would have wanted to believe that Enno had behaved forwardly, i.e. that he had simply invited the girl out of her room. Such methods had certainly become second nature for him while visiting boarding-school girls for his newspaper column. Nyura, as a polite host, didn't have the heart to say no; the long-running inequality of the Uzbek women and their submissiveness to men's wishes also played its own part. Think again! Over the course of the following days, Fabian only encountered Enno at mealtimes. This couldn't still be a feudalist remnant. Their official hosts gladly observed the local girl playing guide to a foreigner all on her own. They knew that their guests would be left with a very good impression of their country, in any case. At the lunch table, they smiled understandingly at Enno and clicked their tongues; in their free time, they focused all of their attention on Fabian, who groaned under the weight of that care. He didn't even meet the girl again before their departure. Nyura came to the train station to see off her new friend. The Uzbek writers smoked on the platform beneath an open window, and continued to compliment Estonian poetry. Enno and Nyura stood at a slight distance, hand in hand and noses touching, like horses in a symbolist film. The train was just about to start moving. Fabian couldn't stand it anymore, and, abandoning his former dry politeness and icy disdain, called out irritably: "Get on!

What're you standing around for? I'm sure you'll get (here, he added a vulgar word) at home again . . ." The tone of Fabian's voice contained something that made Enno obey. He swiftly climbed into the train car. But the Uzbek beauty, who without the slightest doubt made sense of the situation and what Fabian had said, looked directly at him with her incredibly large eyes fringed by calf's eyelashes, and said with all her heart: "A person shouldn't be spiteful!"

At night, when the train had already been clacking along the rails for a long while, Fabian lay on his bunk, his eyes wide open. His companion's soft, simpleminded snoring sounded below him. Doubtless he was dreaming about Nyura, whom he had impertinently snatched out from under Fabian's nose. The man didn't honor subordination! Fabian ground his teeth and quietly banged his fists against the mattress. Why? he pointlessly repeated to himself over and over again. With what right? The lights of whistle-stops flashed past the window. After a while, Fabian calmed down and slipped into a meditation over the meaning of life. He asked himself: But, truthfully, why do I hate? Is there a cause for it? Because a more inferior individual trumped me in a sphere as cheap as that of male-female relationships? What business of mine should that be? Do I really admit that I give a damn about it? If so, then what is my actual goal in life? Do I truly work, create, and collect fame merely in order to get lucky with women? How do I then differ from an ordinary playboy or a common libertine? Or is creative work nevertheless essential for me, and I'd be involved in it even if there wasn't a single woman in the world? Am I capable of embodying a profit-free principle? Have I the strength to rise above the flesh? Fabian dozed off to these thoughts.

Sometimes when telling about his Uzbek trip in a social setting, Fabian would conjure up the expression of a precocious sage, stare off into the distance intently, and smile in astonishment, as if in disbelief that he could truly have ever doubted the absolute spirituality of his being. And the women around him remained anything but indifferent to it!

OLD FABIAN'S LAMENT

THINGS ALWAYS BEGIN sooner than one thinks, although one need not realize it, Fabian thought to himself. The signs had been there for some time, but no one could see them. In retrospect, it was the only way things could have turned out. You've got a strong desire to sputter condescendingly: "It *couldn't* have turned out otherwise! All the circumstances pointed in that direction!" But at the same time, we are surrounded by new warning signs and are unable to read those, either. Otherwise, we *would* behave differently. But then again, maybe we wouldn't, Fabian sighed, and picked up a spoon to stir his coffee. He and Elen were sitting in their tiny kitchen and eating breakfast. It was a beautiful summer day outside (their fourth summer, Fabian suddenly recalled); the white, half-length linen curtain hanging over the kitchen window stirred imperceptibly; a wasp buzzed on the other side of the glass; the slamming of car doors and men's shouts came from the street below. There was a service station down there. The male voice droning from the radio placed on top of the laundry basket turned fuzzy, and Fabian rotated the dial to adjust the frequency. Elen didn't care all that much for the foreign-language daily news, but she didn't bother him with empty prattle. Fabian had a day off today. Elen would leave for work by ten o'clock. Because of this fact, she was wearing a light-green bathrobe over her shoulders instead of her at-home clothes; a bathrobe that was associated with so many shared memories for the two of them. Mm-hmm, Fabian thought to himself. He watched his wife take her mug of coffee between her fingers, raise it to her mouth, and sip it. Her gaze was focused on a point somewhere above the table, where she appeared to be eyeing something over the rim of the mug—intently and yet absentmindedly, frozen, actually seeing nothing. That was her habit. For as long as Fabian could remember, she had always stared like that while sipping. That frozen gaze irritated him, and he turned his head away to hide his grimace. All the same, he was well aware that it hadn't bothered him so strongly before; that once, at the very beginning, he hadn't paid it any heed, and merely smiled at his dearest's idiosyncratic quirk. And that knowledge bothered him even more: why did everything tend to go this way?

Elen rose. She's pouring herself more coffee, Fabian thought. And so she was. Elen took the pot off the stove. When she sat down again, Fabian couldn't help but sneak a look to see how much she had poured herself. But of course—half a mug! Elen always drank one and a half mugs of coffee each morning. Not one or two, but one and a half, without fail. It had made Fabian chuckle during their honeymoon. Back then, everything about his dearest had made him feel tender. After a year, it left him indifferent; after two, it put him out of sorts. Now, however, he sometimes felt that he'd like to seize that one and a half mugs and fling it against Elen's head. That's madness, he thought. Why can't a person drink precisely one and a half mugs? If her body truly demands it? If her body is made that way? He didn't even dare mention that her one and a half mugs aggravates him, in fear of sounding ridiculous. So it is with those things, Fabian sighed. Instead of speaking, I suppress. And it's not as if that one and a half mugs is the only thing. Last night, they had taken a taxi back from visiting friends. Elen gave directions, as always. How many times had Fabian had to hear the words: "To the right here, between the buildings, that nine-story one there in front, middle door." Fabian remembered how his sweetheart's way with words had once made him feel elated; how after a couple of months, he had simply been content with the fact that he himself didn't have to give the cab driver directions. But lately, especially when he happened to be in a bad mood, he felt like tossing his wife out of the taxi and zooming off because of those words she said. Zoom off to where? No matter where. Just away! It's strange how those kinds of repeated instances (which are ridiculously trivial, in reality) can turn you off someone who is otherwise quite pleasant, Fabian mused. Trifling things like that actually cause more harm in a relationship than serious discord or full-blown arguments. In the latter case, the couple snaps at each other and says everything out loud to the other's face, the tension lowers, and the thunderheads dissipate. When bad blood is kept to itself, then it quietly seethes into hatred over time. There they are, those termites of wedlock, Fabian thought.

Is it really impossible for that *not* to happen; for your partner not to start getting on your nerves? he asked himself in exasperation. Why can't I hear my wife calling me to dinner in exactly the same tone of voice every day, year after year, and gladly go, regardless? Or observe how she always lights her first morning cigarette with an identical motion (which Elen was doing right now) and not have it irk me? Is it just me, and I'm *abnormal?* Or has it been that way always and with everyone; is it a law of all humanity? Does Elen possess it? Perhaps even *she* is annoyed by some of my own constricting and stereotypical patterns of behavior. Fabian considered what these might be for a moment. Actually, he doubted it. Wouldn't Elen have told him about them? As frank and childishly trusting as she was, for the most part. But, no—Fabian didn't begin deceiving himself. He wasn't young, and hadn't been a fool in a good long while; he had seen the world and people. The fact that someone got along well with someone else didn't immediately mean anything. People interacting warmly and cooing like doves in private, away from the eyes of strangers, didn't necessarily count, either. Hasn't it turned out often enough that, for years, one "happy" spouse has been hiding the fact that there is something obnoxious about the other? Fabian could picture it perfectly. For example: a man reasons that "I certainly don't like a couple of things about my wife, for instance how she reads those stupid women's magazines, but my foolish little kitty seems to love me blindly and without reservation. Better *I* stay silent about it, then; that way, I'll have a nice little advantage over her." And the woman, on the contrary, thinks: "My lovely little doofus apparently doesn't see a single thing wrong about me, and it's not my job to start opening his eyes to them. He himself has quite a lot of those flaws, for instance his awful habit of hawking up phlegm in the bathroom every morning. But better I don't say a word about it to him. Let me have a few trumps up my sleeve." On the surface, everything is absolutely shipshape, and the nice little couple can cohabitate for a long time. None of their acquaintances believes that lightning might strike their relationship. Until one day, the thunder rumbles. They lose control in a conflict and start speaking their minds. No doubt both will be amazed at the number of critical remarks each has to make about the other. "Why on earth didn't you tell me earlier that that little thing gets on your nerves so much?" both ask, astounded. "I would have stopped it at *once!*" But both of them hid and nurtured in their soul the knowledge of the other's weakness like a secret weapon.

Fabian sat down in his armchair, the latest issue of *Theater. Music.Cinema* in front of him, but he didn't read it, only stared at the cover . . . Truly—it didn't have to be anything great and exceptional, anything outstanding. Like, for example, a carefully concealed criminal passion, a falsified will, or a physical flaw, which turns the relationship between a man and a woman on its head when it comes out into the open after cohabitating for a while. Those things function completely differently; gradually, like drops of water eroding a stone, Fabian thought to himself. He knew this from personal experience, and had regarded it as

natural for life to take such a course. But oh, woe is me—
acknowledging that inevitability didn't buoy his spirits one bit
right now, nor was it relevant in the slightest degree. For Fabian
didn't covet an advantage or trumps up his sleeve; he wasn't
even planning to one day throw something in Elen's face, not in
court or on Judgment Day. On the contrary: he wished that
taxis, half-full coffee mugs, lighter clicks, and absentminded
gazes didn't get on his nerves or darken their relationship, and
was unhappy when they nevertheless did. The fact that he
currently couldn't come to terms with his tiresome reaction and
that the instances pained him seemed strange at first glance. But
taking everything from the past into account, it was entirely
justified. In what way? He definitely wasn't in the first blush of
youth anymore, but rather had experienced quite a lot and felt
wonderfully extraordinary. He had observed himself sufficiently
over his thirty years of life, and knew how his own romantic
affairs worked. The scenario didn't vary—the exact same stages
only repeated. From the first leap of his heart with the feeling of
recognition, to intoxication and losing himself, up until sobriety
and annoyance finally arrive. If you observed those relationships
more closely, the main characteristic was that they remained
unchanged, in spite of a certain degree of variation on the
surface. Sensitivity makes even the most trivial of moments
appear of the utmost importance, allows even the tiniest detail
to become a source of inconsolable desperation and intoxication.
The same applied to stupid acts. Fabian had, of course, wasted
time and money on those occasions; had wanted to watch sappy
melodramas; had longed to hold a certain woman's hand or
simply sit and stare. And when in love, he has always had an
overwhelming desire to talk, to confess. Sometimes, in
retrospect, it seemed as though the best moments in the
relationship really were those long conversations he had in bars,
on park benches, or in homes, when talking to his partner about
their former life and about their life in general. He speaks a

good deal more, of course, because he is usually more eloquent than the girl. With a smirk on his face and a shrug of his shoulders, he pictured how his face becomes more animated and his eyes glisten on those occasions; how his dear partner listens to him reverently, curiosity and excitement dancing on her face. Oh, how important it all is! At that moment, it seems to Fabian *himself* that he is saying something extraordinary. The atmosphere is such that even the most trivial detail becomes rich in meaning and worthy of emphasis. He is exalted, and he brings his partner to a heightened state of mind as well. How thrilling! These are the bright memories of an extraordinary person that pour forth, the truth about himself—painful and genuine! Before, he was convinced that he said something new and interesting on every occasion. After his third or fourth time in love, he realized that he was actually repeating the very same thing all the time, revealing his complexes, describing the fates of relatives living abroad, exaggerating his ancestors' accomplishments. Each one of them, it turned out, had managed to accomplish something exceptional! He talks about a few of the secret adventures he's had in his life, and constantly embellishes them in the telling. He confesses the dreams of his youth (he once wanted to become a great writer), and his erotic preferences (yes, even those, for boundaries no longer exist between him and that other: they are completely one, and the frank discussion of such "forbidden" things seems like the utmost expression of affection). And the climax is at hand. This lasts for some time. Then, a gentle descent follows. They become accustomed to everything. Gradually, boredom tiptoes nearer. They continue going out together and having a relatively great time, but already he starts subconsciously searching for opportunities to go out on his own. Half-unintentional deceptions and white lies about trivial things begin to creep in. And the cycle completes. Fabian had believed it was inevitable. He at least observed that it was practically the same for others.

Falling in love is like an addiction, Fabian drummed into himself. It creates the need for repetition. And with ever greater frequency. One time, when he started calculating how long a relationship with one girl or another had lasted, the result cast him into deep thought. His cycles of romance had grown shorter and shorter! Ever faster did he arrive at spiritual affinity; ever faster did he seize from his partner everything that she had to offer. He was in a great rush to access secrets, to uncover her most intimate details. What a decade ago had taken an entire fall and winter—over half a year—now had to transpire in a week. He seethed with a strange impatience that propelled him forward. Replaying his relationships in his mind, his love life took on the appearance of piecework. In that way, he knew that the increased brevity of his relationships wasn't just apparent; it didn't derive from the overall acceleration to which the lives of his generation—those approaching middle age—seemed to fall victim in every field; it wasn't solely in his feelings of affection. The brevity could be connected to it, could somehow be a condition of it. Inasmuch as his heightened perception of the current speed of life favors superficiality in and of itself; it cultivates an inability to have intense and rewarding relationships with less emphasis on exceptionality. Thus, in more or less all of us emerges a person whose motto is "Carpe diem!" but who counts on the inevitability of future disaster—who feels that the second bell has already tolled, but the third won't ring out soon. But at the moment, it was more important for the brevity to also be objective. He recalled the most significant turning points in his relationships, the brightest moments, and could compare the length of time between them, almost to the very date. Yes, he had accelerated. There was no doubt about it. What will I get out of this? Fabian had asked himself. Is my goal *truly* just to get as many notches on my belt as possible? That prospect had frustrated him. He hadn't regarded himself as being so shallow. Recently, he had finally dissolved his official marriage that dated

back long ago to his youth. Seven months later, he cut off all ties
with the woman, who had made the decisive push for that step
after having been a good friend over the previous years. Life
seemed more absurd than ever. And Fabian had decided that he
wouldn't tie himself down to anyone so easily anymore; wouldn't
give in to temptations. Exactly—for when he looked back, he
couldn't seem to find fault only with himself. The women were
also definitely to blame! When he thought about it, they had
been relatively trite, regardless—some more so, some less.
Fabian resolved to have nothing to do with women like that
anymore. He saw through them ever more quickly, anticipated
the end already at the start, and it was getting harder and harder
to take *himself* seriously. He had to admit that love is also like a
drug in that sense; that the doses have to be increased little by
little, otherwise they won't have an effect anymore. And a desire
had matured within him . . .

"I want to meet the ideal woman," he had confessed to
his friend Kobra, whom he sometimes consulted on romantic
affairs. "Nothing else appeals to me anymore."

"But what about love?" Kobra had asked doubtfully.

"That'll come on its own," Fabian replied, confident. "There's
nothing more natural than starting to love the ideal woman.
There are simply a whole lot of reasons for loving her."

But isn't that businesslike, all the same—to love someone
for something? he had simultaneously asked himself. Shouldn't
that noble feeling stand higher than any other considerations?
He recalled how Aet, his ex-wife, had spoken about it. Love
takes odd paths, she said. It was appointed from on high, a
gift from heaven that is born of who-knows-what and can hit
you in the head on any street corner. It's completely irrational.
It establishes some mystical "pull" toward another individual,
and that's it. Mysterious fate guides your affection. Throwing
yourself under that fate was *sublime*; romantic, in any case. No
other circumstances can affect the spark of love. It can't be earned

or summoned by any possible preconditions. If it exists, then it exists. Totally contrary to logic. Despite all kinds of differences in character, education, appearance, and other things that may hold sway between two people. For love paves all roads. And it was precisely that kind of love that Aet poeticized.

Oh, yes, Fabian mused—he agreed: *all* kinds of love manifest. Undoubtedly also the aforementioned types. We're all romantics, magnanimous, and receptive to noble spiritual movements, at least when we're young. Fabian remembered one girl from his school days. He had taken a real liking to her. He walked her home from parties a few nights, and they had gone to the cinema together a couple of times. They just chatted. Fabian probably sensed instinctively that something was in the air, but what exactly, he couldn't say. Back then, he hadn't known himself well enough to discover the early signs of love in himself, and much less in someone else. On one of those winter nights, when they were walking hand in hand down a quiet street bordered by wooden planks, the sidewalks flanked by snow banks glinting bluish in the darkness, he asked in conversation—without any ulterior motives—who her parents were. The girl replied that she didn't have a mother. "But a father?" Fabian asked. The girl fell silent. The topic sparked Fabian's interest. The girl doggedly withheld the truth. Finally, Fabian pried the answer from the girl: her father worked as a garbage man. She appeared dreadfully ashamed of the fact. However, her shame was exceptionally moving for Fabian. All of a sudden, he felt as if something had pierced him, the layers of his soul had rearranged, and he realized that he was truly in love. And right up to his ears in it! In retrospect, he knew that never before nor after had he wanted to be as infinitely gentle toward the girl as he did at that moment. In any case, Fabian kissed her passionately on the lips in his outburst of tenderness, and since he was still an awkward beginner at kissing back then, the girl became startled: Fabian had apparently nearly forced his teeth down her throat.

That was then. He has been Aet-minded, too. But now, after all of those relationships, so many discoveries and confessions, rushes of emotion and intoxications, such an admission coming from the mouth of some young woman wouldn't stir any spiritual movement within him. Fabian was sure of it. Which doesn't mean, of course, that he leans toward the other extreme now, or that his greatest dream is merely to court the only daughter of an important Papa. No, but neither would the existence of such a father-in-law drive him away (*that* could have even happened in the negativism of youth); quite the opposite. He simply no longer saw a point in poeticizing compassionate, pitiful love. He could no longer bear to ennoble a misalliance, the union of unequals—be it a shepherd's fondness for a princess or a film star's relationship with her stableboy. Nor the kind of love that searches for difficulties specifically in order to be toughened by them; hardships, which make it stronger the less support there is to be found from its surroundings. Life has run me over, Fabian acknowledged. I account for my surroundings and the opinions that come from them. I conform. I don't defy. He doesn't possess that much strength anymore. Not in *any* sense. He no longer has it in him to climb to a library on top of a mountain. That demands immense effort and willpower. But how easy it once was! He could have gone to sit in the library's reading room every other day.

Fabian perked up his ears. Someone was bumping around in the bathroom. It had to be Elen. The clock on the wall showed nine thirty . . . Or take appearance, for instance! Who hasn't realized when they're young how their beloved's flaws become oddly dear after a while! At least as dear as her attractive qualities. Naturally, a young woman is most ashamed of her shortcomings when standing before the very man whom she loves, and strives to conceal her flaws at any cost. She deceives us with creative ways of dressing to give the optical illusion of slimness; refuses to lie down in bed while the table lamp is on;

avoids the beach and mixed-sex saunas, using all kinds of excuses, and so forth. But her shortcomings shine through anyway, and the very manner in which the given person attempts to conceal her flaws makes her even lovelier to us, in turn. Fabian knew this from his own repeated experiences. Who hasn't, in a surge of tenderness, kissed his loved one's hairy birthmark, stroked her bony shoulder blades or her scarred stomach, pinched her bat ears hidden beneath tufts of hair! Oh, yes—the charm of flaws . . . But now he knows that when the initial spell wears off, when the fog that clouds your mind has lifted, then he sees those bat ears for what they actually are—a cosmetic defect. What's more: now, they earn more disdain than they deserve, since he is subconsciously angry at himself for having loved those same ears so much before. And he turns ruthlessly spiteful. But he didn't *want* to be spiteful! And so, he didn't even start pretending to himself, but acknowledged frankly: I've had enough of that ambiguous "something" that schoolgirls hallucinate about and chaste, novel-reading wives dream about. Enough of the "pure feeling" that strikes you as giddiness; the impact of which passes ever faster. Enough of those will-o'-the-wisps that at first seemed so ridiculously tantalizing, but in the end leave you disappointed and at a loss before becoming a complete flop. He wanted to go with what was certain, he had told himself. To build his affection upon something more real. He doesn't promote eugenics, marriage bans, or mandatory sterilization—oh, no! He only recognizes that he's no longer capable of loving for nothing, or for love itself. He wants the woman to be worthy of it, too. He is sober-minded, yes; he's a rationalist (he had made himself completely conscious of this momentary mindset), but he is so on purpose. He wasn't ashamed to admit that he wanted to love a perfect woman, who has a wealth of all kinds of good qualities: both beauty and education, pride and goodness, et cetera, et cetera. He wanted it if only because one usually has no other choice than to try to be better when in such a person's presence. Thus, the more of those fine qualities the woman had, the better, Fabian had thought, disappointed in ephemeral spiritual movements.

"Who even answers in complete sentences?" his friend Kobra taunted.

"Yeah, yeah, sure—who even answers in complete sentences," Fabian said, bristling. "Even *that's* worth it."

And it appeared as if his plea had been heard on high, for soon after the discussion with Kobra, Fabian had met Elen at a social gathering by complete chance. He saw her a couple more times, already not lacking in initiative on his own behalf. He had observed, listened, and marveled, believing that he was seeing a chimera. Why doesn't she have any flaws? Fabian had wondered, scratching the back of his neck. The laws of probability suggest that everyone has to have them. Whether it's a crooked tooth or the habit of using parasitic loanwords. Even so, he noticed the girl didn't possess anything of the sort. At first, he couldn't believe his eyes and ears, thinking that the increasingly attractive overall impression would nonetheless burst like a soap bubble in the next moment. He adopted an ironic stance, deliberately striving to see flaws in Elen. He had believed that such women only feature in literature. His suspicions were greatly deepened by the fact that the girl wasn't taken. He heard from Elen's girlfriends that she had been married once, but long since divorced and childless. She never appeared to have a single suitor trailing or across from her. Why is that? Fabian had wracked his brain. Why had no one put his hand on her if she really was as valuable as she seems? There had to be *some* reason for it, didn't there? But there wasn't. He supposed it was just one of life's little paradoxes when the guy who personally didn't look around is left sitting alone (no matter how alluring that person might be otherwise), at the same time that the less attractive but more eager individuals manage to score. Wary, Fabian hesitated, like a diamond merchant inspecting to see whether a stone is genuine, and eventually arriving at the conclusion that it was. He invited Elen out on a date one Saturday. And it became clear that she possessed an additional fascinating quality: she seemed to be very fond of Fabian! This strengthened his premonition of success, which was confirmed before long. To this day, Fabian could remember how he and Elen had strolled together, holding hands for the first time; he remembered his joyful incredulity. He knew, of course, that women generally liked to hold hands. But with Elen, it was something new. No one had held Fabian's hand that way before. The girl was just the right length shorter than him, and seemed to slide neatly into the crook of his arm, rubbing against his side in such a way that Fabian's left ribs could sense the proximity of her breast. They fit perfectly, like the parts of a toy construction set. Elen had radiated trust, as if she knew nothing more natural than belonging to him body and soul. We were made for each other, the thought flashed through Fabian's mind right at the beginning. A strange sense of happiness flared up within him—he became euphoric and was extremely content with the entire world. That hardly ever happened to him. He pressed the girl closer to him while sneaking a look out of the corner of his eye to see what kind of an expression she was wearing. Elen's face was filled with the delight of a little child. Even *now*, when Fabian recalled it, he couldn't help but smile.

And that had truly been just the beginning; merely the opening measure. Fabian had gotten his longed-for ideal woman. And he hadn't tired of repeating to himself: the mysterious "attraction" might pass, but everything that is erected upon firm ground—that can't end. When you have a guarantee, then the feeling won't go anywhere either. A guarantee most definitely existed with Elen. She was the embodiment of values. Therefore, Fabian became more convinced by the day that he was lucky. And hadn't things with Elen turned out differently than with all the rest? Even time-wise? Nearly four years already!

All their tales had been told and secrets exposed, but still they remained contentedly together. He had disclosed his childhood complexes, his dreams, escapades, and erotic preferences, but it was *still* interesting. Their relationship had long since climaxed and should have been forgotten, but no matter whether the peak was simply gradual or the angle of descent was so small, there was almost no boredom to be felt. Fabian did want to go out socially, but not alone; together with Elen. Not out on an escapade, because he *still* didn't have a noteworthy interest in any other women: he couldn't even be bothered to observe them, as men should do. *He*, who by nature was supposed to have libertine blood coursing through his veins! He didn't regret his lack of interest in others. Elen was far superior to them. That, apparently, was precisely what made Fabian immune to unknown temptations. He felt like someone who has rich relatives abroad, people who constantly send him care packages so that more likely than not he will refrain from combing through shops and standing in line from morning to night to acquire deficit goods. Why, then, did he so readily enter social settings, if not to spy? Because even though he loved Elen, he also felt wholeheartedly *proud* of her, too. He couldn't deny that his vanity was fed when he spent time next to the girl. And when he thought about his luck, about the fact that *he* had been the one who discovered Elen, then even now, he felt like someone who managed to secure front-row seats to a major and long-awaited theater performance at the last minute. And still, *still*, that was the very reason why he was now distressed by those lighters and half-full mugs of coffee that he would have taken as natural and inevitable in the event of any other woman.

Elen came out of the bathroom, sat down in front of the mirror, and started applying her makeup. They didn't have a boudoir—a tiny white dressing table stood in the corner, partway concealed behind the wardrobe. How nice that it's behind the wardrobe, Fabian thought. And how nice it is that I sometimes have to go to work in the morning and can't watch my wife putting on her makeup like this every day. Who knows what displeasure I would start to feel again.

The sound of Chopin's nocturnes emanated from somewhere. In *this* building, Fabian marveled. The only explanation was that someone had forgotten to turn a radio off. Through the wall, he could hear the curtains being pulled back in the neighboring apartment. The metal hooks rattled along the track. But birds were singing outside. They flew to the yard from the hundred-year-old trees in the nearby cemetery. The birds' trilling and twittering mingled with the squealing and screeching of some machinery or winch on the construction site that sprawled next to the building. Strike work was underway there. Elen was ready to go, and walked up to him. Fabian stood. They pressed against each other for a moment and kissed briefly, but affectionately. And in that same second as he felt his wife against him, the memory of how they had kissed for the first time flashed through Fabian's mind. Even *that* had surprised him. Elen had slumped entirely against him, so Fabian could sense her against his own body from her knees to her forehead—he even felt her nose!—and pressed her shoulders forward, as one is ordered to do in an x-ray. Two warm, dense points pressed against Fabian's chest through the sheer fabric of her dress. He settled onto a chair, fumbling around for it with one hand, and drew the girl down onto his lap. They were incredibly quiet about it. And not only so that the other tenants wouldn't hear (it had happened in Fabian's rented room). Fabian felt that he could give his mouth a rest. He no longer needed to explain, elucidate, spell out anything—to conceal, boast, or leave himself an exit. He was grateful. He felt the girl's warmth gradually radiating into his knees. He placed one hand under the girl's arm and the other between her palms, and to him, it seemed as if he had sealed an electrical current. Fabian closed his eyes. They hadn't said even a single word yet. A few moments later, he peeked out through his eyelids. Elen's eyes were closed. Fabian started to feel ashamed for peeking, for all of the peeking in his life, and closed his eyes again. All of a sudden, he felt something warm and moist brush his neck, then his cheeks, his eyelids, and his forehead. They were Elen's lips touching him, gently skimming across his face—like a blind person's fingers when they meet a new object.

That memory fleetingly surfaced in Fabian's mind—now, at a moment when they were embracing, so the hug became longer, which Elen interpreted in her own way, pressing against him even more firmly, even more trustingly. Back then, everything was as it is now. Those very same knees and lips, nose, and two warm, taut points poking through her sheer dress. And even so, it wasn't quite the same.

"Two o'clock, then," Elen said, drawing away.

"Two o'clock," Fabian nodded. They were going to meet for lunch. The door closed. Fabian was left alone. He mechanically sat down, but stood with a start and made for the window. They always waved to each other, had done so day after day. (Fabian had, of course, forgotten on a few occasions, and although Elen had never called him out for it, he was personally embarrassed.) His wife was indeed standing there, waiting between two chestnut trees on the other side of the street. Fabian waved a couple of times, smiled brightly, and then sank back down into the armchair. He couldn't deny the fact that it was pleasant to be at home alone. Aren't I being overly sentimental or dramatic in general? he asked himself. Why am I all out of breath? No doubt Elen has formed her own criticisms of me throughout all this time, too. More likely than not, she doesn't hold me in as high regard as she appears to show. Recently, a close acquaintance had told Fabian the following story. The acquaintance had forever believed that his wife loved him dearly. According to the man, this was demonstrated in many ways, both big and small. Among other things, the acquaintance had drawn this conclusion from the fact that his wife never fell asleep before he came to bed: she would always wait up for him, even when the man occasionally worked late at night. The clock struck past midnight while he was still hunched over his protocols and reports, poems, essays, and diagrams. The woman bravely endured, reading with her elbow propped up on the pillow, and would merely cast weary glances toward the desk from time to time. The man regarded this as a sign of exceptional affection. Afterward, when they separated, it turned out that the woman had simply been unable to fall asleep while the light was on in the room. This story made Fabian laugh, although he knew that great truths could be concealed even in funny incidents.

He stood up energetically, shook himself from head to toe as if wanting to get loose of something, and sat down at his desk. He engrossed himself in work, and his thoughts didn't pester him. When he looked at the clock, an hour and twenty minutes had passed. There were two hours and forty minutes until their lunch date. He would manage to do a lot in that time. All of a sudden, Fabian recalled what their dates had been like four years ago. Elen had been living far away, in another city district somewhere in the green belt. When they had plans to get together, she would take the train to Central Station, and Fabian would go there to meet her. He remembered that the closer the agreed-upon time came, the more restless he would become. His thoughts flitted around in his head and ultimately always arrived back at Elen in some roundabout way. He could be sitting and working when he suddenly discovered that he'd merely been staring at a sheet of paper or out the window, and even *there* he really saw nothing, as the image of Elen's face always materialized before him. Sometimes, he was unable to sit still for the last hour. Then, he would take the bus back to a station on the border between the newer and older parts of Tallinn at which Elen's train would stop. He knew the time of the train Elen would take. Fabian knew the schedules of all the trains with which she could arrive; he knew when one or another was stopping somewhere. He had recorded all of the times in a notebook. When her particular train arrived, he would board it and walk from carriage to carriage until he found Elen reading at a window seat somewhere. It was one of Fabian's boyish tricks, but it gave him heaps of pleasure.

By doing so, he won the additional seven minutes that it took the train to reach Central Station. In his mind's eye, Fabian could see himself in perfect detail in that distant time, four summers back. That time, they were supposed to meet at Central Station at four forty-five in the evening. His excitement had started to grow already around noon. He ate without really chewing, and a moment later was unable to recall what the food had tasted like. Returning to the editorial office, he specifically picked out a piece of duller work so that he wouldn't have to strain his brain muscles. His mind would have gone off wandering before long, anyway. He spurred himself on, but it was no use. Nothing came of it. He gave up, swept the papers into piles on either side of the desk, and rose briskly so as not to change his mind. Eagerness got under his skin, he became recklessly exuberant like someone who has decided to give in to a temptation, and he locked the door behind him. Fabian scurried off toward the city center. The trip was long, since the bus circled back around, and there were also a lot of stops and stoplights. Getting off the bus, he perked up his ears. The railway station was a stone's throw away and just six minutes' more walking distance, but he was dreadfully afraid of running late. Thus, in his state of heightened anticipation, he couldn't tell whether the leaves on the willows that grew along the tracks were swishing rhythmically, or whether the wind was carrying into his eardrums the song of rumbling train wheels, far off at the previous stop. Something pulsed within him. His blood throbbed mercilessly. He sped off.

Now, that seemed dolefully beautiful. Why am not I getting

excited right now? Fabian wondered. There are two and a half hours left, but I could distract myself with whatever I want, be it the date or not. He sighed and focused again. But then, the rumble of a rising airplane (the airport wasn't far) filled the air and bore Fabian's thoughts off into the past once more.

He recalled how they'd gone for a stroll in Kadriorg Park one night. Not quite in the park itself, but alongside it, among the wooden houses in the neighborhood's sleepy streets. It might have been past ten o'clock at night, since a concert-request program was playing on the radio. A heat wave had gripped the city for several days, and windows were opened wide. They were the windows of respectable persons. They walked the entire length of yet another street, and the very same song sounded from nearly every window. The entire street echoed with it. *She* was showing signs as if it were time for her to leave. Today hadn't been their day—like it or not, she had to get home at some point. Fabian was prepared to keep her there by force, to delay that moment. He asked that she not go yet. He said: "A person isn't given many of these kinds of evenings in their life." At the same time, he'd been struck by the fear that Elen might ask how many of them he had already had by then. But no—Elen merely nodded and held his hand more tightly. The cafés were starting to close, and they couldn't get in anywhere anymore. However, Fabian was full of ambition and would have wanted to work something else out. They could have walked to the city center and descended into some bar throbbing with noise and full of tourists and youth, but he felt that wouldn't be the proper place at that moment. "Let's go to the airport," he proposed. Elen didn't ask why *there* in particular. Fabian knew the airport had a café, where he could have a dash of cognac added to his coffee despite the nighttime sales ban. They waited for the bus and rode up the hillcrest. Before entering through the sliding doors, they had stood and stared out over the lake that stretched from the other side of the road almost up to the horizon. Half of the red, descending disc of the sun shone between the buildings on the opposite shore. There wasn't the slightest wisp of breeze in the air. The surface of the water glittered like a mirror, the ripples upon it sparkled in various tones; only in the distance, near the far shore, did the surface turn matt. A coach bus driving down the road caught the rays; bright patches flashed on its roof. Visible within a small grove of trees to the left was a lone window—the evening sunlight falling upon its glass reflected blindingly, like a searchlight. It was hard to believe the hour, although it was no longer as hot as it had been in the daytime. Daylight saving time had been newly enforced, and summers now lasted an hour longer than they had in the days of Fabian's youth. A group of tourists was waiting for their late flight. Based on their clothing and the large backpacks lying on the ground next to them, one could guess that they were mountain climbers. There were a surprising number of people there for such a late hour. Many appeared to be waiting for someone, but a few had certainly found their way there just for fun, the way *they* had. Two television monitors buzzed in the corners, and the clusters of people standing quietly were solemnly watching a sports broadcast. Fabian would have wanted to jet off—together with her. Where? It didn't matter, as long as they left. But they had no tickets, no money to buy them; not even their IDs. Elen had to get home to her elderly mother sometime, and Fabian had to go to work the next morning in order to submit an edited manuscript. At that same moment, an airplane tore itself free from the airstrip and rose with slow rage, buzzing and piercingly droning over the lake and into the heavens. What's not possible, Fabian had thought in wonder, and gained courage. Who knew what still lay ahead! Life felt long.

Fabian, nevertheless, had enough money to take Elen to the bar and have a dash of cognac with their coffees. The plump, motherly waitress eyed them with good-natured understanding. They mounted their stools and drank in little sips, not exchanging a single word. Soon, Elen rose to go make a phone call. Fabian didn't ask to whom. He didn't want to know. Instead, he thought about whom they could go visit afterward. Which of his friends or acquaintances might be open-minded enough to receive them at that hour, to co-experience their happiness, treat them to food and drink, and offer lodging for their love.

And right at the end, he could remember the next morning—he simply couldn't *fail* to remember it. Fabian himself had been the first to wake up that time. Birdsong could be heard through the open window, exactly like it could right now, and chilly air penetrated the room through the curtain. He didn't rouse Elen, and turned off the alarm clock so that it wouldn't start blaring half an hour later. And he sat watching her. Elen didn't make even the slightest noise when she slept. She didn't wheeze, moan, or grind her teeth, not to mention snore. Even in that state she was perfect, looking quite pretty as she slept, her mouth closed, tranquil, an almost joyful expression gracing her face. Otherwise, one might have taken her for dead. Fabian leaned in close to hear her breathing. He saw the tiny holes in her ear (the earrings she had taken out lay on a stool in front of the bed), and studied the pattern of her skin. He must have kissed her eyes at night because her eye shadow was smeared. One might even think that Elen had been punched a short while ago, and that the bruising was only now emerging. A moment later, Elen opened her eyes and reached her hand out toward him . . .

How lovely it all was! Then why the hell those lighters and taxi directions? Fabian asked himself irritatedly. Did it come from excessive proximity, from over-interaction? It could be. Fabian was conscious of the fact that he didn't lack a certain mania. When he loved someone, he wanted, by all means, to be together with her as much as possible. No matter what the cost, although he knew that he would grow tired of the relationship that much more quickly, and the end would come faster. He ordinarily didn't consider consequences. How, then, was he supposed to hold himself back when he met such an attractive being as Elen? He hadn't been able to bear periods of separation at all anymore. And here he was, all on his own now. Hadn't Elen been wiser all the same when she timidly proposed that they could live separately? As *if*—Fabian had been offended by it like a child! Perhaps it would have been more reasonable to delay the arrival of routine, to lengthen the transition period. Why couldn't they have kept their meetings to three or four times a week? Especially given the fact that he liked Elen so much. For that very reason, he should have taken care to ensure that their relationship stayed fresh. Why did he rush headlong to meet his future like a masochist? Hadn't the previous occasions taught him anything? Or was he already too weak, too lacking in willpower to pull himself together? No, he wasn't, and he had learned a thing or two, as well. He'd learned that routine would come anyway; one can't delay it indefinitely. Still, the existence of one other opportunity had ripened within him as the fruit of long considerations. It was contrary to the previous ones, in some sense. One must cross the entire path at breakneck speed! One must rip off all the masks. Not leave uninvestigated areas of the other person, where he might later find space for illusions that would crumble anyway. Bring truth to the surface so that it's all clear as daylight on the palm of your hand. For only then, Fabian had reasoned, when you see right through a person, does it become apparent whether or not it will be possible to be with them stably.

It was a gamble. By doing so, one could effectively lose out on a year or a year and a half that would otherwise be guaranteed. Therefore, only a person who plays it safe can risk intense interaction. Fabian had done so. He had been convinced that even when he came to learn the taste of Elen's lip balm and the glow of her body in fever, when he had seen her in curlers and mopping the floor—that even then, he wouldn't be sick of it.

Yes—when he had grasped that standing before him was the ideal wife, he had played it safe; had wanted to build something lasting.

But did I really? Fabian now probed himself mercilessly. Had he believed they would someday be buried in the same grave? He would so much have wanted to answer "yes." But at the same time, he had to admit to himself that several of his tiny, semi-involuntary acts and subconscious attitudes had not allowed him to take his own belief seriously, or condemned it outright. Fabian's gaze fell upon the desk, where his fingers were mechanically picking at the edge of a book. Take for instance those very same books (although he strove not to think about it)! It went as follows.

When he and Elen started going out, he had already been divorced once and he knew that one of the worst things about separating was dividing up books. In the case, of course, that both have an interest in the possessions. His first wife did. Thus, they couldn't escape that depressing procedure. First of all, they had to determine which titles were subject to being split up; whether one edition or another had been purchased before or after their union. That part was simple: the year of publication was right on the title page. The trouble was that when they wed, they had also stacked the books on the same shelf. And neither could remember which was whose anymore. They should have made some kind of a marking in each book, pasted ex libris in each, or simply initialed a corner. But who thought at the beginning that they would one day need to set their books apart again! That sort of mark making would have been equivalent to jinxing himself. Fine—they had to be divided. They had tried to be polite to each other, especially Aet, since she had watched more TV than Fabian and had seen how educated people should behave when splitting up. Fabian couldn't be bothered to remain delicate, and occasionally erupted into shouting. They reached agreement over most of the books, because both Fabian and Aet ultimately had their own field, their own series; there were two copies of some books, anyway. But in some cases, both were sure that *they* had been the ones who had bought it. Who knows. No matter—in the end, each of them probably received the better part of their own titles. But what to do with the rest? Naturally, both of them started to justify why they had a more considerable need for one book or another. And of course, it turned out that each of them needed the majority of what had been acquired jointly. This was entirely natural as well, of course, since the heart certainly bleeds when you imagine that you might never again see a particular good book.

Fabian stared out the window. What did that have to do with anything now? With their life? It meant that he'd *known* all this back when Elen moved in with him. *She* had brought her own books into their home, also, and they were stacked on the same shelf as his. Fabian's own collection now had ex libris. Although they had bought *more* of them, naturally. Both he and she had. They put everything together. But when Fabian himself bought one, then he couldn't help but simply make his own mark in the new book. As if it were the Devil's own doing. At first, he didn't even admit to himself why he was doing it. He didn't dare acknowledge the act. To start with, he wrote his name on the title page. Why? Not to practice his autograph, was it? He wasn't famous, who needed it? How long could he deceive himself like that? Then, he stopped writing his name, and instead made a little mark next to the impressum at the rear of the book, which didn't catch the eye and only he could recognize. Specifically, he crossed out one zero from the print total. And oh—the way he did it, to boot! Not by picking up the book, opening it to the back, and crossing out the little zero. No, it all transpired casually. Sometimes, he would read the book to the last page, and then as if by its own will, a pencil would end up in his hand at that very moment, and he would seemingly absentmindedly allow its point to lower into the necessary position. Oh, how he performed theater! Recently, though, he had even started to feel embarrassed about *that*. Now, he simply bought two copies of every valuable book. But not publicly! He *still* used clever means. He wouldn't place two of the same titles side-by-side on the shelf, since then Elen could have started inquiring as to his reasons. No—he stuck one here, the other there. Fabian was forced to admit that he *had* been leading a double life, in some sense. Slowly but surely, he had been guaranteeing his future. I really am quite the asshole, he thought. This entire time, he had subconsciously accounted for the possibility that they would break up. Somewhere in the depths of his soul, somewhere in the hinterlands of his consciousness, that reckoning had perpetually existed. The stamp of the possible end—on every word and movement. In reality, he wasn't building a lasting relationship, but still something temporary; still something halfway.

Or, no—all the same, he had been quite honest during the first years. At least during the first months—sincere as a lump of earth, genuine unambiguity. Was I *really?* Fabian asked himself.

He considered his life and cast judgment upon himself. He realized that he is still just as carefree, acting like a capricious child, merely acting on whims . . . That won't do, he decided. Life is life. If he was incapable of getting his act together now, then he would likely never be able to do it. But losing Elen— that perspective seemed depressing. He needs to rethink his attitude before it's too late; before Elen sees through him. What would happen if the woman discovered those tiny crossed-out numbers? How would Fabian explain them? By saying that was how he protests the book industry's print-run policy, since too few of the good books are printed and too many of the bad ones? Ridiculous, Elen wouldn't believe it. How embarrassing! I've collected dynamite under the chair on which I'm sitting, Fabian cursed himself. And who could guarantee that the chair wouldn't be blown sky-high *tonight*? Fabian was gripped by panic. To arms, without delay—to destroying all traces! He grabbed an eraser and bolted toward the shelf, yanking off it the first book he came across. His hands, obeying him poorly out of agitation, opened it to the last page, discovered a tiny line, and liquidated the treacherous mark with a single stroke. The next book didn't have one, but the fourth did. Erase! Destroy all traces! Live a new life! Fabian recited the mantra to the rhythm of his work. Then came a couple of foreign-language works, which he could skip because they were field-based and had been sent to him. Besides, print numbers weren't marked in books printed abroad. After that, the eraser was needed a number of times, until one clean book after another started to come. Fabian was already replacing one such title, when his hand suddenly stopped halfway to the shelf. He squeezed the book between his fingers and sensed that something was strange. But what, exactly? He flipped it over to the front cover—yes, the smallish format hadn't deceived him, it was in fact a book of poetry. He looked at the print total again. Why was it so large? Who wasn't aware of how little poetry was printed; people argued about it openly. True, there were singular exceptions, but this collection's author could hardly be one of them or lay claim to a run of forty thousand like an author of some popular novels. Fabian took a magnifying glass out of the desk drawer and studied the impressum. Having taken a good long look, his eyes peered enquiringly over the rim of the magnifying glass, and came to rest somewhere between the window and the floor—concentrating intently, but not actually seeing anything. Fabian returned the book to its place, eyed the colorful row of spines that stretched from the floor to the ceiling, was lost deep in thought, and appeared to recall something. Then, he grabbed a book from a completely different place on the shelf, opened it, brought it close to his eyes, let it drop down, and stuck it back between the others. Then he took a third from just a little farther away, looked at the back cover, and impatiently cast it aside; then the next, then another and another, until it seemed to be enough. He finally set the magnifying glass on the desk and wiped his brow, a blissful expression upon his face. He hadn't been wrong. In some of the books that had seemed a little unfamiliar to him for some reason, someone had carefully added by hand a little zero at the end of the print total.

Whistling, Fabian started selecting a more cheerful tie for his lunch date.

MY FLORAKIN, MY FAUNAKIN

PEOPLE CALL ME Red Rose. I'm a large woman even by the rising global standards of obesity. I attracted attention while on an internship in East Germany, even though many of the young women there are total cart horses. I'm certainly large, but harmonious. I have titanic hips and wide, pale breasts. My skin is rather pale in general, and lightly freckled. Some say I have a classical profile. Both top and bottom. My teeth are a little stubby and sharp-pointed, so I can't allow myself the dazzling smile of a film star, but instead have to limit myself to a secretive Mona Lisa smirk.

Already in grade school, I noticed that I liked certain kinds of men above all others—ones who didn't seem to be interested in other girls at all. My girlfriends dreamed of tall and rugged guys, of tough cowboys, of muscular secret agents. Their hearts beat for jocks and professional boxers. I'm not saying that men like that left *me* feeling entirely indifferent, but my affinity, my secret sympathy lay with frail, weak little men. That feeling intensified the more that my inner development progressed. Lately, though, I've matured to the point that I am completely besotted with wimps. Tall men make me laugh and give me a feeling of distaste. (It's so comical to imagine how women who are shorter than me have to arch their necks to look them in the eyes!)

At the same time, to my pleasant astonishment, I've determined that those kinds of men are drawn to me. Maybe it has to do with a need for compensation. They lust for me because their own wives are almost always built the same as they are: small and pale, sometimes even anemic. It's as if they don't even really walk, but rather float fairy-like a few millimeters off the ground. They suit their husbands in everyday life, but are unable to offer them everything. The men harbor secret, inescapable desires, and so they stalk me. I allow it all to happen with glee, as such men can offer exceptional thrills even at the beginning of an affair. Machos nearly always hit on you the same way. You can, of course, always play it safe with them, and that creates a sense of security (which people say about marital sex, for instance). Yet, you already know everything beforehand: the manner in which they approach you is simple and straightforward, and overall, it leaves me indifferent. But those others—they make nuisances of themselves in their own annoyingly idiosyncratic ways; with them, it's interesting. They tell exciting stories, are well traveled, speak other languages, and have a lively spirit (especially when slightly tipsy) that makes entertaining jumps and associates things in a way that would never have dawned upon me personally. One of them, for example, recently told me that only dubious sorts of guys come up with anything original. I repeat that little pearl of wisdom to myself daily.

Usually, they invite me over for a nightcap in some fashionably seedy room somewhere in the city center, or on the top floor of an apartment building. They make witty remarks for a while, then turn on some music. They dance with me in odd steps and do artistic twirls. It's purely bodily inspiration, because they don't *actually* know how to dance, for the most part. I happily go along with that inspiration, and then pretend to go limp in their feeble arms. Then, they forget their entire surroundings, nuzzle their noses into my cleavage (since the two are at the same height), and simply shift from foot to foot in some kind of a trance, like in the last quarter of a dancing marathon. They're unpredictable. Just imagine—one time, one of them pulled off my nylons, poked holes in them, and pulled them over his head! I'm amazed by how they do such tricks, and can't always tell whether they're doing it for their own enjoyment or think that they have to entertain me. It's also possible that they don't have the courage to go any farther until they've hyped themselves up with some tricks.

They remove their glasses and strip down naked. Often, they don't even notice that I'm still fully clothed. I make their task easier, and carefully remove my own clothing.

Then, they simply plunge down with me somewhere.

I watch how the geniuses crawl their way up me. As if they weren't actually people, but some kinds of cute bugs. Little white maggots. With tentacles. But bugs that possess supreme intelligence. Little maggots with powerful intellect. Little maggots with sexual organs. I feel something gently tickling me as they crawl up like that. It's certainly barely perceptible and not even worth mentioning to my girlfriends. For what does the Earth feel when a tiny mouse pushes its plow across her field? Or what does a floor feel when a baby turtle crawls across it, dragging a tiny carrot tied to a stick behind it? But that feeling is incredible, exquisite and fine.

From time to time, they snuffle; from time to time, they yell; sometimes they do swimming strokes on top of me. Occasionally, they get stuck behind something; occasionally, one falls in some cavity and is unable to climb out right away.

But climb, they do.

I encourage their scrawny knees and stroke their goosebumps. Their little hooked fingers cling to my white flesh. They crawl ever upward. Sometimes they reach their destination, sometimes not. Sometimes they simply leave their fragrant little stream upon me; their moist path; their gray spoor. The trail of their intellect, I'd call it. Because if you stretch your imagination a little, there's not that much of a difference between that stream and their brilliant gray matter.

The stream dries up before long. I'd like to warm that spot

upon me with an iron, so that the trace would be visible and stay on my skin like writing with milk as invisible ink.

But if they should arrive at their destination regardless and empty themselves into me, I know nothing more sublime.

They shouldn't act too macho. Then, everything is ruined and turns ordinary. The out-of-the-norm charm fades. One time, I was disappointed by a man in an especially harsh way. He was just like *that* by appearance. I was convinced that he *also* belonged to the brotherhood of little maggots. But far from it—he acted like a normal man when he was with me. Imagine that: he pushed and pulled, turned and lifted. He *took* me! I was unable to resist him anymore; I'd let the right moment go by. But when it was all over, I threw him out at four in the morning (even though it was his apartment).

Luckily, such mishaps don't happen all that often. My eye has become ever sharper. I choose carefully. Everything goes the way I want it to, for the most part. At my high points, I even feel as if men don't *possess* an existence; that *I* am the one who gives it to them. They're simply *inside* of me. I contain men. Isn't that great?

My florakin, my faunakin is what I'd like to whisper into their ear in a rush of tenderness.

An orgasm *is* full of life, only visible with a microscope, you know.

Luminescence cascades into the room as Selene drives her chariot across the heavens.

DODGEBALL

He stops in front of a wall. It's cracked. Dust has collected in the grooves of the bumpy plaster. The road that leads past here is asphalted and shouldn't get all that dusty, at least not in rainy weather. You could imagine that it's the dust of time itself, fallen here over the span of a couple decades. And the wall has seemingly become shorter—your hand can reach over the top edge. The wall is suddenly darker in one place. A shard broke off from it, and the area has now been patched. The repaired area reminds him how they climbed over it there. The wall has a broad iron gate, too. Back then, it stood a little ajar. It could be pushed open, in any case. But going through it didn't suit the kids. One had to climb over it, by all means. One's portfolio or satchel was firstly lobbed over in a wide arc. Like a bomb tossed behind enemy lines. Then you yourself went over, accompanied by hollering, naturally. Now, the gate is firmly shut. He stands in front of it and stares at the briefcase in his hand. It's made of good leather, new, and still fragrant. Next to the handle is a combination lock that opens with a code known only to him. He looks up. His generation doesn't lob briefcases or razor-thin portfolios. On the other hand, they squeeze themselves through every chink in walls, no matter how narrow. Is it even worth hollering?

He turns the corner and walks along the wall toward the river. The large, bizarre yard enclosed by the bumpy wall covers more than a hectare. He can't seem to find a way in. But there *has* to be one somewhere, since an entire complex of buildings is visible off in the center of the square. Certainly not apartments, but places where people go to work. One more turn, and he reaches the entrance. He's carrying a briefcase and wearing a well-tailored overcoat. The security officer doesn't ask anything, doubtless deeming him a big shot. He crosses the square and inspects the structures. Tall smokestacks, pipes, cisterns, squat windowless sheds. Halfway across, behind the structures, the asphalt sidewalk ends and a wasteland begins. It's fall, the grass is yellowed and sparse, and the blades lie flat beneath one's shoes without resistance. He reaches the wall again, the same place where he was standing on the other side earlier. The ground here is also covered by turf, even more so than elsewhere. And a couple of old stones still stand next to the wall.

The yard is situated near a schoolhouse. He just came from there. Twelve buildings on one side of the road, even fewer on the other. Back then it had seemed like there were more. They came to play ball here on the square after class. He lived farther away than the other boys, and it took more time to get home. Therefore, he always had to be among the first to arrive. Heaven forbid he got there late. His parents didn't forbid it, of course, but allowed it no more than once or twice a week. And for no longer than forty-five minutes to an hour at a time. That's why there was often trouble. Most of the kids went more often, some every day. Those forty-five minutes were nowhere near enough, either. That was why he had to rush. Or come up with a clever excuse and fib a little later. The way home via the square was longer than when he walked to school in the morning. But a bus went past the square. He could get home even quicker by taking it. If he later told his parents that he had lost his uniform hat and had to look for it, or some other circumstance causing his lateness came up and he fibbed having come by foot, then he could win an extra quarter of an hour for playing. But if he took a risk and just hoped that the bus would come exactly on time, then even more.

They played dodgeball, which people in Estonia then

called "people's ball." The name hinted at something great and important. In reality, it was mainly little boys who played it. Two teams were formed, two captains chosen, and each side tried to hit the other with the ball in a way that the player couldn't catch it. And that was it. It was played during Phys Ed at school and sometimes on the playground at recess, too. Then, there was always so little time and each player had just one life, captains two. Whoever failed to catch the ball once was out. But there, beyond the wall, they played with at least two, sometimes even three lives. It was exciting. He played well, in general. Not the very best, of course, and he was team captain on extremely rare occasions (when a couple of the tougher players weren't there), but still. He played with zeal, in any case, because he had less time than the others. Some who lived closer to the square would run home first and change their clothes. He didn't have that opportunity. His school uniform became coated in dust, since the ball frequently hit the dirt. On top of that, he mostly caught the ball the old-fashioned way—against his chest. One could also catch it using only his hands: that way was more impressive, but not all that certain, since the ball could slip through your fingers. With his way, though, he always had to brush his stomach clean. Girls only caught the ball in their laps. The boys would mock them, watching from the door of the gymnasium the way they hustled around in their spandex. Like chickens carrying eggs about.

He usually had a watch with him. It was his father's old timepiece. He was allowed to wear it during the academic quarters when he didn't have any threes on his previous report card. He would take off the watch for the duration of the game so that it wouldn't get smashed, and hid it in the very smallest slot in his portfolio. Between games, he would go to his bag to see what time it was. He usually had enough time for two games. That's how much he could manage.

On that occasion, the first game took unusually long. The

teams were even, everyone was catching well, and lives were lost slowly. What's more, each had three. When the end finally came, he could sense without even looking at his watch that a lot of time had passed. But when he opened his portfolio and checked, the outcome made him anxious. What should he do? Leave after the first game today? Or still stay for the second? Maybe it would go quickly? They had lost by just a hair. Revenge hung sharp in the air. He didn't have time to decide for himself. The others were calling out: "What're you waiting for? Come on, already!" They had taken up their positions and the captain was holding the ball. He ran towards his own side. I'll leave as soon as I'm out; I won't stay till the end, flashed through his mind when he caught the first ball. But he was playing well today. Probably even better than the captains. Today was his day. A few moments after an exceptionally well-caught ball, he even wished that he would have failed, but couldn't arrange such a thing on purpose. When the opposing captain entered the game, he still had all of his lives. Then, a clever toss hit his leg. Even so, they got the captain several times in a row. The captain was a big, strong boy, who had been held back a grade. He didn't especially bother to duck and dodge, but his throws would leave a mark. He sidestepped, but was hit with one, and although his entire body reverberated with the blow, the ball still fell to the ground. The captain also had one life left. He made a couple more quick attempts, and then unexpectedly got the captain out with a curveball. They had won. However, he had no time to stay and celebrate. He snatched up his bag and bolted toward the gate. He didn't clamber over it, but rather squeezed his way through. As if mocking him, he could see the bus's rear windows from the bend in the road. He'd have to wait five more minutes. He didn't dare look at his watch. He knew that he had stretched it too far this time. At least half an hour had passed since the limit at which he should have been at home. What should he do? He couldn't just tell a white lie today, saying that he came on foot, and thereby reduce his lateness just a bit. Their building was located quite close to the bus stop, and his parents could see from the front window when the bus came. When he was little, he himself had often stood there and waited to see whether or not he could spot his mother or father when they approached. Now, his mother would stand there on occasion. No doubt she was doing it now, too; merely staring off toward the city. There was only one option left . . .

When the bus stopped, he quickly leaped from the rear door. He knew that at that moment, the bus was standing in a line that ran straight from their building to the bus stop, and blocked the view. He needed to get across the road before the bus jerked forward and everything became visible. He hunched down and shot across the road, eyes closed. He stormed straight into his mother, who was just going out to look for him. "You can't *run* like that—you could get hit by a car," his mother exclaimed, pale-faced. Then she covered her face with her hands. There were tears in her eyes. That rarely happened with his mother. She said nothing else, only stood with her hands in front of her eyes. He was overcome with fear, his heart sensed a big row brewing. He needed to justify his actions, but stood cramped and speechless. "But Mom, I still had one more life left, I couldn't quit *then!*" he finally blurted out, and started to cry himself. And so they went home.

He circles back around to the front of the wall and looks at his watch. There was still time, it was lunch break at the funeral office. The bus stop no longer existed—they were being reduced in accordance with local residents' proposals. He walks toward the city limits. He has walked that highway shoulder many a time upon arriving in his hometown. The road is wider and more elevated. And it feels as if it has gotten shorter. He already finds himself at the fire station, and a familiar intersection comes into view in the distance. The ditches on either side of the road have long since been filled in and covered with asphalt.

The bus stop changed its location here as well, moving from in front of one house to another. He stops and stares. The once small trees at the far corner of the garden have grown to the height of the power lines, and cover the front window. No one here could see whether the bus was stopped outside or not. Not even in winter, as they are tangled blue spruce trees. The traffic is just as heavy as in the capital, or even worse. The ring road past the town hasn't been completed yet, and most of the transit tankers drive through here. What then was like compared with now! A few "Moskvitches," a "Pobeda," a smattering of flatbeds, or a horse and cart. And even so, when he has to cross the road at the same spot, he clenches his hand just as tightly around the handle of his briefcase, looks both ways with the carefulness of an old man, before darting across the strip of pavement. And doing so, he is always startled: that one life he had left—he is living it to this very day.

THE OBITUARY

RIGHT IN THE middle of the pedestrian crossing, in the midst of people bustling back and forth, of hundreds of engines grumbling, spluttering, and snorting impatiently in four lanes on each side, Poobs had to grab his quacking telephone from his pocket. Softly cursing, he pressed it against his ear. It emitted someone's voice out of breath and at a distance, as if the caller was anxious or had run a long way.

"What?" Poobs asked, not understanding. "Talk louder, please. I'm outside . . . it's noisy . . ."

"Radymanthes is dead!" he finally heard. The news stunned him, nailed him right there onto the island in the middle of the boulevard.

"Holy shit . . ." was all that he could utter at first. Finally he realized who was calling, too. It was the office secretary, Marju, who repeated:

"That's just what *I* said, too—holy shit. Nothing else you can say to news like that . . ." Marju was tactfully silent for a moment. "And that's the reason I'm calling—for you to write the obituary," she continued. "We figured that you would be the best person to write it—you knew each other such a long time, you know."

"Yeah, yeah, but . . ." Poobs began, nonplussed, "how soon do you need it? I said I'm outside."

"We've already discussed it with the editors, they can wait until evening—till about six or seven. If you tell them the word count beforehand, they'll save space for it."

"Yeah, I'll do it," Poobs replied. "What else—definitely!"

"We'd be very grateful," Marju said, and hung up.

Poobs interrupted his path to the supermarket's oriental sweets section (his weakness!) and made a beeline for his desk at home.

Poor Radymanthes, he though as he created a new file on his computer.

The fact that he had just given Marju his consent wasn't due solely to natural receptiveness or a sense of duty, even though those also figured in—Poobs was a *functionary*. As a result, he had already written obituaries for colleagues on several occasions. But right now was something different, something completely different. Now was, in fact, one of those few times in his life when he actually wanted to write the obituary himself, voluntarily. That feeling was quite natural for Poobs, but it would have taken an eternity to explain, and wise old Poobs knew it. On the one hand, it was difficult to write about Radymanthes; on the other, it was easy. Easy because they truly had been old chums. And although one was merely a young beginner at the time and the other already a seasoned master, they had nevertheless grown close over time and spent countless hours together. Poobs knew Radymanthes through and through, and had meditated upon him a great deal. Sometimes while discussing world affairs, they had also analyzed each other's character, accomplishments, and unfinished projects, and had outlined their possible future roles. As a result of those discussions and ruminations (which had inevitably started to repeat themselves a little over such a long period of time), in Poobs's mind, Radymanthes's persona had long ago metamorphosed into a text all its own in addition to the living person. It comprised word-based formulas that Radymanthes had personally spoken about, and that Poobs had said and thought about his friend, and which had turned elastic from being carried in his head for a long while. Poobs had no trouble committing these to paper—everything flowed independently, in a single piece. It was born naturally, justly, and sincerely.

On the other hand, however, the writing of every sentence unleashed dreadful torment within him. It felt as if in that very way, by spelling out his old friend in words—that only then would he perish for good, and Poobs would truly lose him.

The piece was nearly finished. Poobs knew that the deceased would have been pleased with it. Radymanthes would have even gladly added his own signature at the bottom—the playful soul that he was. Yes, that's exactly what I am; that's how it has to be, Radymanthes would have said, chortling, and would have proposed that they open up a bottle on the occasion of the successful prank. How very like him!

The clock in the corner of Poobs's computer screen showed four. He didn't submit the piece immediately, just in case. It was still possible that he'd have the desire to add, remove, or reword something.

His telephone started to quack. He hadn't turned it off on purpose, not like how he usually did while doing rush work, because important notices might have come from the editorial office, or even in connection with the funeral arrangements just ahead.

Juup was calling from their sister organization and asking whether or not they might be able to add the institution's name to the obituary. "Not like they're going to publish two pieces, anyway," Juup reasoned. "You know *them*. Culture's not in style."

"Fine," Poobs said when he had considered it for a brief moment. He had cooperated that way before, too.

"But I've got a request, in that case," the man continued. "Add one little sentence about us, too. Just one! It'll show he really was associated with the organization. No doubt that'll probably be stated in the body anyway (I reckon you *did* mention it), but just in case, put it in all the same—so that it's more certain."

Poobs was only rather vaguely aware of that connection, since it dated to a period when the young Radymanthes had been more closely associated with theater circles, but he trusted Juup.

"Fine, tell me the sentence."

The sentence was very long, but the general point was: "and who, with diverse contributions, has enriched Estonia's theatrical repository even in the spotlight."

"Listen, I won't make that a stand-alone sentence, but the continuation of another sentence—is that okay? It'll be stylistically better that way?" Poobs proposed.

"As you please," Juup agreed. "I fully trust you with this. Thanks! I suppose we'll see each other soon. Where's the funeral, by the way?"

"I don't know," Poobs replied. "I only heard about the whole thing two and a half hours ago. But I guess it'll be held where all the others are."

"Yeah, suppose that's how it'll be . . . Listen, that's all—stay strong," Juup said, and hung up.

Poobs started to wonder what publications would release his obituary, and whether anyone apart from him might write one, too. It wasn't out of the question, as Radymanthes had been an extremely multifaceted person. In addition to being involved in literature and the arts, he had been an instructor, belonged to boards and councils, and was likewise an active member of charity and historical societies. Could his peers still be alive? Some might be, although they were constantly dying. A man with that kind of a profession and lifestyle burns out more quickly than others, Poobs sighed. Radymanthes had been seventy-one. Robi, for example, could perhaps have written one— something very personal, in the form of a colorful eulogy—"in the name of his schoolmates," we'll say, with whom he studied in Moscow back in the day. Poobs could ask him about it; might so much as prod him. He had Robi's number. Poobs was already turning to look for it in a notebook lying on the shelf behind him when he was suddenly struck with doubt: is Robi still alive? He could easily be dead, too. Not just recently, of course—such an event certainly hadn't reached Poobs's ears, but about a year ago, back when Poobs was working on his third volume—he could have perished *then*. Poobs hadn't read the newspapers or listened to the radio during that period, wanting to completely disconnect from his surroundings. (He hadn't disconnected while writing the second volume, had continued running the organization part-time, and the second volume had indeed been weaker than the first, in the critics' opinion.) He knew that these days, no one speaks about a death or a funeral a week after it happens—that's how busy lives are. He strained his memory, and the more he strained, the more it started to seem as if he *had* heard something about Robi's death somewhere. It rang a bell, in any case. On top of that, he hadn't seen Robi in what seemed like forever. Well, naturally—Robi suffered the health problems that many people his age did. And nothing new by Robi had come out in what seemed like forever, too. That cleared up that matter. Well, so where should that eulogy come from now, huh? From the grave? Poobs sighed. What's gone is gone—poor Robi, even though he sometimes cursed excessively . . .

His landline phone jingled. It was Robi, drunk as he usually was at that hour, ever since Marta had died in a car crash. He expressed his sympathy and rambled on loosely about this and that, added a couple of crude remarks about a female artist, and ultimately proposed that they get together to drink Vana Tallinn liqueur in memory of the deceased. Poobs listened to him politely, and then used a pause in the man's train of thought to bid him farewell and hang up. He descended into thought again. Who else could write it. Maybe Karla? It was rumored that the old fellow had worked himself to the bone, but he had seen Karla on a corner in the city center just a week ago. He had been walking, holding a box, his face dull, his back bowed. Karla had lifted kettlebells his entire life, but you can't fool the Reaper forever now, can you! Karla had suffered a stroke, the heavy weight had dropped from his hand and crashed to the floor. Now, Karla had to take care of himself. Poobs sighed.

Why am I sighing, he asked himself at the same time. I myself still have plenty of time, maybe even a few dozen years.

His telephone quacked again. It was Gaur from another sister organization, who had heard from Marju that Poobs was writing the obituary, and would now like to have his own guild's name mentioned in the piece, as well.

"You do understand—he was certainly more on the theater stage, but he sang a little, too; in a couple of operettas. It wasn't much and it wasn't his main thing, at least not to the degree that it'd force us to write a separate piece because of it now. But you *could* mention it! Even just to educate the young generation. But the practical reason is that we have so many members who've danced and sung their entire lives, and for a long time already, we simply haven't had the resources to write separate obituaries for them all. We write some of them in pairs; we wait for the next one to die, too, and then join them together. But some of the less important ones we even do in threes—our secretary calls it 'dead-man clusters.' That's why it wouldn't suit now for us to write about someone who was only partly one of our own. Although, when the old man opened his mouth when he was a young lad, he was better than many who've made their living from it their entire lives. A nightingale, I tell you—a nightingale! Still, it won't suit, because you have to honor *your* dead; even when they're still living. You get what I'm saying? The deceased's relatives and those who intend to kick the bucket themselves before long would start to protest. They already suspect that we won't manage to write about them separately, either—in pairs, in the best case; so why now an entire piece about someone who wasn't really even *one* of us? But we'd still very much like to give him mention, since he did have a divine spark. A nightingale, I tell you again—a nightingale."

What could Poobs say to that? "Just send me one sentence," Poobs requested. Gaur kindly promised to do so—Gaur was artsy, in his opinion.

Poobs shifted his gaze to the window, out toward the steeple of Toompea Church. Yes—Radymanthes would probably be buried in Metsakalmistu Cemetery if he hadn't by chance requested to be buried where he was born, somewhere in a rural cemetery, far inland. And all the better—others were already waiting there in Metsakalmistu before him, birds of a feather. And it would be easier for the organization to go and maintain the plot when his relatives died one day, which could happen before too long—Radymanthes didn't have any children; Marju had only contacted his niece about the funeral arrangements. Companies would have to be hired to tend the plots, and if there were more graves, then they could get them at a group rate. Poobs also had to consider things like that in his job. What would happen at the wake, he wondered? If anything at all? Would he be buried by a priest, or would it be non-secular? Radymanthes hadn't been religious, but a burial was more sacred with a priest, in Poobs's mind. Or more ceremonious, at any rate. Although, thinking about it, one might not be significantly more authentic than the other. Some priests also discharged such drivel that—oh, cover your ears. Poobs could count on one hand the number of people who would be able to bury the intellectual in a way that wouldn't embarrass others. The wisest thing an undertaker could do on such occasions was to be discreet and undemanding—creative-minded mourners *already* have an excess of thoughts and feelings. An undertaker must die in his deceased, Poobs mused on Barthes. But no doubt the niece had more precise directions.

His mobile phone started quacking again. Poobs couldn't hear anyone on the other end at first and was just about to hang up, when a soft voice from beyond the grave started telling, without any lead-in, the story of how he and Radymanthes had gone to the fair in Pechory when they were young.

"I don't really think it'll be much use to you in writing your obituary right now—I was calling more just to call; to feel better," the voice politely apologized.

Poobs felt a wave of emotion swell, and an idea dawned on him. "Listen, sir—how about you write your story down? Write down everything that you remember about him and send it to us. Then, we'll look together to see what to do next with it. One way or another, people are going to start collecting memories of him soon."

"You mean *me?*" the voice asked warily, and hung up.

Poobs opened up his inbox, found the sentence that Juup had sent, fit it into the right place in the obituary, and sighed.

Who would attend the funeral? There were ever fewer old people left. Creative types had drunk a dreadful amount of vodka at the end of the Soviet period or had gone kamikaze otherwise, had aged early, and gone to the grave before their time. The difficulties of adjusting to the new society and feeling like outcasts only helped it along. There were very few of Radymanthes's kind anymore—true princes of life who crowned the top by nature, under any regime, and didn't suffer from any sorts of complexes.

Poobs started counting on his fingers the number of people for whom he himself would still need to write obituaries. (This did, of course, partly depend on whether or not he would still apply for another term in his post as well.) He had buried one other friend, Immertaal, a year ago and had written a piece about him; now Radymanthes; and he really didn't have a third friend who was that close. But that meant nothing—he would certainly have to do more, being the functionary that he was.

These would definitely include some for unpleasant individuals, outright assholes, but *he* didn't have a choice. More likely than not, he *would* have to write one for a complete asshole: agreeable people are able to get by on their own; they have supporters and others for remembering them. But with assholes, it could always be the case that Marju the secretary would have called here and called there, have rung up old schoolmates and retired companions, but wouldn't have gotten anyone to agree to it. Some refuse because they see the departed as having been too big of a pig; others, who have personally been the same kinds of people, quake because of their reputation, fearing that the departed's bad shadow will also be cast upon them. Then Marju comes to his, to Poobs's office and says in exasperation: "What'll we do now, then, Poobs?" Then Poobs himself would have to bite the bullet and write it. The departed couldn't be deprived of an obituary, so what if he was a pig and an asshole. It had to be written even just for the guild's honor. Strange—the fact that someone was a pig and an asshole bothers the next generation less than honest individuals failing to write him an obituary. As if leaving it undone would cast a suspicious light upon all the rest of them, too. Oh, yes—the dead had to be honored; that was one thing still left. And so Poobs will have to go to *their* funerals, also; will have to put on his black suit that tended to be a little tight at the waist, his white shirt with a slightly yellowing collar (be it summer or winter), give a brief but solemn eulogy, and afterward mingle with the funeral-goers, wearing a holy expression.

The landline telephone rang and Manivalde wanted to know whether the pensioners' Christmas party was going to be held this year or not.

"It will, it will," Poobs reassured him. "There's *worlds* of time yet; it's only just going on spring."

"I love to make long-term plans," Manivalde said slyly. "I'm an old-school man, that's why."

Poobs continued musing where he had left off. Rumor had it that Ants was on his way out, for instance. *He* was that kind of a pig in particular, and Poobs was already tormented by the thought that he would have to write at least one page about him. He instantly dreaded the idea. Things were always the most difficult with those types. He had to word things in a way that didn't directly praise the person, but at the same time refrained from saying anything wholly bad about them, either. In such a way that a wise man would more or less get the point, and that someone unfamiliar with him would also be satisfied. It was like dancing on a tightrope. Perhaps I'll take unpaid leave when Ants is just about to pass away. The idea flashed through his mind, and was just as suddenly extinguished, for, after all, was it gentlemanly to shrug an unpleasant obligation onto the shoulders of his subordinates? Even some of his younger colleagues were sick and might not live for long. Take for example that Ludvig, a great careerist who had once shoved Poobs aside—people said that he was "on his last legs." But Poobs certainly didn't long for the man's death. On the contrary—he wanted Ludvig to live a long life, for then he would see Ludvig himself being shoved aside one day, just as the man had once done to him. Only that *he*, Poobs, wouldn't even mind—he would manage, but Ludvig would be nothing without his high position; doubtless he would sink like a stone. And how!

His mobile phone quacked. Helga expressed her sympathy. She was a sensible woman who had known both Poobs and the deceased quite well back in the day, but who had then suddenly withdrawn from public life and lived all alone on an island somewhere. Poobs perked up—he almost proposed that they meet up, but then remembered from how far away the other was calling, and limited himself to thanking her.

Who could write an obituary for *me*? Poobs wondered. His first thought was, of course: Immertaal. Immertaal was an incredible person who was able to write about anything, and able to do so very well. But he was dead. Then Radymanthes, of course. But it was the same story with him. Poobs settled into deep thought, paging through the names of his acquaintances in his mind. Then, he picked up a little book that contained, among other things, the list of their organization's members, and checked there. He certainly felt a greater spiritual closeness to some of those people than to others, but his path had crossed most of theirs only recently. He *had* known some of them from the time before, from deep behind the lines of the Soviet Union, along with the twists and turns of their careers and the inner spiritual struggles over whether or not to join the Communist Party, but they hadn't been friends. Certainly not enemies, either, but simply different kinds of people.

Relatively few of Poobs's peers interested him. No matter how hard he tried, he couldn't shake the feeling that the past had done its trimming of them in spite of everything, even though their maturation already coincided with glasnost. He liked a few of the much younger individuals much more— Poobs was moved when he observed them, although he was certainly wise enough to hide it. Younger people had their own activities. There's a slack in history, Poobs felt; but he wasn't the one who could manage to pull it taut. On top of that, there was the fear that some of those more talented youths whom he liked would drink themselves to death before he himself perished.

He did have a couple of friends, all the same, but they weren't adept writers—they were in different fields. They might perhaps put in a couple of good words for Poobs with St. Peter—they definitely would; but they would be too personal for a eulogy.

Schoolmates? They had grown too distant.

Thus, some were unsuitable because of one quality, others because of another.

Maybe someone from a sister organization will write it (Poobs had done favors for people in many different places), and will ask someone from their own institution to sign at the bottom, together with a little half-sentence, Poobs thought. You never know. He started pitying himself.

It'd be awful if some younger-generation person who knows nothing of anything at all wrote it.

Apparently, he would have to start looking around more widely; to mingle more in social groups, at fashionable bars and clubs in order to see where the sharper young people went. Some might think that Poobs was looking for a new partner; it wouldn't cross anyone's mind that he was merely setting up the future author of his obituary.

The time was five fifteen, and his landline rang again. A woman whom Poobs didn't know shrieked hysterically that she had been Radymanthes's lover, and that she intended to cast herself into his grave at Metsakalmistu.

And who will bury me? Poobs wondered. That event could certainly be far off in the future. It was possible that whoever it would be had not yet been born, or was still only in preschool. And so, he would be buried by people of an entirely new age. Poobs recalled giving a speech next to a coffin for the first time. It had been so long ago, deep in the stagnation period. Then, Kuhmann—an eighty-year-old coryphaeus or something of the sort (in any case: an old man with a white shock of hair)—had approached him afterward and said that he certainly hadn't been able to stand the deceased; he had emerged from home only in order to see if young men know how to bury! "Don't worry, it turned out really well," he had said, nodding in appreciation. But did the youth of today or of the future know how to bury? Bury and cry?

Poobs's thoughts had run out for this occasion. He looked at the clock—there was still a full hour left. He moved the mouse and combed through files containing half-finished works—maybe something would inspire him to continue? Yet, nothing beckoned him to do work today. Even so, Poobs was a hardworking person who wasn't accustomed to sitting around idly. He created a new file, considered for a brief moment, and began:

"In memory of Poobs—a colleague, friend, and teacher . . ."

A SHORT FABLE

ONE DAY A WOMAN didn't want to have intercourse anymore. She told her husband she didn't like him, and that she didn't want to sleep with him.

"Why?" the husband asked.

"I don't, and that's it," the wife replied.

"Maybe you've got someone else?" the husband asked. "Maybe we can clear things up reasonably?"

"I don't have anyone else," the wife snapped. "How can you even *think* that of me!"

"Sorry," the husband said. "But if you're not interested in sex anymore, then will you allow me to do it with others?"

"Are you crazy?! I'd never forgive you for that," the wife declared.

"But I'll stay with our family. On the outside, everything will be exactly as it was before. We don't have to tell the kids. They're still just teenagers—it's a tender age, that much is clear."

"You watch out," the wife said, wagging her finger. "If you do that, then I'll report you to Brussels."

The husband was struck with fear. The wife worked for local government and drafted projects—who knows, maybe she *would* report him to Brussels.

"But what'll become of us, then?" he asked the wife after a while.

"Nothing," the wife answered. "I suppose we'll put up with it."

"For how long?" the husband asked hopelessly.

"Till death do us part," the wife replied, elated.

THE LADY WITH THE WHITE BERET

KROBERT THE WRITER was traveling to meet his readers. He might have turned down the invitation because there were loads of other things to be done, but one night, his father, a former academic, appeared to him in a dream—the gray-haired expert in Scandinavian studies, Vanevild, who (before he melted into the bluish fog of pre-waking consciousness) told him: "You mustn't only scratch out powder at home, happy ears." Krobert interpreted those somewhat ambiguous words as a scolding, telling him that it was important to carry forth the torch of intellect into a crowd of the more ordinary, too. Vanevild had been an avid environmentalist and heritage protectionist back in his day, and even a member of the pro-independence Popular Front (which had emerged from the former movements) prior to his death. And so Krobert had accepted the invitation, and tried to rest up and fortify his spirit before the given date and hour. He read through the previous weeks' newspapers, and strove to recall what problems were being handled in the parliamentary committee on culture; what words of wisdom the prime minister had spoken recently; what was topical overall in cultural life.

In reality, he quite liked going to meet readers, because by speaking with individuals freely, he took part in their thoughts and their worries. He had met intriguing types and had even gained motivation for his own creative endeavors. Occasionally while conversing with them, Krobert felt he was keeping his finger on the pulse of his nation; was breathing in the same rhythm as it was. True, those occasions had become more a thing of the past; Krobert hadn't gone to meet his readers for some time. He felt that it was a condition of both his own age and the general spirit of the era. The older a person becomes, the greater the pull toward more eternal hobbies; the more he wants to be involved solely in what is most important. Let the youth go now, Krobert thought to himself. He *had* read in a newspaper that some young poets frequently gave lively public performances. They cried out their verses to the audience, blew horns, banged shaman drums, having painted themselves in a kaleidoscope of colors beforehand, and handed out condoms to the audience between haikus.

The car glided almost soundlessly across wintery Estonia toward Viruvere, the white flatlands quickly started to turn a shade of blue, and red digital lights flashed reliably on the dashboard, measuring the temperature outside, how many calories the driver was burning by turning the wheel, and through the seat upholstery also measuring the cholesterol content of Krobert's patriotic blood.

Everything filled him with a pleasant sense of tranquility. Transportation costs were being covered by the event organizers—Krobert had made that a condition after he gathered up his nerve to go. Otherwise, he had been unpresuming on such occasions and arrived by bus, for the most part; only requesting that he be met at the stop. But Viruvere was an unfamiliar place for him; certainly not backwoods, but more like a small township that had already amalgamated with a popular summer resort town. It turned dark early this time of year, the weather was cold, and it would have been something of a task to find the meeting place. He had no acquaintances in Viruvere. A couple of artists and a half-writer—the scandalous and pea-brained bard Jammer—did live in the resort town. Still, Krobert didn't believe the man would make the effort to come and listen: writers no longer attended each other's events, but every writer did look to see where he could hold one for himself. And all the better, Krobert thought. Even he had heard rumors that Jammer had tried to urinate in front of the audience at some recent literary event.

The driver, who was named Mait and had introduced himself as the husband of the director of the Viruvere Literary Club, made polite conversation at first, and then each had sunk into his own thoughts. Krobert pleasantly relaxed. He imagined for a moment that he was a school inspector at the time of the first Estonian Republic—an enlightener of the people, who travels around assessing schools; then he envisioned himself as a traveling salesman far away in Russia—someone who treks beyond the Arctic Circle to sell galoshes. All the payment I need is the knowledge that I'm out there for the right reason, he instilled in his brain before dozing off briefly.

They arrived at an open gate. Glinting in the depths of the park beyond it were the windows of a renovated neoclassical manor house. According to Mait, a ritzy hotel operated in one wing of the building, while the other contained a conference hall and a couple of smaller rooms designated for the promotion of local cultural life.

"We got here a little early," Mait said apologetically when he had parked the car next to the building's grand front entrance. "But better early than . . . You yourself know how things can be with traffic sometimes." They had left the city at rush hour, but miraculously hadn't gotten stuck in a single traffic jam.

"All the better—I can stretch my legs a little," Krobert said amiably, and stepped briskly into the building first.

The hotel porter—a young, respectable man with a round face and light-colored cropped hair—greeted them kindly and, hearing who Krobert was, came out from behind the barrier to show him to the event space. On their way there, Krobert eyed himself in the mirrors that lined the walls. He had thought about what to wear for a long time. Naturally, it wouldn't be suitable for him to come dressed casually in jeans, since he was a dignified individual and a respected author all the same; not some howling condom-distributor. But wearing actual evening dress would have been over the top, also. Thus, he finally settled on a blackish-gray velvet jacket. It was as if velvet had been created especially for artists: elegant yet liberal. Yes, you could always wear velvet.

The porter opened a door in the opposite corner of the foyer, which led to a large oval-shaped room that could even have been regarded as a small auditorium. Coffee tables and chairs were positioned along the walls and in the center; a buffet table set up with coffee cups and plates of cookies was next to one wall. A chair with comfortable armrests stood separately at the back of the room, next to a lush potted palm. Krobert grasped that it was meant for him. Although there was still a good half hour left before the event started, a whopping two people were already in the space. The women, probably aged about forty-five, were sitting at a table next to the wall, coffee cups positioned before them, very quietly, almost motionless— you could have mistaken them for mannequins at an open-air history museum. The audience is probably going to be above average, Krobert thought, his spirits high. He decided to go for a walk in the manor park—it was enclosed by a fence, so there was no risk of getting lost.

When he returned about twenty minutes later, Mait the driver was sitting in the foyer's designated smoking area, holding a cigarette between his fingers and conversing with a short, gaunt old man. The latter had a high, bald forehead, a white goatee, and was wearing a blue suit that had seen better days. Krobert nodded to them and went to check out the auditorium. To his slightly unpleasant surprise, he discovered that no one else had come apart from those two unmoving women.

"They work here—blind twin sisters," Mait the chauffeur said, catching Krobert's look with a little bit of guilt. "They weave brooms and baskets."

"Are they Soviet medal-winning laborers?"

"No, not exactly . . ." Mait appeared to want to say something, but was tongue-tied. However, Krobert had noticed and didn't leave it be: "What are they, then?"

"They were sent here as punishment," the scrawny old man interrupted in a whiny, high-pitched voice. "Someone was supposed to come and give a lecture. We here ain't lecture-lovers. Then someone higher-up decided that they'll go, so that *someone'd* be there. You came to the lecture then, too? Whereabouts're you from? Can't seem to remember you. You from around Väätsa?"

"I *am* that writer who is speaking here today. Or, as you said, giving a lecture," Krobert said with an air of dignity, and adjusted the button on his collar.

"Oohh, I'm a big admirer of your talent," the old man exclaimed eagerly. "True, I haven't read any of your works, you know—but your name was in the papers real often at one point. That's when it stuck in my head."

Krobert didn't reply. The old man made a sucking sound with his lips, took a pocket watch from his coat pocket, glanced at it, and shook his head. "Just that the time ain't the very best," he sighed.

"What's wrong with the time, then? It's an hour just like any other," Krobert said, trying to take a lighter, more familiar tone.

"Yeah, ain't the very best, it ain't," the man repeated, as if he hadn't even heard Krobert. "Picture's starting on the tube in just a minute. That 'Forbidden Love'—that's our favorite show around here. From Argentina. Real good, it is. About love and men's love, too."

"Why don't you go watch it, then?" Krobert remarked. "If it's so good?"

"I'm retired, you know," the old man said emphatically. "I always watch my soaps in the morning. Then I've got the whole day free."

What do I have to offer that can beat the love of Argentinian men, Krobert asked himself.

"On top of that, there was a party at the club yesterday," the old man continued. "A band from the capital played. What *was* its name, now?" He turned toward the chauffeur, but Mait only scratched his jaw. "Oh, I just can't remember. There it is, that old-man memory . . . But there was a whole horde of people there! A good six hundred heads showed up. Suppose some're sleeping it off today."

"How many people live around these parts, anyway?" Krobert asked.

"No more'n seven hundred, if we're talking about our little township," the old man sighed. "They've all gone. Headed to bigger places. More live in the city, of course." The old man fell silent for a moment. "We here can throw a party for three whole days in a row, too," he announced triumphantly. "Though we sleep for three whole days in a row afterward, too." Krobert could feel his willpower starting to fade.

"But that's not what's most important," the old man added after a pause.

"What else, then?" Krobert asked.

"What's worse is that *that's* why the people who're the cultural enthusiasts won't show today," the old man explained confidently.

"Why's that?" Krobert asked, not understanding.

"Well, 'cause there was a cultural event just yesterday, of course. People've had their dose of culture for this week. Not as if too much culture's good for you either, you know," the old man reckoned.

"Why not?" Krobert protested. "Some band and a literary evening—how can you group those two together?"

"Oh," the old man sighed windily, dismissing the question. "Not being able to—that's how it looks from way up there, from your point of view. But from *ours* down here, things look entirely different. A band or a writer—there ain't such a big difference at all. Still got to wash up before, pull on your going-out clothes, see people you know and chat with 'em, there's some opener as well, and the night's a goner."

The chauffeur's wife—the literary club's director—breezed in through the front door: she was a plump brunette around the age of fifty wearing a green skirt and white-collared jacket, and was strongly perfumed. Krobert remembered that she had introduced herself on the telephone as Sirje. Sirje seized both of Krobert's hands and held them in her own for a long time, speaking in an artistically melodic tone. "At last, at last . . . We've *so* been looking forward to this . . . People around here are great, you know—really great . . . Just that sometimes you can't get them moving at first; afterward, though, you can't get them to stop."

People were indeed starting to gather. They came quietly, half dressed up, took a cup of coffee from the buffet table and a couple of cookies from the plate, let their gaze wander over the room, searching for a place to sit down, then took a seat and froze there or spoke briefly with their neighbors. Including Krobert, literary-club director Sirje, Mait the chauffeur, and the old man with the piercing voice (whose name was Elmar), altogether over a dozen people collected in the space, so only about half of the chairs were occupied.

Not bad, Krobert convinced himself. What had he really hoped for? For a throng of the enlightened public to form at the door, so many that others would have to stay in the hallway, peeking with sparkling eyes over the heads of those in front of them, yearning for a share in the writer's presence? Those days (if they had existed at all) lay far in the past. Now was a different era. And this was one of the most ordinary places in Estonia, where people toiled from morning to night to get by in their daily lives, and filled the hours left over with simple pleasures. In the town nearby, there was no college; no local newspapers or a radio station; no art galleries, community theater, or other cultural hearths; according to Mait, even books were only sold from a couple of short shelves in the shopping center. Where was one to get those book enthusiasts for this event? Not bad, Krobert repeated to himself once more: so it had to be.

He gazed at the audience, trying to insert as much good intention into his expression as possible. Almost all of them were women. No, not quite: one man was sitting in the corner, too. He was older, wearing a folk sweater, and his restless eyes stared out from beneath bushy eyebrows. Krobert intuitively sensed, based on previous experiences, that he was the local oddball. The kind who goes everywhere, no matter what is happening—from political rallies to theater performances. Such people *are* the only reliable crowd—they are loyal attendees, Krobert thought sourly. He could tell that the oddball didn't attract the attention of those around him; everyone appeared to be used to him. The oddball dislodged a bundle from under his sweater and removed a piece of bread from it. "Oskar, do you want coffee? Should I bring you a coffee? Have you already had coffee today?" the literary-club director Sirje asked, and when the man didn't respond, brought him a cup of coffee and two oatmeal cookies from the buffet table. The oddball immediately hid the cookies in his pants pocket.

"We should probably start," Sirje whispered delicately to Krobert, who nodded bravely. Everyone in attendance stared at him, true, a little indifferently. Or was it simply out of weariness? Two more people slipped into the auditorium at the last second: a middle-aged woman dragging a man by the hand. The director was thrilled. "Let's see—do we still have any seats left?" she asked rhetorically, even though it was clear that there were far too many open seats.

"Here today is our next visitor, a living Estonian writer— Krobert K.," Sirje formally declared. "Everyone knows Krobert K.; if not personally, then certainly by his works. His books have accompanied us from the paths of youth up to the mounds of mature middle age. And now, we will give him the floor," she said, turning to Krobert exuberantly.

Why "give me the floor," Krobert wondered. I'm not a lecturer who goes around the country giving his perpetually repeated speech, now, am I? I don't know how to do theater, and I'm not a buffoon. When agreeing to the event on the telephone, hadn't he requested the director to ask him a few questions to start with—to be his warm-up act, so to say? But apparently, the director had forgotten it or had thought he was just saying it out of fashion.

Krobert delayed a while longer. He hadn't forced himself into coming here, he had been invited. Consequently, these people had to know what they were expecting of him. It would have been simplest to ask: "What do you want from me for having invited me here?"

But he knew that he would offend these people if he were to speak like that. Over the years, they had become accustomed to someone coming or being sent from somewhere and giving them a lecture.

And so, Krobert started talking, through briars and brambles, picking one thought from here, another from there. He droned on about how culture had helped Estonians stay themselves over the centuries, and how it would come in handy in the future, too. No one argued his claims, but nor did anything give any indication that they might agree with him. They didn't encourage him, didn't nod wordlessly, didn't even smile. The audience listened to him in silence and merely stared. I'm speaking too complexly, flashed through Krobert's mind. Perhaps they don't know what "identity" is. He attempted to go over the same point more simply, but still not a single eyebrow rose, as if there was a wall between them. Finally, Krobert expressed his thought yet a third time, and this time so simply that what came out was complete crap, and even *he* was embarrassed by it. After that, he decided that from that point on, he would speak just as he saw fit—whether or not the audience understood was their own problem. He snuck a look at the clock. Only ten minutes had passed! There was still at least an hour ahead.

The literary-club director was looking in his direction and nodding hopefully, as if to say: "Look, you're getting it now!"— like to a child answering a question at the chalkboard.

Krobert's gaze drilled into the faces across from him one by one. When his eyes met someone else's, the latter would look away in modesty and Krobert started to feel embarrassed. What a pity for these people, what a pity, what a pity, the thought banged away in his head.

He decided to read them something from his book, which he had prudently brought along. That usually had an effect. He took the compact volume out of his jacket's breast pocket. And that's when he noticed her.

There was a woman. She was indistinguishably middle-aged and with a pale face, the lines on which gave an exceptionally refined impression. It was difficult to judge her weight since she was sitting down, but she was more on the side of frail than chubby. A white beret covered her dark blonde, shoulder-length hair. Strange, Krobert thought, that I didn't spot her right away. Had she maybe slipped in while Krobert was trying to mold his complicated thoughts into a simpler form, and had turned his gaze to the ceiling for help? There was something ethereal and absent about the woman, her eyes seemed veiled and her lips slightly parted. A book lay on her lap. Which book exactly, Krobert couldn't tell, but he decided in an instant that it was one of his own works. And what was most bizarre of all— the woman was stroking that book lightly and delicately, in a circular motion from left to right, while at the same time staring off somewhere into the distance, her eyes dreamy, not seeing the earthly world. Krobert couldn't say whether the woman was beautiful or ugly. It didn't seem at all important. Yet something about her madly fascinated him and gave him a spiritual boost.

He enthusiastically read out a short, funny story, in response to which the first rustling broke out among the listeners. Krobert looked around triumphantly and started to talk about the work of writing; its problems and joys. Here and there, he digressed into the wider context, making references and drawing parallels. And what do you know—he had gained gusto, his fantasy turned more vivid, his form more pliable, his thoughts worked sharply and boldly, and it was as if the words appeared on his lips all on their own. The invisible current of energy that passed through him appeared to gradually carry over into the audience. Here or there someone nodded, someone snorted at one of Krobert's witticisms, pressing their hand over their mouth or even emitting a peep. Krobert inhaled and furtively peeked at the woman in the white beret. It appeared that a glint had sprung up in her eyes, that she was following closely along in her quiet manner, pleased that Krobert was performing so masterfully. He released all tension.

Why are some anguished faces so lovely? he wondered, drawing in a breath. Who could she be? It's strange how she's stroking that book. It doesn't even matter whether it's mine or one of my colleague's. What's important is that it's a book—a concentrate of intellectual enlightenment. That person is attached to the word. She's already on her way. And Krobert just let his own words flow forth.

He was like an actor, for whom it suffices when there is just a single person in the auditorium who knows how to appreciate his art, and to whom he can act. All else is unimportant.

However, Krobert had celebrated too early. He had decided to read one more story aloud, but it didn't have the same effect as the previous one. Of course, it wasn't short and funny like the first; it was sad and complex. In any case, it was obvious that it wasn't pulling the audience along—people's attention was fading. Krobert strove to liven up his performance by using external measures, declaiming a phrase from time to time, embodying the voices of the different characters during dialogues, and even standing up on a couple of occasions. It seemed to help at first, but then Krobert realized that the audience wasn't following the point of what he was saying—rather, they focused on his escalated demeanor and mimicry. I'm an idiot, he thought to himself.

When the story came to an end and he wanted to move on to the next topic, to speak about dignity and nationality, he became convinced that his words were no longer reaching anyone.

Meanwhile, a new slice of bread had appeared in the oddball's hand. He nibbled on it, but then stopped his chewing, stared blankly ahead, and sputtered menacingly: "Puhf . . . puhf . . ."

Krobert peeked at the time. Thank God—the hour was almost up. He gave up on talking about nationality and dignity.

"Thank you for that interesting talk," literary-club director Sirje said. "Now, all of us certainly have many interesting questions." She peered demandingly out over the audience. No one made a peep. "While the others are still thinking, I'd like to ask you something myself . . ." Sirje began, but before she could get to the question, the auditorium door was thrown wide open. Standing on the doorstep was a tall and spindly man of about thirty, with gigantic radar-like ears dangling out from his light-colored, bowl-cut hair. It was Yammer—a local celebrity and former protest-poet.

"Welcome, welcome—we are going to be wrapping things up here soon, but there are still some free seats," the director said briskly, not letting herself be disturbed, and prepared to pose her question. But Yammer stormed in as if there was no one around, came right up to the potted palm next to Krobert, unbuttoned his pants, and prepared to urinate on the plant. Everyone stared at him, frozen. The silence that lasted for a couple of seconds was broken by someone in the hallway roaring into their mobile phone: "Come quick, Big Yammy's gonna piss on a palm!"

At that instant, director Sirje yelled: "Mait, help!" And together with her husband, they escorted Yammer toward the exit. He didn't even resist.

"I wasn't *really* gonna," he whined in the doorway. "I just wanted to cause a little excitement. Literature has to be *sold*, you understand? It's got to be attractive. You're all just sitting here, one person's mumbling up in the front—what's that, now? That won't do. Let's make the thing *jump*, huh? Make a *happening*! But, meh, if you don't need it, then you don't need it." And he was gone.

Krobert sensed that everyone present in the space was pleasantly surprised. The director appeared deeply offended, but he felt that even *she* was a little proud that an original personality the likes of Yammer lived in their vicinity.

"So, what is the mission of literature today?" she asked, finally voicing her question.

Krobert readied himself to reply, but before he could open his mouth, two panting teenage boys barged in through the door. They looked around eagerly, but then disappointment appeared on their faces. They pivoted, and through the door they slammed behind them while exiting, Krobert could hear them exclaiming to someone, apparently a companion who'd rushed to the scene: "Yammy's not there anymore, it's just that writer . . ."

Krobert directed an imploring look towards the corner. It appeared that the woman in the white beret hadn't been rattled by the incident. She continued to stroke her book, her enraptured gaze focused off into the distance.

A serious-looking young woman in the audience stood and asked why young people weren't interested in literature anymore.

Before Krobert was able to reply, an old woman, who

introduced herself as a lifelong handicrafts teacher, and who was sitting next to the younger one, unexpectedly opened her mouth.

"Literature should be more attractive. Why do writers appear on TV so rarely? Why do they appear in public so rarely?" the handicrafts teacher asked. She explained that a writer *had* gone to her school one time, but apparently asked money for his appearance. The audience livened up as it always does when money comes under discussion.

Krobert explained that writing is work, and a writer lives off it. And that literature isn't a sideshow and a writer isn't a showman.

The serious-looking young woman stared critically at Krobert, sneered, stood, and left without hearing the answer to her question.

What goddamned attractiveness?! Krobert wondered, feeling that the woman in the white beret was still the only link connecting him to that group of people. Everyone else was of no consequence. Krobert derived spiritual strength from her; for her, he was prepared to face such an ordeal.

There are still people interested in free spirits. They're everywhere, even in a backwater place like this Viruvere. They *are* the citizens of the republic of the written word, of which Voltaire spoke, he thought to himself.

One old geezer in the middle of the audience stood up. "I've been listening to you with great interest. What you're saying is correct." Oh-ho! Krobert thought, flattered. "And therefore, I'd like to offer you some interesting material. Namely, I'm a freedom fighter. Look: Kalju Konist—you must have heard of him. He was such a famous person—you see, you should write about how he wanted to join the Tsar's imperial court. That was in forty-three. They had a boat ready in forty-two already. Kalju Konist was a tough freedom fighter, too." The geezer sat down and was imposingly silent.

The crowd stirred and started to buzz. First one person, then another shifted as if intending to stand up.

"Does anyone have any more questions?" the director asked the audience. "Are there truly no more questions?" The director's tone was harsh, almost angry. The silence lasted five seconds, ten, fifteen . . . But no one had any more questions. I won't say anything, either, Krobert resolved, hardening. The man whose wife had dragged him there by the hand then huffed, pulled his wife up from their table, and shuffled out together.

"Very well, then we'll start to close," Director Sirje declared, and the audience joined her in applauding.

"We have a gift for you as well," the director announced.

A tablemat or a photo album? Krobert wondered dully.

But he was given a pineapple! "May this pineapple symbolize the enlightenment and love for literature that can be found in every corner of Estonia," Director Sirje spoke, handing Krobert the knobby, oblong fruit.

Krobert sniffed it. The pineapple smelled simultaneously like a pumpkin and a strawberry.

"And what's more—this isn't just a pineapple that can be bought from any supermarket." The director's tone turned sly and pompous. "We grew this pineapple here at home. Yes— pineapples can even be grown in *Estonia*! The famous wrestler Õuger, who himself sprouted right here in our neighboring village, gave us the seed. He brought it back from his latest competition abroad, which led him to Polynesia, where he defeated all of the famous black wrestlers."

Krobert nodded solemnly to signal that he understood.

"Who wants an autograph?" the director called out.

A woman of fifty-five, who was made-up to look younger, approached him briskly. "That character in the story of yours that you read—that *was* actually you yourself, wasn't it?" she asked, thrusting a book toward him and winking conspiratorially.

"What does it feel like to age alongside your characters?" a frail, pink-faced old man next to her demanded. "Probably feels great, huh?"

Krobert gave five autographs, all in old books that he had written back during the Soviet period. He felt choked up when he saw them, so he forgot about the woman in the white beret for a moment. She didn't come to ask for an autograph. When Krobert realized this, his eyes roved the room in astonishment and he even ducked out into the foyer to check. But the mysterious older woman had disappeared into thin air.

Mait was going to take him back to the city. They were already sitting in the car and Mait was putting it into gear when Krobert saw that old Elmar, with whom they had conversed in the foyer before the meeting, was dashing toward them. Krobert opened the door.

"What is it?"

"Little Calf!" the old man shouted, out of breath.

"What little calf?" Krobert asked, puzzled.

"The band's name was Little Calf, that's right!" Elmar crowed happily. "That's all I thought about through your whole lecture, everything else just breezed past my ears. Little Calf, of course it was!"

Krobert pulled the door shut.

"Yeah, around these parts, things are the way they are," Mait said, turning the wheel, and letting Krobert make what he might of the statement.

"No worries," Krobert stubbornly resisted. "There are readers among them, too. Not all of them, of course. Like that oddball who was eating bread . . ."

"Hasso? He was the salt of the earth here way back when. Recorded folklore and the local dialect. The president himself gave him a medal. Now, he hasn't read anything in a long time."

"But that serious-looking girl, on the other hand . . ." Krobert recalled.

"Marge? She's from out east, industrial town. Got out of jail on parole, used to inject and steal before. Now, she's a social worker—works with delinquents. I don't believe she reads all that much. She's seen too much life, from every angle."

"But that woman wearing heavy makeup, who looks at you sort of squinty-eyed?"

"Katrin? She's got big debts, pays her husband child support," the driver commented curtly. "When's she got time to read? Lot of suitors. Her time's running out, too."

Krobert stared blankly at the pineapple in his lap. He had one trump left up his sleeve!

"But what about that mysterious woman who was sitting in the corner? Had sort of a veiled look to her?"

Mait couldn't put his finger on who it was at first. "Can't think who it . . ." he excused himself. "Who could that be, now . . ."

"Wearing a white beret. It seemed like *she* had read a lot and is a lover of literature. She was even *stroking* her book, you know. I've never seen anything like it in my life." Krobert still smiled tenderly at the thought. Finally, the driver figured it out. "Oh, that's Alma. Her . . ." Mait trailed off, turning on the windshield wipers for a moment to clear the muck that sprayed onto the windshield from the back wheels of a daredevil car that had sped past them before he finished his sentence: "Her cat died just recently."

NAUSEA

ERNEST FELT THAT Moisha was undermining him. Not in general, not the company, but rather the ground precisely beneath *him*, Ernest. True, maybe not on purpose, more subconsciously, instinctively, with the unbridled force of a young male; but the fact remained a fact. In Ernest's opinion, Moisha wasn't by nature a bad person with sadistic tendencies, who finds fun in striking blows to others. Far from it—at times, Moisha even gushed grandmotherly softness and ladylike sentimentality. On top of that, he came from a respectable home: his parents were accountants, normal people who had instilled in their children (Moisha's brother nearly ten years his senior was a vice-secretary in some ministry, and his sister seven years his senior was a flavor analyzer for a multinational corporation) the values suitable for common existence. Yet despite this, Ernest clearly felt that he was being undermined, and the more time that passed, the stronger he felt it. By now, Ernest and Moisha had been working together for nearly two years, and Ernest could swear that, at first, when Moisha entered their company, there had been less undermining. Oh, much less! In truth, Ernest could even put up with the present level of undermining somehow. He was a good communicator, and was able to look away and not hear everything when necessary. But being experienced in life, he knew that any kind of subconscious undermining can turn into *conscious* undermining one day, which painted a dire picture for the future. It was better not to think about it.

Why is Moisha undermining me?—the thought plagued Ernest

when he couldn't fall asleep some nights, and for time to pass more quickly, he would get up to turn on the VCR and watch his favorite film, each and every detail of which had already been etched into his memory. In Ernest's opinion, the main reason lay in Moisha's unusually high need for activity, which was in turn spurred on by exceptionally great ambition. Naturally, these characteristics were accompanied by an immense urge to dominate, for how *could* Moisha carry out his ambitious plans if he wasn't able to completely control his surroundings and get down to business, unimpeded? Moisha possessed an immense reserve of energy. He wanted to seize the reins at every moment, to command, to get others to follow his lead. If, for instance, he spoke with someone who was on the same hierarchical level as him, then equal conversation only lasted for a couple of exchanges. Progressing from there, Moisha would already interrogate his partner, probe him, continue to put him in his place, and then deliver an energetic monologue about new projects, to which the other person could only nod along.

If, however, Moisha's conversation partner was situated higher up in the hierarchy, he would initially keep politely quiet, nodding and giving the impression that he was listening eagerly. In reality, though, he couldn't bear to listen, and was instead restraining himself and waiting for the opportunity to pipe up. And when it was his turn to speak, he couldn't stop: he would light up and chatter away until he suddenly realized that such behavior really wasn't proper, and then excuse himself and fall silent, blushing, because he had good manners all the same. But fifteen minutes later, or the time after next, the exact same scene would repeat itself: Moisha was incapable of holding himself back.

Ernest had never seen anyone with such a great desire to work his way to the top. True—he hadn't really seen all that much of the new generation, either. Specifically, Moisha was young—awfully young; under twenty-five. Nevertheless, he had already gotten quite far in life. Both officially and unofficially. He had reached the assistant director's chair early even by the criteria of the new age, and a wide range of publications wrote more and more frequently about his diverse hobbies, which included karaoke and floor hockey. Why did he want to climb higher even faster? He had *more* than enough time for it.

Moisha was genuine and well-meaning, with a slightly naive-looking face, a somewhat bulging stomach, and relatively thick thighs. Looking the way he did, it was hard to believe that he was extremely frisky, trying to form relationships and hit on women everywhere. And when that wasn't successful, then he would pat and pinch their bottoms all the same, without any deep ulterior motive. It had turned into an extremely disgusting habit, in his opinion. Ernest couldn't understand why women didn't see it the same way, but instead almost *tolerated* it, even if they were technically feminists.

It was hard to be angry at Moisha, but Ernest felt that there was no other way. The right thing to do would be to fire him, the assistant director. Ernest realized that soon there wouldn't be enough room for the both of them in the department. He could sense how Moisha was longing to take his own job. To Ernest, it seemed that Moisha was already making insinuations about him behind his back. No, he didn't contrast himself with Ernest in terms of nature or views; didn't come out with a new platform. It was a little hard to imagine it, too, because they almost never conflicted on work issues; they understood things the same way, both conceptually and in regard to methods, both in tactics and strategy. The contrast was in terms of *generations*. Moisha constructed himself as someone who was energetic, young, and an ambitious serpent, in contrast to Ernest, who—although tenured—almost seemed to represent a man of yesterday; someone clinging to the past. Moisha seemed to believe that the time of the forty-four-year-olds was over: they'd certainly had their fair share already. Now, let it be the turn of people like

Moisha. *Was* it so simple, then? Ernest couldn't figure it out. *They* had been *repressed*, there *hadn't* been any freedom during the Soviet era. Didn't that mean they had the right to be and to work now, too? They did, oh how they did!

Yes, Ernest should do something about it before Moisha himself does. New tensions had been added to their relationship lately. The most unpleasant part of it was that while Ernest suffered under those strains, they seemed to roll like water off a duck's back for Moisha. Ernest sensed that Moisha wasn't fully subordinate to him, and even scoffed at him. He certainly completed his tasks, and did so well for the most part, but didn't he do so lazily, half-assed? Didn't he even make it seem sometimes as if the option Ernest proposed had actually been his own idea? When Ernest said something at a meeting, Moisha would look at the other lower-level employees (mainly at the young women) and smile meaningfully, as if to say: Let the old guy harp on; *we*, the young people, certainly know for ourselves what's right and from which direction the wind is blowing. And when Ernest gave a long monologue or said something important, Moisha would be scribbling stick figures on a scrap of paper and seem not to be listening. Only when Ernest raised his voice and tapped his pencil on the table would Moisha look up and stare at him obediently. But wasn't it perhaps *too* obediently? True, Moisha was a little hard of hearing, and hadn't even been accepted for mandatory military conscription because of it years before, which had saddened him deeply. Like many people with poor hearing, Moisha also tended to speak at a high volume. In his case, though, people had regarded it as a sign of musical talent, since he had been a rapper at one time. On the other hand, he was very good at concentrating, so he was able to switch off from the surrounding racket and work in unbelievable conditions. Therefore, it wasn't impossible that he was doing work at the meeting, also. But what was he working on, then? Shouldn't that time belong to the company?

Moisha cracked jokes all the time. Ernest felt he himself had a very well-developed sense of humor, and got old Brezhnev anecdotes just as well as he did "dot-com" humor. However, he generally didn't like Moisha's jokes. They were somehow careless and boorish. On the one hand a little hickishly crude and too old for someone his age, while on the other hand insolent and told with a lot of nerve—the kinds that a young servant-boy would use in the company of servant-girls to disparage their master; meaning seemingly respectful on the surface, but actually having a twist. Yes, occasionally, Ernest felt clearly that Moisha's jokes were like a pup's playful nipping—before it starts to bare its teeth at the old pack-leader.

And so, for a long while now, Ernest had felt that he should bring Moisha into line, or at least come up with a sharp come-back; still, something held him back—it was as if every time he should shoot back at him with something, he lost the ability to speak. It was truly strange, and his angst grew ever deeper. Would he really resign himself to failure without putting up a fight? Would he let himself be walked over while he was still the department head? Why were those young people in such a rush? Couldn't they just wait for their time, just as Ernest had waited for *his* back in the day, and others before him? That *was* the course things should take . . .

On top of it all, Ernest was jealous of the fact that, although Moisha drank a great deal and maybe even used recreational drugs on occasion, he could take a lot and never seemed to be afflicted by a hangover. As the years piled up, however, Ernest's own hangovers had become ever nastier; ever more unbearable.

But as they say: beware a patient man's anger! Ernest had been patient. But one day, when Moisha cast him an especially cheeky look during their morning meeting, Ernest decided he'd had enough of it. He felt that things couldn't continue that way.

It was either him or Moisha. What should he do? He decided that he had to talk to his boss. Not complain—that would've been undignified—but rather speak about the situation in their department more generally and hint that there were problems with Moisha.

He needed to do it before Moisha got in before him. Today. It has to happen today, Ernest felt when the employees had left the meeting. He took a mirror out of a drawer. Looking back at him was a childishly angry man with a pained expression. He put the mirror back in the drawer, took a tie out of another one, and tied it, since their boss had been brought in from a company where the wearing of ties hadn't gone out of fashion yet.

Ernest called ahead.

"Hold on, I've got one person here right now," his boss Oomer answered. "Come in half an hour."

What's half an hour, Ernest reckoned. It's just good that he found some time for an appointment at all. Namely, Oomer had an immense amount of work to do—everyone who walked past his soundproof booth, behind the glass wall of which you could see his worried expression, could be sure of it. Oomer was constantly having endless and productive telephone calls, moving his mouth like a fish in an aquarium. Tousling his full-grown, light-brown beard with one hand, he tortured the computer mouse with his other, monitoring the screen distrustfully from behind a pair of thick glasses.

Ernest strove to come up with the order in which he should deliver his speech to Oomer. In his opinion, Oomer was certainly not an intellectual giant, but he did highly appreciate Oomer's frankness, succinctness, and modesty. These were the very qualities that Moisha lacked. But did he have enough imagination, enough of an instinct for self-preservation? For it was clear that Moisha didn't intend to just sweep him, Ernest, to the side, but rather Oomer *himself* one fine day, and then ever onward and upward and who-knows-who-else. Ernest should hint at that, too. He stood and walked over to his left, into the main office space. His subordinates were hunched over their desks. Moisha's chair was empty.

"Where's Moisha?" he asked.

"Dunno, he went somewhere," someone answered.

"Someone called and summoned him," another employee added.

Just can't sit still, can he, Ernest thought a little scornfully. Suddenly, he was gripped by a dreadful suspicion. What if the person whom Oomer was meeting at the moment *was* Moisha?

His heart sank to his shins. That meant he'd still gotten in first, the fucker.

He seized his mobile phone and dialed Moisha's number. "Can't talk right now," the man replied softly and curtly. The voice seemed to come through the line immediately, as if Moisha was talking from within arm's reach. Ernest naturally understood that this meant nothing, that physical distance couldn't play any role, but even so, he had a deepening suspicion that the man who answered was only a dozen feet away. He could have gone and peeked through Oomer's glass wall. However, he was unable to force himself to do so. Instead, he sat down at his desk and watched the clock impatiently. So—the half an hour was just about up. He decided to get going.

His suspicions were confirmed. When he knocked, the person sitting across from Oomer rose and walked toward him. The door opened, and Moisha walked out. It was impossible for Ernest to read anything from his perennially optimistic expression.

Ernest's boss gestured for him to take a seat while he answered a call on his mobile. Then, he turned toward Ernest:

"It's good that you came, because to tell the truth, I did need to talk to you about one issue. Allow me to begin. Because I had Mr. Peega here just now, and after our meeting, the matter has become more acute than I thought." (Peega was Moisha's surname.)

Oh, Lord—what's going to happen now, Ernest wondered.

"It concerns Moisha," his boss continued. "He's a good worker."

Well, just come out and say it—you want to put him in my place, the thought flashed through Ernest's head, burning a hole in his mind. He found he was having a difficult time following what his boss was saying. It's over, over, over, the thought hammered in his head. What'll become of my loan that needs paying back; what'll become of my relationship with Kristiina, which has just reached the phase where I need to decide whether to have a family for the second time in my life or abandon the idea? He was reminded of the name of the social group to which he would belong: men on the market for their second time. His attention was drawn to a pin on Oomer's lapel: "Advanced National Defense Courses." Hilarious! Ernest's boss was speaking, but to Ernest, it felt as if a song was resonating from somewhere instead—like the sound of an organ and choir echoing from a country church out into the churchyard. He almost wanted to start humming along.

". . . cannot continue like this." Oomer's words started to penetrate his consciousness again. Of course it can't, Ernest thought sarcastically. Nevertheless, something made him pay closer attention.

"I have reliable information that he consumes alcohol excessively," Oomer was saying worriedly. "He got into a fight with a bouncer, and during the altercation, he shouted that he works at our company. That was definitely the *last* thing we needed now that our ties with the People's Republic of China have become very complicated. Specifically, he was brawling at a Chinese restaurant. But that's just the half of it. I've always emphasized that I have little interest in our employees' private lives. We're not politicians. I'd look past all of Moisha's mischief if he were giving his whole heart and soul to our company, dedicating all of his energy to it. But he's *not*. In addition to here, he's also working somewhere as a copywriter, and furthermore provides information to our competitors, writes little pieces for porno mags under a pseudonym, performs in foreign punk bands, and gives lectures on Estonian culture at Estonian Houses around the world. Even if he were to actually know something about it, it'd *still* be too much! Wait . . ." He raised his hand thinking that Ernest wanted to say something, even though he hadn't intended to. "I understand that a young man has energy. But he's spreading himself too thin. I'm not sure whether our company can allow that. He's doing more work on the side than he is in his own company. There's no balance. And therefore, I'd like *you* to have the decisive say. I've checked out several people who could take that job, by the way. You yourself are certainly aware that right now, unemployment among creative intellectuals is higher than ever before."

"Wait, I don't understand," Ernest said haltingly.

"Exactly—I want *you* to say whether or not we fire Moisha," Oomer spoke worriedly. "You, I trust, because you give your job one hundred percent and are a company patriot."

"I . . ." Ernest stammered before collecting himself. "I agree with your criticism of Moisha. Even so, there are mitigating circumstances, as well as arguments against letting him go. The company has benefitted greatly from Moisha's energy, regardless. He has given us new ideas. He's really a talented person. Our team has started to breathe differently."

"Ooh, is that so . . . ?" Oomer asked, raising an eyebrow.

"And as for the alcohol, I won't deny the fact that there have been problems with it. I've even seen a bottle right on his desk from time to time."

"What kind of bottle?" Oomer asked, becoming alert.

"Vodka," Ernest confessed without blinking.

"Good Lord," Oomer sighed, signaling that Ernest should continue.

"However, I have categorically forbidden him from drinking

on the job. If at all, then only a bottle or two of the lightest lager you can buy, and only in hot weather, so that we don't overburden the air conditioner. Fine—if someone's having a really hard time, then he or she can drink discreetly in the old break room. Moisha has generally accepted that rule. And, by the way, he hasn't left a single work assignment incomplete, even when he's drinking."

"But those side jobs . . ." Oomer growled.

"Yes, he works a lot outside the company, that's true," Ernest agreed. "But I can understand it, because he sorely needs the money. He has a young wife and a small child, and it's rumored that there's another one on the way. He just took out a large mortgage. And everything that concerns kids *is* very expensive these days; not like back in our day, so . . ."

"So you think he should still be given one more chance?" Oomer asked.

"Yes, I do," Ernest exclaimed almost eagerly.

"Fair enough, I appreciate your expertise. I'll raise his salary a little," Oomer grunted. "Fine, then it'll stay that way. Wait, but what did you need—you wanted to talk about something, didn't you?"

"Oh, there's no hurry," Ernest said, dodging the question and getting up to leave.

"Whatever you say," Oomer said, raising his eyebrows and turning back to his computer, implying that their conversation was over.

Ernest exited Oomer's office. He pricked up his ears. Someone's very familiar-sounding laugh was coming from somewhere. People were having a jolly time somewhere. He felt oddly relieved. At the same time, he felt he needed to steady himself against the wall. He felt a terrible nausea sweep over him. Terrible nausea.

THE INNER IMMIGRANT

I'm an inner immigrant. You heard me correctly—an inner immigrant, an "inny." I'm a foreign body in this society. Not an active enemy—oh, no; I'm not that stupid. I don't covertly set bombs, don't sever cables, don't poison wells or hack into closed databases. I don't channel my sewage into the groundwater, don't toss my cigarette butts into dry forests, don't infect anyone with AIDS or do any other shenanigans. I vote when I need to, I hoist the flag, I comment on online articles, and I go to church at Christmas. But I admit without any ambiguity that I don't *like* this society, I don't regard it as my own—yes, I don't tolerate it all that much. The only thing is that I don't *talk* about it. I don't tell anyone that this thing doesn't sit well with me. Not my relatives or my acquaintances, my superiors or my inferiors. I don't even lose my composure in the company of jolly drunks. Yes, I could have become a spy; that's how well I keep my composure. True, I even speak up critically on occasion. Certainly not in the newspapers, but for instance at some informal gathering that follows a training course or a conference. I do it so magnificently that a fervent sweat even beads on my forehead. Sometimes I speak words of fire, the verbal rod flicks, tongue in cheek, wry-mouthed, kissy-kissy, tail between legs, chest to chest, painstakingly, welteringly, smeltering tea, minaret lee, Amenhotep . . . You see—I've got the gift of gab, but I don't let *that* show, either. For that would arouse suspicion. In everyday life, I speak clearly and simply, occasionally shifting my weight from foot to foot, and swaying my upper body from side to side, kneading and squeezing my hands as if they were knotty, cracking my knuckles as if I can't find the words, even though I have more of them than necessary (words, not knuckles). Only on extremely rare occasions do I employ my full verbal harmonics. No, erupt "with the entire richness of mother-tongue beauty" (wow!). Then, everyone thinks that I'm awfully intrigued by something. They say that old Juhan (naturally, that isn't my real name) has a low pain threshold. My pain threshold, if you wish to know, you apes, is just as low as the Great Wall of China!

But maybe I don't shift my weight at all? Maybe I slap my hand over my mouth? What do *I*, a stupid woman, have to say . . . (You'll never guess my true gender—you'd have to have a *supremely* rich imagination for that.)

Even so, I occasionally even speak so critically that a comrade citizen looks at me in dismay: He's not an inner immigrant now, is he? But already in the next moment, I murmur something painful and patriotic, so the doubter starts to feel embarrassed and treats me with even greater sympathy than he did before. That's how easy it is to fool people. I'm a respected individual. Highly respected. But nonetheless, I don't like that thing one bit. For I am an inner-inner-inner (oh, how deep can one burrow?) immigrant.

One time, I nearly lost my composure, all the same. A small group of acquaintances and I ended up discussing politics. I said that X and company (politicians) are as stupid as can be.

"Yes," the others agreed. "They're far from being as smart as Y and company, for example."

"No," I shot back. "Y and company are even *stupider*."

"What are you, then—with Z and company, huh?" they snickered. *Everyone* knows who Z and company are!

But I replied coldly that Z and company are downright bastards.

At first, they just sat staring at me dumbly.

"But whose side are you on, then?" they asked.

"No one's," I replied.

"Listen, don't you like our country then, huh?" they probed, becoming guarded.

Then I realized that I'd crossed the line a little. Of course, they'd hit the nail on the head when they asked if I didn't like the country. But you shouldn't say that, especially to narrow-minded people like them; they might descend upon you in their holy loyalty to the state. And kill you to boot. They'll pound you into the ground and rake leaves on top of you, autumn leaves, colorful reddish-yellow ones, which might have an acorn or a nut among them as well.

"No," I said. "I'd form my own party, instead. Together with people in whom a true fire still burns." Even though that is the last thing that I'd like to do. For only a fairy-tale teller believes that any sort of a flame is still left somewhere. But they stared at me with the utmost reverence and afterward approached me one by one to whisper that they think the exact same way as I do; that everything we've got right now is good for nothing, that things have totally degenerated. And if things "should get going," then they'll join my party immediately.

One story that's somewhat similar, but even funnier, took place in those very days. The elections were coming up, campaigns were underway, and all kinds of groups were working away at them. Someone from an opinion-polling company even came to me with a questionnaire. One of those "questionnaire-Mafiosos." Their poll concerned citizens' political preferences. Naturally, I'd thrown away all of those questionnaires that have been stuffed into my mailbox over the past fifteen years, with total peace of mind, not even looking to see what exactly they were asking. It doesn't interest me in the very least, you see. But lately, the Mafiosos have become cleverer. They've realized that all normal people throw their questionnaires into the wastebasket, so they don't send them by post anymore, but rather dispatch their own workers to the scene. How can you evade types like that? They've gotten your mobile number from somewhere or ring the buzzer at your door with cretinous persistence. The worst is when they come to your workplace—how long can you really get your secretary to lie about you not being there? You come up with a stupid excuse, like you did with summons to mandatory military reserve trainings (*pardon*, they weren't delivered—don't pry!). Well, she came—that sort of brainless, fake redhead, a female intellectual snob, wearing non-prescription glasses, who (it's immediately obvious) had her nose stuck in the social sciences for a few years, and maybe even holds a master's degree in the field. Someone like that asks pointless questions, robbing your life of at least three quarters of an hour in order to collect money for their company and personally earn a few thousand a month. (Although, to be honest, what would people like you really need that forty-five minutes for? *I'd* need it, but people like you—never! You'd just pack some kind of shit together again. Over that length of time, *I* on the other hand can down a mug of beer and visualize the young neighbor chick's tits, which is an especially beneficial activity in societal terms.)

Oh, yes—that questionnaire-fetishist sits down across from me, holding a piece of paper in front of her. She doesn't let me fill it in on my own, of course. They're probably afraid that I might bungle it. (Which I *would* naturally do.) So, she personally polls me and personally marks down answers. By the way, how do *I* know that she's really marking down my answers the way I say them? Maybe she has instructions . . .

And so, the redhead begins:

"Whom do you prefer? Right-wing politicians?"

"No," I reply.

"Do you prefer left-wing ones?" she asks in the exact same tone (they're trained to act like machines so as not to lead the respondent).

"No," I answer in an identically unvarying tone of voice, demonstrating that *I* can act like a machine, too.

"Do you prefer the center party?" she presses.

"No," I snap back.

"Uh-huh," she says in the professional drawn-out tone of someone involved in the work of understanding, and starts to mark something on the questionnaire. "So, we'll mark down the Greens."

"No, no!" I exclaim. "I'm not a Green."

"What do you *mean* you're not?" she asks, baffled.

"That's your problem," I say, smirking nastily.

"Listen, don't joke around," she snaps angrily.

"I'm not joking. I'm a very serious person," I reply. "But I hate the Greens."

"Excuse me, but please understand—I need to go through twenty more people today. They're waiting," she pleads.

"That's your problem," I say to the fake redhead, implying how little I think of her as a woman.

"What, so you're saying you don't *have* any preferences?" she asks, turning serious and even sad.

"Yeah, you got it—I don't have any preferences," I say, nodding.

"Oh," she exclaims, pouncing on what she believes will put an end to the situation. "Then you're an anarchist. In that case, you fit nicely into the option that reads 'And other miscellaneous.' Of course. We'll write 'anarchist' here."

"I'm not an anarchist," I counter, instantly cooling her sense of triumph, and even take her pen away from her. "I *abhor* anarchists."

"Nice try," she retorts, getting irked. "You've at least *got* to fall under the 'and others' category—you can't refuse to, because it's such a broad concept."

"I *don't!*" I roar. "I'm not 'and others' and I don't fit into your tables at *all!*"

"Then I don't understand you at all," she admits, and removes her glasses.

"I don't have a worldview," I say teasingly. "Just like how some people don't have a hole in their rear. Can that fit into your plaster skull?"

"But you could be dangerous then," she says, staring at me fearfully.

At that moment, I end the game and pull back. I patronizingly explain to her that a questionnaire like that isn't secret, and cite the freedom of conscience as a constitutional right. We leave as friends. She has started to see me as something between an inner auditor and a veteran soldier; a hardened fellow; a theoretician of revolution. I ask her to leave the questionnaire with me so that I can fill it out in solitude. I promise to send it back. Which I don't do, of course.

Why don't I like this society? It's impossible to explain in detail. Nothing here is in detail. But there's more of it put all together. If you take it apart, then I could almost even *like* all of the parts. They don't make me nauseous, in any case. It makes me nauseous as a whole. It's like with people. Each person has his own story, he confesses it, justifies things, you start to understand why he's a dullard, and in the end you even start to feel sorry for him. But all of those dullards put together—there's nothing to understand or sympathize with. You can't explain everything together; it's awful, explaining is pointless anyway.

Why don't I state all of this openly, using my real name? I repeat: I'm a respected individual. I have a position, which now, under the new regime, is quite a pleasant thing. Why should I forego it? None of you can guess, can believe, can even *imagine* how high a position I actually hold. In my field, rising higher is practically impossible. (What field is that? Ha ha, you guys . . .) And especially given my past. (No, I wasn't in the *nomenklatura*! No, I wasn't in Siberia! Perhaps I was a top artist, instead? No, no I wasn't . . . A top athlete? A Siamese twin?) And given my education. I studied . . . No, I can't say. In any case, I'm in a position with the kind of orientation where no one would even suspect that I don't like this society. Sitting in such a position, a thing like that shouldn't even come under *consideration*—it's a sacrilege; the person at a desk like that should love his society down to the last ass-hair. But that *is* the beauty of it, when he *doesn't*.

To me, living in this society and putting on the expected masks is like copulating in a telephone booth in plain view of everyone. No one believes that someone is copulating in there; everyone thinks that those two people are taking turns speaking through one receiver to a third person. But instead, you're actually copulating in a public place with a sizeable, chubby, nationalist woman, who is wearing a ribbon the colors of the flag in her ethnically-pure blonde hair. And you know, the funniest part is that even if it were all like that (since it goes without saying that I'll never start messing around in any telephone booth), that woman might even personally believe that she was being copulated with out of great patriotism. I am taciturn (the sign of a true hero!) and that copulation would be a lie, a little thanksgiving mass for our country. Well, what do you know—I strayed too far into fantasy. Eroticism generally doesn't interest me all that much; that was just for fun.

In any case, the fact that I'm respected and rich (I have an entire hiding place full of money stashed under my double-floored cellar—all of it has been acquired by completely legal means, I haven't killed or robbed anyone) couldn't hold me back from openly acknowledging my inner-immigrant status. We *do* have tolerance and freedom here in Estonia. Well, tell me: what could be done to me aside from kicking me out of my position? I wouldn't be put in prison, in any case; they wouldn't find a legal loophole in order to try me. I wouldn't even be beaten up. That really is so nice with a liberal society: you can be the ultimate outcast, a stinking pinhead, but you can't be made to take responsibility for it anyhow. Freedom like that downright *incites* you to turn nasty. You wake up in the morning and you think: today, I'm going to go out and be nasty! I'll slither up close to the smart and the beautiful and let idiocy and ugliness flow at full blast, with all my might. Let the smart and the beautiful suffer a little, too. Their lives are too easy, anyway. They aren't allowed to display their distaste for stinking pinheads like us openly. Whatever they explode, pant, and sputter among themselves leaves me feeling completely indifferent. When you've been respected for thirty-five years (that was a random number, don't even hope to guess my true age by it: I could easily be twenty or eighty), as it's been for me, then you couldn't care less if someone despises you for a few more years. What'll I do with that respect? Will I take it to the grave? On top of that, I've been well aware this entire time that people respect me for the wrong reason. But please—hadn't my work been beneficial, objectively speaking? Well, it certainly had a little, but so what.

But even so, on the other hand, why openly acknowledge that I'm an inner immigrant? What will change because of it? Everything will stay just as it was and as it's always been. The mills will keep on grinding. The idiot will get beaten up, no matter where. The smart man will live well, no matter where. I know that. I live well because I'm smart. But what should I do if I don't like it? On the other hand, I wouldn't like it if the idiot lived well and the smart man was beaten up, either. My whole life, oh Lord, I've experienced heartfelt compassion for the weak, but have still held more compassion toward the strong with my sense of reason! But what does that "Lord" have to do with any of this? I don't know any Lord. I said it just because; as a figure of speech.

I lied. I *do* like one thing, regardless. The frame of a young woman (forgive my prosaism, but it'd be even more awful to say "torso") that I watched through a window every night, back when I was still young. I crafted a spyglass out of the contents of a Tinkertoy box to do so. (Don't get too excited, secret police: I could just as easily be gay, or enjoy pleasuring chickens, too.) That is my bible. Tits. *Seins.* Do you see how an element encountered in my youth has become the motivation for linguistic study for me? I know what "tits" are in eighty languages. I feel like I would like them better in some other society than I do here. I'd like to travel to England (specifically England, but not to some United Kingdom or United Arab Emirates; in short, I'd like to travel to United England) so I can perform observations of neighbor-girls' tits from the second story of a double-decker bus. That's it, that's my paragon; oh, Satan—with that, I give myself unto you! But there *are* no more of those double-decker buses or double-decker tits, the latter have been done away with—that was one of my last bastions. Because, look—a neighbor-girl's tits in the subway aren't the same thing anymore, they're not the same at all (weeping and wailing). But without a doubt, that's no reason for going into inner immigration.

Mankind has degenerated. At my workplace, there's a bimbo, easy on the eye, a total airhead, who wants to go to a warm country every winter. According to her work contract, she also has the right to take vacation time in winter. And so, she booked a trip to some hot, nasty place where you have to wear dark sunglasses all the time. I asked her why she was going there. She stared back at me, baffled—What do you mean, *why? Everybody* goes. Her acquaintances would have been the ones looking at *me* like I was a weirdo. Those poor people—they feel as if they're living life, as if they *are* citizens of the world now. But I'd gladly say to them: you're all little drones. Naturally, though, I don't, so as not to give myself away. I urge the bimbo: Why don't you get traveling already; isn't it about time to clamber into a plane and start flapping your wings?

I personally don't want to travel to somewhere warm. And

I don't intend to. I come up with all kinds of excuses to avoid going. Because only boneheads go to warm places in winter. They don't understand that in winter, you should be sitting in a snowbank, hunched up in a poorly heated, drafty house, trembling, getting sick. That's what a proper man does. Then, people understand that it's *winter*. You mustn't run away from winter. The cold is better for being an inner immigrant. But the bimbos—they twitter on about their impressions afterward, sigh, and reminisce about how they liked the warmth, show you their photos and souvenirs.

Yes, those souvenirs . . . One bimbo came and showed me her fire-red moccasins. Why are souvenirs always some kind of specific thing? A souvenir is what I *want* a souvenir to be. A souvenir can even be a house if I bring it back with me. I'll bring back an outhouse together with its cesspit if I want to, and will say it's my souvenir. I'll bring back a full trash can. The ideal souvenir could even be a rotten banana. Don't stuff me full of your glass knickknacks and your red moccasins. You see? No matter where I look, all I do is get angry.

I've been an inner immigrant for a relatively long time. I became conscious of it gradually. There was no leap, no breakthrough in consciousness, no wool pulled from my eyes or other crap like that. Let this be stated in case someone considers composing a work on the pathogenesis of the inner immigrant. By the way, I've even considered doing that myself. Conceivably, there's something wrong with me. Perhaps I should talk to a doctor. Why aren't I capable of singing "hallelujah?" Why don't I grow emotional? Why don't I hold a beetle in the palm of my hand or moan tenderly about how lovely the world is? I don't even feel mountaintop-high happiness, not at *all*.

As you might have realized, I'm prone to emotional outbursts; I have mood swings, mental quivers, and spiritual cramps. But maybe I'm just imagining them in order to be more interesting.

A little almost intellectual-ish, even. Oh, how I'd like to be an intellectual. The kind who is greeted by everyone standing up when he enters a room. So it is: I wanted to become an intellectual, but I became an inner immigrant instead.

I must debunk one more chance for misunderstanding. Specifically, one might be left with the impression that I thoroughly enjoy my own critical attitude; that I love gloating, and thus, that I put people in their place out of principle. Far from it. I outright loathe those types. Because I perceive with quite a good deal of certainty that at least half of them don't have a critical attitude in the very least. In reality, they don't give a damn. They put people in their place in order to make a living. How *banal*. In reality, they maybe even love all that surrounds us. But since they have a sort of ability to put people in their places easily (it's the same kind of anomaly as an exceptionally large shoe size, hair that grows from your ears, the ability to quickly calculate cube roots in your head, and other such things), they apply their ability. It's soulless technicalism. Professional place-putters like that will never oppose the system. They go with it, just like pollen goes with a blossom.

My inner-immigrant status can't be substantiated. I've been a winner, both materially and morally. All this put together should have given me a sense of happiness; should have refreshed me; should have provided new impulses for living. Nothing of the kind has happened.

Now, you're thinking that my rambling has exhausted itself— look, the style is already getting looser, a little more and I'll actually reveal myself. In your dreams! That was just temporary.

Even a Great Man can chitchat with a random person in the restroom. Just like you and me. Attention, I'm tightening up again!

The refrain begins.

You'll never find out who I am. I could stand right next to you, and you wouldn't recognize me. If you end up sitting next to me on the bus by chance, you won't be gripped by a flash of fear. If I pick up my groceries from the conveyor belt next to you in order to start bagging, your gaze won't rest on me suspiciously. If I stand barely a few inches behind you at national celebrations, you won't feel an icy breath upon the back of your neck, or fall into a panic. I could be the plumber who renovated your bathroom, the general who salutes a parade, the doctor who sticks a needle in your vein—anyone. I exist, me, the inner immigrant, and I don't intend to disappear. **I'm biding my time.** For what? I guess you'll see. When the time is ripe.

Mihkel Mutt was born in Tartu, Estonia in 1953. He has authored scores of critical essays, short stories, novels, travel essays, and plays. He won the Tuglas Short Story Award in 1981 and in 2008, as well as the Cultural Endowment of Estonia's Award for Essays in 2001 and 2015.

Adam Cullen (b. 1986) is a translator of Estonian prose, poetry, and plays into English. He has translated works by Tõnu Õnnepalu, Mihkel Mutt, Indrek Hargla, and Rein Raud.

MICHAL AJVAZ, *The Golden Age.*
The Other City.
PIERRE ALBERT-BIROT, *Grabinoulor.*
YUZ ALESHKOVSKY, *Kangaroo.*
FELIPE ALFAU, *Chromos.*
Locos.
JOE AMATO, *Samuel Taylor's Last Night.*
IVAN ÂNGELO, *The Celebration.*
The Tower of Glass.
ANTÓNIO LOBO ANTUNES, *Knowledge of Hell.*
The Splendor of Portugal.
ALAIN ARIAS-MISSON, *Theatre of Incest.*
JOHN ASHBERY & JAMES SCHUYLER, *A Nest of Ninnies.*
ROBERT ASHLEY, *Perfect Lives.*
GABRIELA AVIGUR-ROTEM, *Heatwave and Crazy Birds.*
DJUNA BARNES, *Ladies Almanack.*
Ryder.
JOHN BARTH, *Letters.*
Sabbatical.
DONALD BARTHELME, *The King.*
Paradise.
SVETISLAV BASARA, *Chinese Letter.*
MIQUEL BAUÇÀ, *The Siege in the Room.*
RENÉ BELLETTO, *Dying.*
MAREK BIENCZYK, *Transparency.*
ANDREI BITOV, *Pushkin House.*
ANDREJ BLATNIK, *You Do Understand.*
Law of Desire.
LOUIS PAUL BOON, *Chapel Road.*
My Little War.
Summer in Termuren.
ROGER BOYLAN, *Killoyle.*
IGNÁCIO DE LOYOLA BRANDÃO, *Anonymous Celebrity.*
Zero.
BONNIE BREMSER, *Troia: Mexican Memoirs.*
CHRISTINE BROOKE-ROSE, *Amalgamemnon.*
BRIGID BROPHY, *In Transit.*
The Prancing Novelist.

GERALD L. BRUNS, *Modern Poetry and the Idea of Language.*
GABRIELLE BURTON, *Heartbreak Hotel.*
MICHEL BUTOR, *Degrees.*
Mobile.
G. CABRERA INFANTE, *Infante's Inferno.*
Three Trapped Tigers.
JULIETA CAMPOS, *The Fear of Losing Eurydice.*
ANNE CARSON, *Eros the Bittersweet.*
ORLY CASTEL-BLOOM, *Dolly City.*
LOUIS-FERDINAND CÉLINE, *North.*
Conversations with Professor Y.
London Bridge.
MARIE CHAIX, *The Laurels of Lake Constance.*
HUGO CHARTERIS, *The Tide Is Right.*
ERIC CHEVILLARD, *Demolishing Nisard.*
The Author and Me.
MARC CHOLODENKO, *Mordechai Schamz.*
JOSHUA COHEN, *Witz.*
EMILY HOLMES COLEMAN, *The Shutter of Snow.*
ERIC CHEVILLARD, *The Author and Me.*
ROBERT COOVER, *A Night at the Movies.*
STANLEY CRAWFORD, *Log of the S.S. The Mrs Unguentine.*
Some Instructions to My Wife.
RENÉ CREVEL, *Putting My Foot in It.*
RALPH CUSACK, *Cadenza.*
NICHOLAS DELBANCO, *Sherbrookes.*
The Count of Concord.
NIGEL DENNIS, *Cards of Identity.*
PETER DIMOCK, *A Short Rhetoric for Leaving the Family.*
ARIEL DORFMAN, *Konfidenz.*
COLEMAN DOWELL, *Island People.*
Too Much Flesh and Jabez.
ARKADII DRAGOMOSHCHENKO, *Dust.*
RIKKI DUCORNET, *Phosphor in Dreamland.*
The Complete Butcher's Tales.

RIKKI DUCORNET (cont.), *The Jade Cabinet*.
The Fountains of Neptune.
WILLIAM EASTLAKE, *The Bamboo Bed*.
Castle Keep.
Lyric of the Circle Heart.
JEAN ECHENOZ, *Chopin's Move*.
STANLEY ELKIN, *A Bad Man*.
Criers and Kibitzers, Kibitzers and Criers.
The Dick Gibson Show.
The Franchiser.
The Living End.
Mrs. Ted Bliss.
FRANÇOIS EMMANUEL, *Invitation to a Voyage*.
PAUL EMOND, *The Dance of a Sham*.
SALVADOR ESPRIU, *Ariadne in the Grotesque Labyrinth*.
LESLIE A. FIEDLER, *Love and Death in the American Novel*.
JUAN FILLOY, *Op Oloop*.
ANDY FITCH, *Pop Poetics*.
GUSTAVE FLAUBERT, *Bouvard and Pécuchet*.
KASS FLEISHER, *Talking out of School*.
JON FOSSE, *Aliss at the Fire*.
Melancholy.
FORD MADOX FORD, *The March of Literature*.
MAX FRISCH, *I'm Not Stiller*.
Man in the Holocene.
CARLOS FUENTES, *Christopher Unborn*.
Distant Relations.
Terra Nostra.
Where the Air Is Clear.
TAKEHIKO FUKUNAGA, *Flowers of Grass*.
WILLIAM GADDIS, JR., *The Recognitions*.
JANICE GALLOWAY, *Foreign Parts*.
The Trick Is to Keep Breathing.
WILLIAM H. GASS, *Life Sentences*.
The Tunnel.
The World Within the Word.
Willie Masters' Lonesome Wife.
GÉRARD GAVARRY, *Hoppla! 1 2 3*.

ETIENNE GILSON, *The Arts of the Beautiful*.
Forms and Substances in the Arts.
C. S. GISCOMBE, *Giscome Road*.
Here.
DOUGLAS GLOVER, *Bad News of the Heart*.
WITOLD GOMBROWICZ, *A Kind of Testament*.
PAULO EMÍLIO SALES GOMES, *P's Three Women*.
GEORGI GOSPODINOV, *Natural Novel*.
JUAN GOYTISOLO, *Count Julian*.
Juan the Landless.
Makbara.
Marks of Identity.
HENRY GREEN, *Blindness*.
Concluding.
Doting.
Nothing.
JACK GREEN, *Fire the Bastards!*
JIŘÍ GRUŠA, *The Questionnaire*.
MELA HARTWIG, *Am I a Redundant Human Being?*
JOHN HAWKES, *The Passion Artist*.
Whistlejacket.
ELIZABETH HEIGHWAY, ED., *Contemporary Georgian Fiction*.
AIDAN HIGGINS, *Balcony of Europe*.
Blind Man's Bluff.
Bornholm Night-Ferry.
Langrishe, Go Down.
Scenes from a Receding Past.
KEIZO HINO, *Isle of Dreams*.
KAZUSHI HOSAKA, *Plainsong*.
ALDOUS HUXLEY, *Antic Hay*.
Point Counter Point.
Those Barren Leaves.
Time Must Have a Stop.
NAOYUKI II, *The Shadow of a Blue Cat*.
DRAGO JANČAR, *The Tree with No Name*.
MIKHEIL JAVAKHISHVILI, *Kvachi*.
GERT JONKE, *The Distant Sound*.
Homage to Czerny.
The System of Vienna.

JACQUES JOUET, *Mountain R.*
Savage.
Upstaged.
MIEKO KANAI, *The Word Book.*
YORAM KANIUK, *Life on Sandpaper.*
ZURAB KARUMIDZE, *Dagny.*
JOHN KELLY, *From Out of the City.*
HUGH KENNER, *Flaubert, Joyce and Beckett: The Stoic Comedians.*
Joyce's Voices.
DANILO KIŠ, *The Attic.*
The Lute and the Scars.
Psalm 44.
A Tomb for Boris Davidovich.
ANITA KONKKA, *A Fool's Paradise.*
GEORGE KONRÁD, *The City Builder.*
TADEUSZ KONWICKI, *A Minor Apocalypse.*
The Polish Complex.
ANNA KORDZAIA-SAMADASHVILI, *Me, Margarita.*
MENIS KOUMANDAREAS, *Koula.*
ELAINE KRAF, *The Princess of 72nd Street.*
JIM KRUSOE, *Iceland.*
AYSE KULIN, *Farewell: A Mansion in Occupied Istanbul.*
EMILIO LASCANO TEGUI, *On Elegance While Sleeping.*
ERIC LAURRENT, *Do Not Touch.*
VIOLETTE LEDUC, *La Bâtarde.*
EDOUARD LEVÉ, *Autoportrait.*
Newspaper.
Suicide.
Works.
MARIO LEVI, *Istanbul Was a Fairy Tale.*
DEBORAH LEVY, *Billy and Girl.*
JOSÉ LEZAMA LIMA, *Paradiso.*
ROSA LIKSOM, *Dark Paradise.*
OSMAN LINS, *Avalovara.*
The Queen of the Prisons of Greece.
FLORIAN LIPUŠ, *The Errors of Young Tjaž.*
GORDON LISH, *Peru.*
ALF MACLOCHLAINN, *Out of Focus.*
Past Habitual.

The Corpus in the Library.
RON LOEWINSOHN, *Magnetic Field(s).*
YURI LOTMAN, *Non-Memoirs.*
D. KEITH MANO, *Take Five.*
MINA LOY, *Stories and Essays of Mina Loy.*
MICHELINE AHARONIAN MARCOM, *A Brief History of Yes.*
The Mirror in the Well.
BEN MARCUS, *The Age of Wire and String.*
WALLACE MARKFIELD, *Teitlebaum's Window.*
DAVID MARKSON, *Reader's Block.*
Wittgenstein's Mistress.
CAROLE MASO, *AVA.*
HISAKI MATSUURA, *Triangle.*
LADISLAV MATEJKA & KRYSTYNA POMORSKA, EDS., *Readings in Russian Poetics: Formalist & Structuralist Views.*
HARRY MATHEWS, *Cigarettes.*
The Conversions.
The Human Country.
The Journalist.
My Life in CIA.
Singular Pleasures.
The Sinking of the Odradek.
Stadium.
Tlooth.
HISAKI MATSUURA, *Triangle.*
DONAL MCLAUGHLIN, *beheading the virgin mary, and other stories.*
JOSEPH MCELROY, *Night Soul and Other Stories.*
ABDELWAHAB MEDDEB, *Talismano.*
GERHARD MEIER, *Isle of the Dead.*
HERMAN MELVILLE, *The Confidence-Man.*
AMANDA MICHALOPOULOU, *I'd Like.*
STEVEN MILLHAUSER, *The Barnum Museum.*
In the Penny Arcade.
RALPH J. MILLS, JR., *Essays on Poetry.*
MOMUS, *The Book of Jokes.*
CHRISTINE MONTALBETTI, *The Origin of Man.*
Western.

NICHOLAS MOSLEY, *Accident.*
Assassins.
Catastrophe Practice.
A Garden of Trees.
Hopeful Monsters.
Imago Bird.
Inventing God.
Look at the Dark.
Metamorphosis.
Natalie Natalia.
Serpent.
WARREN MOTTE, *Fables of the Novel:
French Fiction since 1990.*
*Fiction Now: The French Novel in the
21st Century.*
Mirror Gazing.
Oulipo: A Primer of Potential Literature.
GERALD MURNANE, *Barley Patch.*
Inland.
YVES NAVARRE, *Our Share of Time.*
Sweet Tooth.
DOROTHY NELSON, *In Night's City.*
Tar and Feathers.
ESHKOL NEVO, *Homesick.*
WILFRIDO D. NOLLEDO, *But for
the Lovers.*
BORIS A. NOVAK, *The Master of
Insomnia.*
FLANN O'BRIEN, *At Swim-Two-Birds.*
The Best of Myles.
The Dalkey Archive.
The Hard Life.
The Poor Mouth.
The Third Policeman.
CLAUDE OLLIER, *The Mise-en-Scène.*
Wert and the Life Without End.
PATRIK OUŘEDNÍK, *Europeana.*
The Opportune Moment, 1855.
BORIS PAHOR, *Necropolis.*
FERNANDO DEL PASO, *News from
the Empire.*
Palinuro of Mexico.
ROBERT PINGET, *The Inquisitory.*
Mahu or The Material.
Trio.
MANUEL PUIG, *Betrayed by Rita
Hayworth.*

The Buenos Aires Affair.
Heartbreak Tango.
RAYMOND QUENEAU, *The Last Days.*
Odile.
Pierrot Mon Ami.
Saint Glinglin.
ANN QUIN, *Berg.*
Passages.
Three.
Tripticks.
ISHMAEL REED, *The Free-Lance
Pallbearers.*
The Last Days of Louisiana Red.
Ishmael Reed: The Plays.
Juice!
The Terrible Threes.
The Terrible Twos.
Yellow Back Radio Broke-Down.
JASIA REICHARDT, *15 Journeys Warsaw
to London.*
JOÃO UBALDO RIBEIRO, *House of the
Fortunate Buddhas.*
JEAN RICARDOU, *Place Names.*
RAINER MARIA RILKE,
The Notebooks of Malte Laurids Brigge.
JULIÁN RÍOS, *The House of Ulysses.*
Larva: A Midsummer Night's Babel.
Poundemonium.
ALAIN ROBBE-GRILLET, *Project for a
Revolution in New York.*
A Sentimental Novel.
AUGUSTO ROA BASTOS, *I the Supreme.*
DANIËL ROBBERECHTS, *Arriving in
Avignon.*
JEAN ROLIN, *The Explosion of the
Radiator Hose.*
OLIVIER ROLIN, *Hotel Crystal.*
ALIX CLEO ROUBAUD, *Alix's Journal.*
JACQUES ROUBAUD, *The Form of
a City Changes Faster, Alas, Than the
Human Heart.*
The Great Fire of London.
Hortense in Exile.
Hortense Is Abducted.
*Mathematics: The Plurality of Worlds of
Lewis.*
Some Thing Black.

RAYMOND ROUSSEL, *Impressions of Africa.*

VEDRANA RUDAN, *Night.*

PABLO M. RUIZ, *Four Cold Chapters on the Possibility of Literature.*

GERMAN SADULAEV, *The Maya Pill.*

TOMAŽ ŠALAMUN, *Soy Realidad.*

LYDIE SALVAYRE, *The Company of Ghosts.*
The Lecture.
The Power of Flies.

LUIS RAFAEL SÁNCHEZ, *Macho Camacho's Beat.*

SEVERO SARDUY, *Cobra & Maitreya.*

NATHALIE SARRAUTE, *Do You Hear Them?*
Martereau.
The Planetarium.

STIG SÆTERBAKKEN, *Siamese.*
Self-Control.
Through the Night.

ARNO SCHMIDT, *Collected Novellas.*
Collected Stories.
Nobodaddy's Children.
Two Novels.

ASAF SCHURR, *Motti.*

GAIL SCOTT, *My Paris.*

DAMION SEARLS, *What We Were Doing and Where We Were Going.*

JUNE AKERS SEESE,
Is This What Other Women Feel Too?

BERNARD SHARE, *Inish.*
Transit.

VIKTOR SHKLOVSKY, *Bowstring.*
Literature and Cinematography.
Theory of Prose.
Third Factory.
Zoo, or Letters Not about Love.

PIERRE SINIAC, *The Collaborators.*

KJERSTI A. SKOMSVOLD,
The Faster I Walk, the Smaller I Am.

JOSEF ŠKVORECKÝ, *The Engineer of Human Souls.*

GILBERT SORRENTINO, *Aberration of Starlight.*
Blue Pastoral.
Crystal Vision.

Imaginative Qualities of Actual Things.
Mulligan Stew. Red the Fiend.
Steelwork.
Under the Shadow.

MARKO SOSIČ, *Ballerina, Ballerina.*

ANDRZEJ STASIUK, *Dukla.*
Fado.

GERTRUDE STEIN, *The Making of Americans.*
A Novel of Thank You.

LARS SVENDSEN, *A Philosophy of Evil.*

PIOTR SZEWC, *Annihilation.*

GONÇALO M. TAVARES, *A Man: Klaus Klump.*
Jerusalem.
Learning to Pray in the Age of Technique.

LUCIAN DAN TEODOROVICI,
Our Circus Presents...

NIKANOR TERATOLOGEN, *Assisted Living.*

STEFAN THEMERSON, *Hobson's Island.*
The Mystery of the Sardine.
Tom Harris.

TAEKO TOMIOKA, *Building Waves.*

JOHN TOOMEY, *Sleepwalker.*

DUMITRU TSEPENEAG, *Hotel Europa.*
The Necessary Marriage.
Pigeon Post.
Vain Art of the Fugue.

ESTHER TUSQUETS, *Stranded.*

DUBRAVKA UGRESIC, *Lend Me Your Character.*
Thank You for Not Reading.

TOR ULVEN, *Replacement.*

MATI UNT, *Brecht at Night.*
Diary of a Blood Donor.
Things in the Night.

ÁLVARO URIBE & OLIVIA SEARS, EDS.,
Best of Contemporary Mexican Fiction.

ELOY URROZ, *Friction.*
The Obstacles.

LUISA VALENZUELA, *Dark Desires and the Others.*
He Who Searches.

PAUL VERHAEGHEN, *Omega Minor.*

BORIS VIAN, *Heartsnatcher.*

LLORENÇ VILLALONGA, *The Dolls'*
Room.

TOOMAS VINT, *An Unending Landscape.*

ORNELA VORPSI, *The Country Where No*
One Ever Dies.

AUSTRYN WAINHOUSE, *Hedyphagetica.*

CURTIS WHITE, *America's Magic*
Mountain.
The Idea of Home.
Memories of My Father Watching TV.
Requiem.

DIANE WILLIAMS,
Excitability: Selected Stories.
Romancer Erector.

DOUGLAS WOOLF, *Wall to Wall.*
Ya! & John-Juan.

JAY WRIGHT, *Polynomials and Pollen.*
The Presentable Art of Reading Absence.

PHILIP WYLIE, *Generation of Vipers.*

MARGUERITE YOUNG, *Angel in the*
Forest.
Miss MacIntosh, My Darling.

REYOUNG, *Unbabbling.*

VLADO ŽABOT, *The Succubus.*

ZORAN ŽIVKOVIĆ , *Hidden Camera.*

LOUIS ZUKOFSKY, *Collected Fiction.*

VITOMIL ZUPAN, *Minuet for Guitar.*

SCOTT ZWIREN, *God Head.*

AND MORE . . .